T0336336

Advance Praise for
The Adventures of Spike the Wonder Dog

"Bill Boggs and his friend Spike the Wonder Dog unleash comedic wizardry in this madcap, highly entertaining, satirical novel. Spike is the newest canine literary hero to take on the world with hilarious results."

—WINSTON GROOM, author of *Forrest Gump*

"*The Adventures of Spike the Wonder Dog* is so smart, witty, and inventive that I had to keep reminding myself that I didn't write it."

—ALAN ZWEIBEL, original SNL writer and Thurber Prize–winning author of *The Other Shulman*

"Don't let the title of the book fool you—*The Adventures of Spike the Wonder Dog* is indeed about a dog, and a wondrous canine at that! But the book is also a highly personal and very compelling memoir of the underbelly of local and national television and fame. Amidst the hilarity, and it is indeed one of the funniest books I've ever read, there is a very touching coming-of-age story for man and dog, with good-natured, lovable characters albeit with some dastardly ones as well!"

—WILL FRIEDWALD, *Wall Street Journal*, author of *Straighten Up and Fly Right: The Life and Music of Nat King Cole*

"Bill Boggs has hit a home run with this highly original and hilarious satire on…everything! A terrific read I highly recommend."

—MARC ELIOT, *New York Times* bestselling author

"Mr. Lee, call your lawyer. There's a new Spike in town, an acid-tripping terrier who savages the media landscape while avoiding death and castration. Bill Boggs takes us on a darkly comic journey through his twisted world. It takes a hero with four legs—and two balls—to survive."

—RICHARD JOHNSON, *New York Post*

"OMG! Who could write such an outrageous novel? Spike the Wonder Dog! With a little help from his pal, the raconteur Bill Boggs, Spike has gotten his memoirs down (on a better grade of paper than most pets get). His dog-eared hearing picks up the bizarre sounds of people being their fallible human selves, and his soft canine eyes see more than is probably good for him. *Spike the Wonder Dog* is an irreverent hoot."

—SUSAN ISAACS, *New York Times* bestselling author

"The wondrous Bill Boggs' *The Adventures of Spike the Wonder Dog* has another big adventure awaiting: climbing to the heights of the bestseller lists. Spike tells us the story of how he and his master, Bud, go from Spike's first appearance on local High Point North Carolina daytime TV, to a big deal appearance on late night TV, to big time NY TV. Spike will keep you laughing—and on the edge of your seat at the same time. Filled with real-life celebs, lots of inside TV info and crazy adventures, this one is made for the big screen. How do you say 'bravo' in dog?"

—LINDA STASI, *New York Daily News* columnist, TV commentator, bestselling author of *The Sixth Station* and *Book of Judas*

"Like Joan Rivers, *The Adventures of Spike the Wonder Dog* is definitely Not Safe for Snowflakes. But fans of transgressive humor like *Family Guy* or Dave Chappelle will appreciate Spike's wild tales, which are raunchy, hilarious, and spectacularly politically incorrect. Bill Boggs has the manners of a gentleman, as does Spike—so they'll both understand if you take offense. Rivers would just have told you to go fuck yourself."

—LESLIE BENNETTS, author, *Last Girl Before Freeway: The Life, Loves, Losses and Liberation of Joan Rivers*

THE ADVENTURES OF
SPIKE
—THE—
WONDER DOG

THE ADVENTURES OF
SPIKE
— THE —
WONDER DOG

— AS TOLD TO —
BILL BOGGS

Post Hill
PRESS

A POST HILL PRESS BOOK

The Adventures of Spike the Wonder Dog:
As told to Bill Boggs
© 2020 by Bill Boggs
All Rights Reserved

ISBN: 978-1-64293-376-5
ISBN (eBook): 978-1-64293-377-2

Cover art by Adam Baker
Illustrations by Jacob Below
English Bull Terrier icon art by Delsart Olivia
Interior design and composition by Greg Johnson, Textbook Perfect

Post Hill Press
New York • Nashville
posthillpress.com
Published in the United States of America

*"I have found that when you are deeply troubled,
there are things you get from the silent,
devoted companionship of your pets
that you can get from no other source.
I have never found in a human being loyalty
comparable to that of any pet."*

—DORIS DAY

*"Never lose your sense of humor,
it's the most valued possession you have."*

—HOWARD HIGMAN

L.H.S. JANUARY '59

"Warning: I got no trigger warnings for you."

—SPIKE

Contents

Prelude 1

PART ONE

Chapter 1: High Point 7

Chapter 2: New York: The First Time 19

Chapter 3: Celebrity 25

Chapter 4: Lombardo 39

Chapter 5: The Visit 51

Chapter 6: Vegas 60

Chapter 7: "The Hebe Named Zebe" 82

Chapter 8: On the Lam 97

Chapter 9: The Phone Call 106

PART TWO

Chapter 10: The Trailer 117

Chapter 11: The Show 134

Chapter 12: Our Life 145

Chapter 13: Tryin' to Get Laid 154

Chapter 14: Disco Fever 159

Chapter 15: Benny and Some Jets 166

Chapter 16: The Gaze 173

Chapter 17: Daisy 190

Chapter 18: Gone Dog 199

PART THREE

Chapter 19: The Hour Shall Come 205
Chapter 20: The Freezer 236
Chapter 21: Dyin' with Your Boots On 252
Chapter 22: A Month Later: The Orange Doghouse 261

About the Author 269

PRELUDE

And so, Spike started at…The Eve of Destruction.

Last week, I'm getting a standing ovation from fans at The Garden for returning Roger Federer's 130-mile-an-hour serve with my head. Now I'm locked in a cage on a filthy concrete floor growling at two guys named Julio.

They stole me off the street. I've had to fight for my life. Tomorrow, these crack-sniffing degenerate morons are throwin' me in against two dogs at once—Monstro, three times my size, plugged with more steroids than the Giants' defense. His hobby's biting anything that moves. Nice résumé. His coworker, Little Tiger, is trained to crack the bones in your back legs. The Julios are betting against me. Everybody is. I would, too.

Where the hell is Bud? Buffy? Lombardo?

How did this happen? How does a good little puppy from a top breeder in Devon, PA, end up a big TV star killed in a rigged fight? I just wanted the simple life of bein' a good pet for Bud.

I'm alone. It's dark and creepy in the middle of the night. Only the sounds of lonely dogs barkin' in their dreams for a master they never had.

I got a hell of a story for ya, and if this is my last night alive, like I figure it is, I might as well tell it.

But wait a second.

If you're as sharp as I figure you are for bothering to read this in the first place, you're probably already wondering, how can a dog tell a story? Fair question. So I'll explain. Anybody who's ever had a dog sees that we understand every word you're saying when you're talking to us. Right? You know that. Don't deny it. Look, we've had centuries of listening to you humans blather on with your every concern, every whim, every worry. We get it.

And yeah, at times, face it—you're tedious. It's, like, deadening for us hearin' all this long-winded drivel when we should be outside running around together playing happily in the sunshine. You see your dog yawning? Consider what you're talking about. Wonder why your dog sticks his head outta the car while you're cruising down the road? Same thing. You're not bowlin' us over with your wit and jocularity.

So we got the listenin' part down solid, but it's a sad evolutionary fact that we're still a long way from being able to bark back in a meaningful two-way chat. The average dog is frustrated by this, and—unknown to you till right now—there's a great deal of canine incontinence that occurs 'cause of this communication block.

But I got lucky, 'cause in the case of telling you this story, my communication was greatly aided by licking some drool off Mr. Boggs' mouth after he'd taken a psilocybin mushroom capsule.

"Why," you ask, "would a stable, charming man like Mister Boggs be taking magic mushrooms? Even a microdose?"

Well, my master, Bud, was doin' a special for his TV show about the benefits of tiny amounts of psilocybin for treating things like depression, end-of-life suffering, or enhancing creativity. So Bud talked his pal Mr. Boggs, who's always up for a little more TV exposure, into being part of the "creativity group."

A nurse who's got two bad tattoos—unfortunate, slightly cross-eyed versions of Taylor Swift's face—inked large on the back of each big calf, gives Mr. Boggs his dose. Of course, he wants more, but she says no. After she and the cross-eyed Taylor Swifts leave, Mr. Boggs searches the supply cabinet and gleefully helps himself to another pill. He goes back to a dressing room, puts on a fluffy white robe, and lies down to relax.

What am I doing there? Well, Bud's busy across the street doin' some editing, so I get left with Mr. Boggs, who's one of my closest friends, a real buddy. We got a great connection, and he's almost like a second master to me. We're curled up together. As he's sleepin', I see a river of drool oozing outta the corner of his mouth, so I lick it off.

Yeah, that's pretty affectionate on my part, but it's also protecting him in case, say, maybe some attractive TV producer walks in. I don't want her seein' Mr. Boggs with his big mouth wide open, drooling all over the pillow. Or worse, what if the photographer who's been lurkin' around the set stops by and snaps a shot of him? I can see the *National Enquirer*: "Dying Bill's Brave Goodbye!" You gotta take care of your friends, and I'm glad I did, 'cause….

About a half hour later, Mr. Boggs wakes up. His eyes are wide open, and for the next ten minutes, he's staring at me, and I'm staring back at him. He's smiling real big. I'm wagging real hard. We're, like, connected but in another world. His eyes are blue like they've never been. I'm looking into these little blue pools feeling like I'm shooting my thoughts into his brain, tellin' him some of the stuff that's happened to me in the last two years. And then slowly, it's like I'm rising up and twirling around and around and around, and I land on a big stage. A giant red velvet curtain lifts and I'm in the spotlight, and he's floating in front of me, like he's an astronaut who happens to be wearin' a white bathrobe with an ABC logo instead of a space suit.

"Spike," he says, "it's like I can hear you in my head."

"Indeed, Mister Boggs. You can!"

"You're talking to me, Spike!" Mr. Boggs says.

"I want to tell you the story."

"Yes, Spike! Yes! Nobody knows what all that was like for you. Stardom? The kidnapping? Those fights? That awful freezer? Tell me," he says.

"Then close your eyes and turn on the picture in your head while you're floating around out there."

"Spike, you're coming in on wide-screen high-def with a Bose soundbar. No, wait…I upgraded myself to three-D with Dolby seven-point…. *Go!*"

"Well, Mister Boggs, it all started 'cause it looked like I was yawning on cue…."

Part One

1
HIGH POINT

Bud took me to the TV station that morning. I'd never been on television. I was nine months old, with the immediate goal of mastering control of basic excretory function. I'd been out of control a lot, so maybe that's why I got hauled to the studio in the first place.

He sits me in a big blue chair on the set and rattles off the day's guests:

A psychic who's boldly predicting that Adele will replace Marie Osmond as a Nutrisystem spokeswoman exactly five years from today.

Lawyer Gloria Allred's proudly displaying two big digital devices that demonstrate the number of men blamed for sexual misconduct is rising faster than the national debt.

Some PC singer's on promoting his new album of songs revised to be gender-neutral. He's gonna sing "You Make Me Feel Like a Natural Person."

There's a doctor warning of a scary new thing plaguing humans called Dormant Butt Syndrome, which has most of the audience goosing themselves to check.

Finally, he's got an interview with Cher that he taped after her show at the Greensboro Coliseum. OK, I know she's so old that she's up there with dead people like Alexander Hamilton, 'cause there's a Broadway show about her, but don't get me started on Cher. Every time I see her on TV, I want to lick those thighs.

Anyway, right after he says "and Cher" in that big, kinda too-loud voice he uses sometimes on TV, he turns to me and says, "Well, what do you think of the show today, Spike?" Now I'm looking at him and noticing he's a little bloated from that big bottle of Delirium Tremens beer he downed last night, and I'm honestly a little drowsy, way off my normal demanding schedule of sleepin' most of the day, so it's a natural thing when I just open up and yawn. It's a long, enjoyable yawn. Draws a lot of attention, 'cause I've got a colossal trap. Bit like a crocodile.

"Really, Spike?" Bud says. "That's what you think of the show?" And I yawn again. More relaxin' with two.

Meanwhile, a great deal of laughter is ensuing from the crew, the audience, the guests, and Bud. Everybody's yucking it up—loud. And these are real laughs, not those forced phony ones morning-radio people use to make you think what's happening is funny when it's not even close.

Bud looks at me and I look at him, and we both know we got something hot going, 'cause Bud and me have had that dog–human connection since the day he picked me outta the litter. So he says, very sincerely, "Anything else?" He pauses. "Spike?" What would you do? Obviously, I yawn again, this time on purpose, and sink into the chair to get some much-needed sleep.

The next day, the *High Point Enterprise* runs a big picture of the incident. Front page—Bud and me. There I am with my jaws open wide enough to bite a football. The headline: "Meet Spike 'The Wonder Dog.'"

Bud loved the ink. When he got to the station the next morning and saw the paper, they said, he sounded orgasmic. And believe me, I know what that sounds like. He drives back to the house, wakes me, shows me my picture, tapes it on the fridge, tells me I'm now The Wonder Dog, and rushes me back to WGHP.

I'm on the show again. OK, why not? I yawn, lick his mouth, and smell he's smoked pot before the show. A Listerine breath strip's not covering that up, pal. At one point he says, "Remember, coming up today, part two—Cher." Of course I bark at the mention of Cher. The bark is not yet my full-throated hammer, but it gets attention. He buys in and says, "Spike, you seem to like Cher. Am I right?" So I let my sizable pink tongue slide very, very slowly outta my mouth while panting heavily. The camera zooms in. So I drool. This is easy stuff, really, but it's greeted with hysteria. You would think I'm Trevor Noah in a dog suit.

The best thing that happened that day was that people found out what I am. Bud explained. I listened like I didn't already know—that sort of fake newscaster-concern listening that somehow earns local anchors millions of dollars. You know, like when the female anchor's being artificially serious trying to wrinkle her cement-hard botoxed brow as she reads the teleprompter about a teenager with multiple stab wounds in the Bronx. The older male anchor's pretending to care by frowning and nodding solemnly into the camera, while he's figuring out where to go for dinner: "Hmmmm…stab wounds? Stab wounds? Knives…ah, sushi would be good."

The audience, by the way, is looking at me like I'm Snoopy lying on his back saying "love me, love me." I have 'em right where I want them, and it's only my second day on the job.

"Spike is an English Bull Terrier, not a pit bull," Bud explains, "and quite certainly not a baby pig like some people have been saying."

He skims over the history of my breed—bred for dogfighting in England in the 1860s, exceptionally loyal to our owners, love people, bred down so we won't start a fight, but sure won't run from one either. All true. I'm smiling broadly, winking the eye with the black patch. But he forgets two important notes. I think it's 'cause he's slightly stoned. Not bragging, but English Bull Terriers are the supreme athletes of the canine world. Sorry, Dobermans. True. We're stronger than any dog as fast as us, and faster than any dog as strong as us. Think Jim Brown, Muhammad Ali, and a sumo wrestler in one hard-as-a-rock package that just wants to sit on your lap, watch TV, and sleep in your bed.

But how, I ask you, could Buddy boy forget this?

In World War II, my great-great-grandfather Brick went with Charlie, his Cockney owner, as part of Operation Tonga, June 6, 1944. He was in a glider platoon with the British Sixth Airborne division that landed after midnight near Caen, France. You could say that what Great-Great-Grandfather Brick did that night was the finest hour in the history of our breed. Well, maybe up to Spuds MacKenzie or that nervous-lookin' Target dog. Spuds made a ton of cashola sellin' beer. You be the judge.

Three German soldiers with three German shepherds charging ahead of them came out of the dark straight at Charlie in a small trench. The way it's told is that Brick leaped out of the trench—"sprinted like a white comet," Charlie said. He sprang five feet through the air and took down the lead shepherd in a heartbeat—crushed his throat. Charlie was firing at Krauts, who were running and shooting. The two shepherds went for Brick just as Charlie finally took down a Kraut, but the others were closing in.

"I fixed my bayonet while Brick tangled with both shepherds," Charlie would say, "and it sounded mean."

Charlie fires, nails the second Kraut, but now as he's tryin' to reload, the last Kraut gets to the trench and aims his rifle straight down at Charlie. He pulls the trigger and Charlie hears "click, click." The German's going for his pistol, which is stuck in the holster, when Brick, "blood-covered as an amputation," Charlie said, leaps at his back and knocks him into the trench, where Charlie finished him off "quite cleanly."

Three dead soldiers and three dead dogs lay on the field as Brick bled to death in Charlie's arms. He's buried in that trench. Even though he was dead, they gave him something called the Dickin Medal, Britain's highest award for what they say is valor by a military animal.

Spuds or Brick? You make the call.

The High Point, North Carolina, morning talk show was a great gig for Bud. His first show. Produced it himself. Called the shots and put me on almost every day.

I started sitting next to a lot of weird guests, all clamoring to be on TV, like the engineer who was introducing a new generation of "artificial stupidity" robots, designed to raise human self-esteem 'cause the robots got no idea where they're going or what they're doing. Or the head of the World Bedbug Foundation, "dedicated to helping America understand a most misunderstood insect."

One show had the inventor of "The Pants Enhancer," which he called a codpiece for the modern male. "Men," he asks, "feeling marginalized? Need to reassert yourself? Want to meet more women and be the talk of every party? The Pants Enhancer's your answer."

As part of the segment, Bud does the talk show demo shtick of putting one on under his jeans. Gales of laughter from the women in the audience pointing at what looks like two tennis balls and a Philadelphia cheesesteak in Bud's suddenly massive crotch wasn't exactly the kind of sexy promo Mr. Pants Enhancer had in mind.

Evangelists get high ratings in North Carolina, and we had one on almost every week. Franklin Graham commanded Bud not to smoke, drink, have sex, watch cable TV, read *The New York Times*, turn gay, or laugh too much. Then he puts his hands on my head and prays for me. Ridiculous, right? Praying for a dog? But you know, the hands got smoldering hot. I raced to the men's room and plunged my head in a toilet afterward. Maybe there's something there?

The so-called Wonder Dog isn't really doing very much, but it's all working—yawning, barking, jumping around, licking guests. My two specialties are sleeping—hot lights, comfortable chair, slow-talking guests with Southern accents; it's a miracle Bud stays awake—and food tasting after cooking demos.

Everything tastes great to me. I'm a dog, not Martha Stewart, so I hafta perform. I can't just scarf up whatever they put in the

Wonder Bowl. For example, spaghetti squash with sautéed vegetables, pine nuts, and marinara sauce with Parmesan. Love it; could down a bowl in under five seconds. But no, I gotta be discerning: a careful sniff, a hesitant small taste. A look skyward, another larger taste, a wrinkled brow during a slow, thoughtful chew. A big affirmative nod—then I inhale it in record time.

This six-step tasting routine came directly from watching Al Roker sample food on *Today*. When Bud made it to New York and I met Al, I rubbed my body against his leg and sat on his foot to thank him. Good man, short legs, big feet, nice shoes.

It's embarrassing to recount it, but my private parts were causing trouble. A couple times, I rolled over in my chair to sleep on my back, making it kinda easy to spot two white, fur-covered balls. That's when everybody in North Carolina realized that you don't see a lot of balls on dogs these days.

Bud gets hauled into his boss Lombardo's office, and Lombardo tells him that Animal Control, as a so-called public service, is offering to have me "reproductively reorganized," which is the stupid term that the crazy woman who runs the place uses instead of "neutered."

She wants to do the surgery live on the show and give a two-for-one deal—which technically is a four-for-one—to people with unneutered male dogs. Then she's sayin' she'll fit me with Neuticles—testicle implants for neutered dogs. Like a Pants Enhancer, but balls. Revolting.

Luckily, I know Bud doesn't want to reproductively reorganize me 'cause of what happened with Brenda when I was a puppy.

Brenda's his hot girlfriend. Oils her legs, law student at Guilford College—not vet school like the other one, or she'd be shoving me full of needles for practice. Brenda and me are mostly OK, but she's on top of Bud all the time—actually she is on top of him all the time; it's her favorite position—because I'm taking leaks all over the house. I'm missing the Wee-Wee pads by a mile and claiming the edges of the couch as prime spots to hit.

"What are we going to do about this puppy, Bud?"

"Huh?"

"You got to get Spike fixed," she says.

My ears fly up.

"He's not broken," Bud says.

"He's urinating all over the house. Get him fixed; he'll be easier to train."

If you're gonna be a lawyer, Brenda, you gotta come up with better than that.

"Nobody has unneutered dogs these days," she says.

Generalization. Proceed, Bud.

"There's no way he's getting neutered," Bud says. "He's from the best bloodlines, and I'm gonna breed him."

Yes!

Now an argument explodes. Brenda's trying to prosecute me with crap like I'm gonna die sooner and get cancer of the balls, blah, blah, blah. She won't let up, and she's pissing Bud off, 'cause my pissing's pissing her off.

Finally Bud says in a different, extra-loud voice than the one he uses on TV, "Love me, love my dog's balls, Brenda!"

Brenda takes her framed autographed photo of Marcia Clark, her luxury sex toy catalogs, her Agent Provocateur thong collection, and moves out.

Case closed at home.

But at work, Lombardo's the boss and he seems real sensitive to the concerns of the Animal Control woman, 'cause she's married to Mayor Gordon, the crooked slob who's supposed to be running the city of High Point. At WGHP-TV, Lombardo gets what he wants.

So he, too, may be out for my balls. Basically, I got no problem with Lombardo; we like each other's strength. He's a big, handsome Sicilian and tough. He makes Pacino's Michael Corleone look like a pizza delivery boy.

But at the time of Ballsgate, Bud's in hot water with Lombardo. What happened is, Bud and old Kris Kristofferson are out back swappin' a big doobie after the show when Lombardo himself appears to partake of a Chesterfield, and he's enraged 'cause they're breakin' the law smoking weed on station property. Kris gets them both outta trouble by singing "Me and Bobby McGee" to Lombardo's wife over the phone. But Bud's still on the shit list.

So, there's this meeting. Lombardo, Bud, me, and the Animal Control woman, Doris Gordon, who's saying it's a community service to cut off my balls as a good example to pet owners everywhere. Lombardo's nodding like they're not his balls we're talking about, when in bursts Brenda, acting like she's Elizabeth Warren in a push-up bra.

She's presenting a legal case for me to keep my balls. Seems that Bud bribed her with a dinner at Pierre's if she'd put together an argument that my balls were Bud's property or something… not sure. So we win but later learn that Lombardo was jerking our chain. He tells us he "just had the meeting 'cause that dingbat Doris Gordon is the mayor's wife."

High Point was simple and fun with Bud at the controls. Nowhere near as much of the shit that would get thrown at us when we went to NYC. I always thought we shoulda just stayed in High Point. Plus, I had a yard. Bud set it up for me to practice things like jumping over stacks of bricks, bouncing around in a circle like Muhammad Ali, throwing truck tires gaily in the air, or using my jaws to hang by a big rope knot for endless hours. Try doing any of that in a one-bedroom apartment at Sixty-Third and Madison.

When I was around age one, Bud had a birthday party for me on the show. This actually leads to us getting on *The Tonight Show* for a dog-trick segment.

The guests are station employees' pets—as if I know them or actually care. There's a big bulldog, friendly but dumb as a chew toy. A just-washed mixed breed, who's an OK dog except for bad breath. A bored cat, two blue parakeets, and an English springer spaniel who keeps barking frantically at the birds and has to be dragged out of the studio.

The first special guest is Lassie with Russ, his trainer. This is big for me. I'm a huge fan of Lassie's work—always impressed that Lassie wore a mange costume to costar as the ratty Sam the Dog with John Wayne in *Hondo*. Oh, and newsflash—Lassie is the first real transgender showbiz star. Yeah, long before your Bruce Jenners, you had Pal, a male collie playing female Lassie. This Lassie is like the eighth generation bred from Pal, and I think maybe they've gradually become more and more naturally effeminate.

So Lassie minces over to me. I gotta say my heart is beating fast—it's Lassie! But I also gotta remember Lassie is actually Barry. And Lassie-Barry plants this long lick on me starting under my chin, then going over my nose and halfway up my head. People are goin' nuts. Things are spinnin' around. The camerawoman says to Bud, "Spike's verklempt." The next thing I know, I've rolled over on my back and I'm wagging the tail, so of course they cut to commercial—'cause, again, my balls are showin'.

Next up is some dog trainer guy named Cesar who wrote a book claimin' you could train your dog in fifteen minutes. Wanna get on TV? All you gotta do is write a book sayin' you can do something complicated, like adding a front porch with solar panels to your house, in only fifteen minutes. It takes Bud longer than fifteen minutes to clean up after me.

Cesar's got some juicy chunks of fillet in his pocket, and he's telling everybody he's gonna train me to offer my paw like I'm shakin' hands. I figure, he gets the paw when the pocket's empty, and after fourteen chunks of raw meat I give it to him. Had so much beef I started passing gas, which woke up the bulldog and somehow offended Lassie.

On the commercial break, Bud says, "Wait'll you see this, Spike." So I'm expecting Cher. But no. Who lumbers out but Pluto on a big leash with Mickey Mouse from the Coliseum's *Disney World on Ice*. I'm underwhelmed, but I bark like I'm trapped in a hot car, 'cause I'm startin' to learn the phony side of the business.

Mickey's waving his hand like he's the Pope. But Mickey's done for me. He's totally lost it. Original Mickey had an edge, would get pissed off on occasion, maybe even punch somebody out. Modern Mickey just smiles all the time like every TV weatherman. Pluto's cool. Been a good friend to Mickey, so he's OK. But I'm hopin' Donald Duck's gonna waddle out, 'cause he's my favorite, hasn't lost it, and basically, I like ducks. But no Donald.

Pluto's clumpin' toward me, and I jump off my chair and lick his face, which smells like a wet cardboard box. The guy inside says, "Hi, Spike. I'm Pluto. Happy birthday." I look in his eyehole, and sweat's pourin' off his head and dripping outta Pluto's nose. "It's way too fuckin' hot in here," he says.

Music comes on. It's Donna Summer's "Bad Girl." They probably played it for Lassie. All of us are dancing around to end the show. Lassie starts bumping his ass against me harder and harder. Not a hump but a major twerk. I growl. He stops cold and runs over to Russ. Bud and Cesar are lookin' stupid dancing alone. Mickey's doing his mechanical Pope-like wave, just as the guy in the Pluto suit throws up straight outta Pluto's left eye. Lassie's covered with barf as the credits start to roll.

17

That night I'm sound asleep in my doghouse in the yard and I'm yanked out, and we're headed to the ice show at the Coliseum. Bud and me have to be there for some kind of cross promotion with the station. My mood is not the best, 'cause I figured I was in for the night.

We get there at intermission. When the lights go down, this big stupid formal voice booms, "Ladies and gentlemen, kindly direct your attention…" We head out on the ice. I'm stickin' close to Bud in case he falls, 'cause he can't skate and looks about as flexible as Frankenstein doing Pilates.

A spotlight hits them as they glide out waving—Mickey, Minnie, Goofy, Pluto, Daisy, and Donald. I see him, and something snaps. I don't know; I love Donald Duck I guess, and plus my paws are freezin'—killin' me. So I take off chasin' Donald. I'm slippin' and slidin' and Bud's yelling "stop," and the crowd is going nuts. Totally, totally nuts. You'd think I'm Bryce Harper rounding the bases after a grand slam.

I'm gainin' on Donald, and unless he's got eyes in the back of the costume, he has no idea he's being chased by a fifty-pound dog. The crowd starts chanting, "Spike…Spike…."

I'm running beside Donald, and I bang up against him to say hi. I don't mean to, but I knock Donald sideways. He's about to fall, so I jump high to catch him by his big yellow beak, but as I come down I got the whole Donald head in my jaws. The little woman in the Donald suit is skating after me to get the head. I'm havin' fun. Glad I woke up. The paws are warm, so why not take a victory lap on the ice with Donald's head?

Bud's crew has the thing on tape, and three days later we're off to do a "pet stunt of the week," on Jimmy Fallon's *Tonight Show* in New York. But first we have to do a goodwill visit to the Donald costume woman in the hospital, 'cause her neck's in traction.

2

New York: The First Time

So we fly to New York. You don't like flying? Try it as a dog. I'm crammed in a crate. You need more legroom? I can't even turn my head. Bud begged, but he couldn't get me a seat 'cause they said I'm too big.

After I get unloaded, we're in a cab. I've never been in a back seat before, and this is like a cage. I usually ride up front with my head in Bud's lap thinkin' about all the other heads that've been down there. The cab driver smells like a falafel stand, and he's honking like a war's over while calling three other drivers "asshole" at the same time.

Out the window I see people running around like it's their last day on earth, and they got faces that look like they're enduring a rectal worm check. Several guys are walking holding hands. Not something you spot much on the streets of High Point, except maybe during the furniture market week. I know plenty of gay dogs—they're a lotta' fun, keep their houses neat. You gotta figure they don't like breeding too much, but they end up bein' very good parents with their puppies.

At *The Tonight Show* there's a table full of food. So I jump up and pull off a tray of chopped liver molded to look like Jimmy Fallon's head. Bud's not happy, but Diana Lewis, the producer who booked us, is hysterical 'cause Jimmy's nose landed on her shoe. She's cute and is patient with Bud.

"Will I get to meet Jimmy?" Bud asks.

"Jimmy usually doesn't see all the guests before the taping."

"Does he know about me and my show down South?"

"I gave him your stuff and…if he reads it…" she says.

"Well, I just thought if he could mention, you know, *Southern Exposure*, the show, it would help us out."

Bud's chatting up Diana Lewis. I'm eating Jimmy's head off the rug when in walks Willie Nelson. Bud's glad to see him, 'cause Willie's been on our show. I bump up against him and Willie scratches my head and sits on the couch. He's a little bit creaky, so I'm not sure he'll be able to get up too easily.

But he hops outta his seat to say hi to Ike Piles, a boxer on to promote his pay-per-view fight. "Call me Money Piles, Willie. I Ike 'I Got Money' Piles," he says, while launchin' a bro hug on Willie that bends him in half. Then he spots me.

"Who dat? Who dat? Look at him! He bad! Look at him!" he yells at the three big guys and four women who came in with him. He's fingering the new black collar with tiny spikes that Bud got me for the show. He's panting heavily just looking at me.

"Money Piles buy this bitch! He tough. He fighter like Ike 'I Got Money' Piles be! Money Piles buy him. Who I pay?"

One of the big guys hands him a pile of cash the size of a catcher's mitt, and he starts rippin' off hundred-dollar bills when Bud tells 'em I'm not for sale.

"Money give you ten thousand dollars for this badass dog right now."

Bud says, "No, sorry, can't do it."

"Money give you ten thousand dollars and whole case of Money's new Money cologne. Wear it, you smell like Money smells. We all wearin' it."

"Yes, I couldn't help but notice that," Bud says.

"What it smell like to you?" Money asks.

Bud sniffs Money, then sniffs one of the girls. I'm wonderin' if he'll get it right, 'cause soon as they walked in I gave it a dog-sniff ID.

"Smells like a combo of gardenias and overcooked peas," Bud says.

"He right, he right!" Money yells. "Money brew first batch in kitchen. We gonna make millions sayin', 'Women love you when you smell like Money.'"

He looks down at me. "He bad! Money give you twenty thousand dollars, give you free Bunny Ranch loyalty card, and you take Cartier, Ra'sheed'duh? and my crew of butter girls home tonight. They butter girls 'cause their legs got that natural spread. They spend more time on their knees than San Francisco Forty-Niners. After a night with them, you're gonna say, 'My erectile tissue miss you.'"

Money finally notices everybody in the room staring at him with their mouths wide open.

"Oh yeah," he says. "Oh yeah, I so bad…"

One of his men whispers in Money Piles' ear. "Shit yeah," Money says. "And plus, for dog, Money Piles give you ground-floor franchise opportunity in Money's new masturbation app, called Palm. It work twice as fast as ordinary masturbation apps, so you finish your business in half the time and you back to loungin' around the house twice as sooner!"

"Huh?" Bud says. "What?"

"Explain that," Willie asks, eyes twinkling.

Money pulls out his Vertu phone to show them the app.

"Money make Palm app use same blue and white color design as Calm app. So everybody think they buyin' Calm, but they gettin' Palm. Real quick they find Palm keepin' them calmer than Calm. The franchise deal be like Tupperware parties with happy endings. Just give me that leash, man. I'm gonna party with this beast. He carry belt to ring next fight."

Money Piles is breathing hard, Bud's staring at the cash, and the girls are looking at him like he'd be a big break from the usual nighttime routine with Money Piles.

Bud says, "No sale, sorry."

Diana Lewis says, "Hey, Bud, Jimmy wants to meet you and Spike."

We don't meet Jimmy Fallon; she just wants to get us outta there. She sits us in a room with no food and comes back later and tells Bud that Money Piles is trying to buy Willie's guitar.

Bud and Diana go over what we're doing. Jimmy's gonna show the video. Some iPhone stuff went viral, but ours was shot by Bud's crew guy skating next to me on the ice. Bud and me are in the audience. Jimmy will show the clip, then we're supposed to run up onstage and I do my trick—which is hanging by my jaws clamped to a big knot on a rope for two segments of the show, around fourteen minutes.

Diana says they're gonna have something on me called Jaw Cam so viewers can see me hangin' there every once in a while when Willie's on. Easy stuff. All Bud's gotta do is lift me to the knot, which is five feet off the floor, 'cause my vertical leap is only four feet. It'll take another year till I can maybe nail a full six-footer.

Bud's pacing around backstage hoping to meet Jimmy and introduce himself. No luck. He has to walk me, which is the low point of my life up till then, 'cause I'm takin' a monstrous smoldering dump outside Rockefeller Center, with the entire *Tonight Show* audience standing in line cheering me and taking pictures. To make it worse, Bud has to scoop it up with two *Cher Show Playbill*s he picks up off the sidewalk.

We're in the freezing-cold studio audience. Diana told us Jimmy likes the place cold as a meat locker. Jimmy tells Money Piles he's the only guest he ever had who never used verbs. Bud thinks this is funny. Everybody in the audience has a self-satisfied look pasted on their face, 'cause they actually got in to see the show, so they're roaring at everything, including a lot of crap that's not close to funny. I'm relaxed, cool, and loosening my jaw for the big clamp.

We're up. They show the video with multiple slow-motion shots of me rippin' off Donald's head. He even has a short clip of the woman in traction lyin' in her hospital bed tryin' to wave a couple of fingers. The hospital shot gets the biggest laugh of the show so far. Diana said, "I knew this would work." I'm wonderin' how the little Donald Duck woman's feeling about bein' set up like that when Jimmy Fallon calls us up.

The only question Jimmy asks Bud is, "Are we safe, or is he going to grow more?" Bud says I'll get bigger and add fifteen more pounds of muscle, which is happy news to me. Bud bends down to lift me to the rope's knot, and on the way up I hear this crunching sound and a muffled screech from Bud. I guess sitting in that freezing-cold audience tightened up his back. And I know the back's been outta whack for a day or two, 'cause he's been goin' at it heavy with his latest, Rhonda, who's working her way through rabbinical school as an aerial dancer at the Taboo Gentlemen's Club in Greensboro.

I'm hanging by my jaw lookin' down at Bud, who's squirming in pain on the floor. Jimmy Fallon's playing this like it's part of the act and getting big laughs. I could let go of the rope and drag Bud offstage, but I know Bud wants me to stay with the clamp trick. I hold on and watch him try to crawl off while The Roots play Sly Stone's "Stand."

Diana gives Bud some heavy-duty Vicodin pain pills, and for a few days he's very happy and doesn't care that he never actually met Jimmy.

3

CELEBRITY

We get back to High Point, and Bud's now got a bug up his ass to get his own show in New York. I've had a bug up my ass; it's horrible. I figure this New York thing is 'cause of the pain pills. Bud's always a dynamo of energy—one of the reasons Lombardo hired him—but with the pills he's having delusions of grandeur about what he can do. The pills are makin' some of his "stoned ideas"—like painting my doghouse orange to match sunsets—look like Supreme Court decisions.

He's talkin' about getting hobbies, like being a trapeze artist, when the guy can't stand on one foot to put on a loafer. Anyway, he runs outta pills, is a zombie for a day, but he's still talking "New York, New York" in his sleep.

Meanwhile Lombardo, who'd be the sharpest pup in any litter, is promotin' the Fallon spot like Bud won a combo Academy Award and Nobel Peace Prize. He's telling every little station in the South that *Southern Exposure* is the hottest local show in America. Seems the idea of a host like Bud in a tiny market like High Point doing *The Tonight Show* is some kind of media miracle. Lombardo's makin' it out like Bud can walk on water; forget the fact that he fell on his ass and Diana Lewis had to drag him offstage.

Before Jimmy Fallon, before I came on yawnin' that day, Bud was doin' just great. He was beating the *Today* show every day, and Lombardo was happy. But now Lombardo blows us up into a syndicated six-market morning show that scores double *Today*'s ratings and is raking in wads of cash for all concerned.

Bud gets a raise, and life is better than ever, except he's still playing that damn "New York, New York" song by Frank Sinatra ten times a day. For a while he was playing the Liza Minnelli version till I bit the CD in half.

He rents a way nicer house down the road in Thomasville, where we've been livin'. So I get a bigger fenced-in yard, and the Budster gets a pool, and with it, his long-awaited chance to study string bikini theory.

Of course, neither of us knows I can't swim. First weekend at the new place, it's hot. Bud's retreated to the house with Alicia, who's in med school at Duke and may or may not work at The Geyser massage parlor.

I figure they went in to get beers and they're not inside boinkin' away at it, 'cause Bud's pack of Burt Reynolds Longest Yard Condoms is on the table from last night when Rhonda dropped by to surprise him. Anyway, I'm boilin' hot, and I got these gnats flyin' around my eyes, so I figure I'll jump in the pool like Bud's been doing. I'm just planning to paddle around for a little while to cool off.

I've seen Lassie forging rivers on his show. Spuds had a pool party in a Super Bowl commercial, so why not? In I go, and I sink like a bowling ball. Paddling the legs, sinking. Paddling, sinking, paddling, sinking. Next I'm standing on the bottom like a hippo. Then I'm walking. Yeah, like I'm strollin' down Main Street, 'cept

I'm eight feet underwater and my chest is pounding like it's gonna explode. I'm not seeing any white light with my mother barking at the end of a tunnel, but this must be what dyin' is.

Next thing I know, Bud's pounding the hell outta my back, and I'm real dizzy but OK. Turns out he was comin' out of the house for the condoms when he spotted me. Thank you, Bud. Thank you, Alicia. Just sorry I missed the sight of Bud divin' into the pool usin' his big woody as a rudder.

Even more than before, Lombardo takes Bud under his wing. Warning him all about gettin' famous and its pitfalls—like winning Best in Show, I figure.

"You're a nice guy, Bud," Lombard says. "Maybe too nice. In show business you gotta cultivate the ability to say 'fuck you' with clarity and precision. And remember what Ailes used to say: 'In this business you can never be too paranoid.'" With all the pot Bud's smokin', I figure he's got that one covered.

Then Lombardo says somethin' that hits me. "And remember, Bud, you never get a second chance to make a first impression." I realize a lotta times when I'm meeting people I'm staring off into space not thinking about much except the next meal or that I'll never see my brothers and sisters again. One day you're an eight-week-old havin' fun wrestlin' around with 'em, and then someone reaches in the pen and your sister is gone. Kinda haunts me.

So now to make an impression I pant, smile, show a little tongue, and wag like I'm trying to go airborne using my tail. I worked on havin' a gleam in my eye like Bud does when he's meetin' some-body, but I was scaring people by looking demonic.

The show's more work now, so Lombardo gets Buffy McQueen to handle mail and help get guests. Buffy's cute, blonde, freckles. She's Bud's type. But sometimes I think any babe with fresh lipstick and personal lubricant in her handbag is Bud's type. Lombardo

27

tells Bud, "Don't get your meat where you get your potatoes," as some kind of food warning to keep things business between them.

Not sure what that really means, but anyway, every day piles of mail are comin' in to Bud. People are sending him books, sweaters, photos of their dogs—which Buffy always shows me. I saw a couple cute bitches there I'd like to snuggle up with on a rainy afternoon. But more than anything else, we're getting Bibles—stacks and stacks of Bibles. "This is the Bible Belt," Buffy says. And that's where I get Bud in trouble.

One morning, I'm lyin' around chewing on one of the Bibles piled on the floor while studying Buffy's shoes. Don't know where she bought 'em, but not from Shoe Town like everybody else in High Point. Got a dog? Guarantee you they possess a profound knowledge of footwear.

I've been lyin' there for a while and all of a sudden, I'm in the mood for one of my sprints around the block. Took Bud a while to adjust to this, but I go out the revolving door and run around the block as fast as I can and come back quite refreshed. So I set out with the Bible in my mouth, 'cause I like carryin' something when I run—good for the neck muscles. But the Bible's not heavy enough, so I circle back to the office and dig out a long plastic thing—it's like a bumpy, veiny bone—from a box of stuff from some sex therapist that's tryin' to get on the show.

I'm out the door and chargin' around the block havin' big fun, 'cause the bone thing's vibrating and tickling my mouth. I stop to take a leak on a couple of rocks on the curb, and this guy with a white collar on backward starts screaming at me to give him the Bible. I spot a big cross dangling from his neck and figure he's a minister, not some wacko going to a Halloween party. Then he sees the bone thing and yells, "Oh my God, that's a dildo!"

He's trying to get the Bible away from the dildo, and I'm thinkin', "Padre, you and your ten disciples aren't gonna pry open these jaws today." He's screamin' and yankin' and yankin' at the Bible. A crowd's gathering and a cop's pointing a gun at me like if I don't drop the Bible, he's gonna do his civic duty as a cop and blast me off the face of the earth. Someone yells, "Don't shoot him; that's The Wonder Dog," so a kid runs to get Bud.

A reporter and crew from channel three, the rival station across the street, shows up to video the hunched-over minister wrestling me for the Bible. Bud comes charging in. I drop the mangled Bible as the dildo goes into overdrive, twisting like a giant pink eel. The minister snatches the Bible and reads, "Dear Bud, care for this holy book. My beloved aunt Marie served in the Sacred Order of the La Leche Sisters. She read this every night in the nunnery. May it also help you fight temptation by remaining celibate."

Bud's got the wriggling dildo in one hand, and he grabs the Bible with the other as the reporter asks, "Well, Bud, what do you have to say about this?"

The station across the street is a CBS affiliate that'll do anything to beat us in news ratings. They even spent a ton of money on a custom-made Scott Pelly anchorman robot. The thing's good—actually, it's way more lifelike than Scott Pelly, which caught the attention of network brass, so they're secretly working on a virtual Walter Cronkite.

They run the story big. The Pelly robot covers the Bible-dildo incident like ISIS invaded the High Point furniture market and set up base camp in the Raymour & Flanigan showroom.

Because of this caper, I'm now a problematic topic, and Lombard's nervous.

"That dog could get us in big trouble," he says. He won't take me off the show 'cause of my considerable fan base. He decides to make me an employee at ten dollars a week, so I'm covered by liability insurance. I never see a penny of that money, by the way.

Lombardo says to Bud, "What are you going to do about this? Minister Jordon and his congregation can't get the picture outta their heads of you with a Bible in one hand; a writhing, half-chewed dildo in the other; and your dog grinning manically into the camera. They want you fired. Whadda you say?"

"Fuck you with clarity and precision."

"What?" Lombardo screams.

"Kidding, Boss, kidding."

"This is no joke, Bud."

So Bud says he'll calm the waters of the Bible thumpers at the minister's church by going Sunday morning to offer a complete apology. This'll be the first time Bud's been to church since he was twelve and got flunked outta vacation Bible school for answering that Mel Brooks was the "King of the Jews," not Jesus. So the Budster takes this challenge real serious. Saturday night he's not at Pierre's for a wine-soaked dinner with some babe. He's home at his little desk workin' on his speech, telling me, "This is gonna be great!"

Sunday morning Bud sets out to deliver the goods. He's tall and handsome and lookin' sharp in his black suit, white shirt, and black knit tie. The George Clooney look, he calls it.

He gets up there in the pulpit with that big smile and slowly starts reading some lyrics from Stevie Wonder's song "As." This stuns the congregation into realizing this is as close as they'll ever get to black gospel music. The nickname for the place is "Church of the Redeeming Albino." The congregation's so lily white, they don't even get tans in summer.

He transforms from TV Bud into evangelist Bud. He quotes his favorite George Carlin line on religion: "As we all well know, 'There's an invisible man who lives in the sky…who sees everything you do…'"

"Amen, he's staring down at me now!" someone yells.

"He saw me do laundry yesterday!" a woman in the first row screams.

"Does he watch me when I poo?" a little boy cries out.

"Not if you flush," his father tells him.

Bud quiets the crowd and begins preaching about the power of forgiveness and launches into his love of small-town life.

Somehow he's making sense touching on the connected spiritual merits of raising the minimum wage, medical marijuana, organic farming, gay rights, Ram Dass, the legacy of President Eisenhower, and the value of saying "you're welcome" instead of "no problem."

He begs everybody to put down their cell phones and connect with their loved ones. "Would Jesus use a selfie stick?" he asks, which makes no sense, but people are yellin' "amen!" He closes with an a cappella version of some old Broadway song, "You Gotta Have Heart," the same one he sang to win an eighth-grade singing contest.

31

The whole congregation is gapin' wide-eyed at Bud. They're ready to elect him president of Liberty University. Problem is, they want more, so for the next couple of weeks he's fighting hangovers while deliverin' Sunday morning sermons. He always includes some inspirational show tune. But after he sings "I Am What I Am," about a cross-dresser from *La Cage aux Folles*, he's not invited back.

Before our big TV success, there was never much payin' attention to us on the streets of High Point, except the summer when Bud was dating Margaret, the engineering major and bathing suit model who wore Edith Lances projection bras under white tank tops. Lotta gawkin' at us then. Had something to do with something Bud called "thrust."

It used to be a wave, a "Hi, Bud." But now people are starin' at him like he's an eye chart. They always glance at me—'cause I'm bright white, built like a statue, and have a certain charisma. I may get petted a little more, but it's not interruptin' my daily routine.

Now, Bud's bein' stopped all the time, accosted by oddballs who think he's got nothin' to do all day but chatter about all manner of drivel, like their collection of limited-edition wet-wipes plastic containers or the wind velocity on the Outer Banks, or how long the fish live in their pond. Pure crap that Bud listens to with his usual rectitude, like they're reciting verse from *The Great Gatsby*. They want him to meet their grandmother at a pie supper, join a bowling team, or get them tickets to the Christmas show at Radio City Music Hall.

They think 'cause Bud's on TV, he has a magic power to do anything. A woman comes to the station for him to get her upgraded to first class on a flight to Acapulco. Bud's never flown first class in his life.

The worst is people tryin' to get on the show. Bud says, "I see this look in their eyes when they spot me. They come over like they're just gonna say hello, but they really just want something. They think TV exposure'll make 'em rich. Maybe they've got a niece I should get on *Dancing with the Stars* or some cousin who's a chiropractor who's gotta be on the show as soon as possible, 'cause he thinks my spine is in grave danger."

I growl to scare them off, but it doesn't work. Why is everybody obsessed with getting on TV?

And Bud's too nice. He's tryin' to make everybody happy, wearin' himself out. Then one day on the show he's got Regis Philbin, and after they go out for lunch and talk about the TV business.

Bud says, "I'm really happy here, great life, but it's not enough. I want to leave this little market and get a show in New York and live the New York life."

Regis thinks and gives Bud the name of 'a guy who knows a guy who knows a guy' who might be looking for a show host. "I don't know if it's New York, but check it out."

Bud tells Regis about this pressure he's feelin' from people who want a chunk of him. "You think these people really care about you?" Regis asks. "One day you'll get replaced, and they'll knock you over trying to meet the new guy. A person who tries to make everybody happy is doomed to failure. Focus on the important things in life, Bud, not fame."

Problem is, Bud doesn't have a lot of the "real stuff"—just me, the show, and a succession of babes who seem to be irresistibly drawn to working in the exotic services industry while studying for advanced degrees.

So Bud calls Regis' guy who knows a guy who knows a guy who's shooting a pilot for a reality show, but he won't tell Bud the idea 'cause they're afraid someone will steal it. But knowin' now what it was, I don't think that woulda been a problem. Bud ships them video of the interviews he shot at the Greater Greensboro golf tournament.

They call him. He's got the job if he can get a week off and come to Fort Myers to shoot the pilot for a show they're callin' *I'd Live with Goats to Be on TV.*

Right away, I get the sense we're not talkin' *American Masters.*

Bud's all hot to do it—to make the extra bread, have some fun, maybe break nationally, 'cause they tell him it's for major syndication. The big challenge is convincing Lombardo to let him host a reality show costarring goats. I'm hopin' the boss is gonna say no—don't get me started on what I think of goats.

Bud explains the premise to Lombardo: "A family signs a contract—they gotta have their home rigged with cameras and then live there with a herd of untrained Caribbean roadside goats for five days."

"People living with goats?" Lombardo says. "What the fuck?"

Bud tells him that the goats will have full run of the house but can't be let outside. "My job is to go in each morning and evening to report on what it's like for people to live with goats."

Right now, I'm prayin' I don't get dragged into this.

"It's hard to interview people when you're wearing a gas mask, Bud, 'cause that's what you're going to need to go into that house. The average goat produces ten pounds of manure a day," Lombardo says.

"How do you know this stuff?" Bud asks.

"Bud, there are some things that are just common knowledge when you've had a liberal arts education at an expensive, obscure college," he says.

"Hmm…well…hadn't thought about any of that, but here's the thing. If they make it through the five days, they win," Bud explains.

"What do they win?"

"That's the great thing; they don't win anything. They just get to be famous for living with goats on prime-time TV. The producers figure the sky's the limit for the winners in pop culture after that—book deals, shovel endorsements, political office. Who knows?"

"I'm saving your career right now," Lombardo says. "You're not doing this. Don't say another word; just get outta here and get ready for your interview with Itzhak Perlman, or should I tell the maestro you've run off with goats?"

That night, it's drinks at The Dive Bar with Buffy and Phil Froth, the gay weatherman. That's not Phil's on-air title, by the way. We're havin' a great time. Nobody's more fun than Buffy after four drinks, and Phil and Bud are pals. Sometimes we go to his house for parties, which are great, 'cause he uses ballet dancers to park cars. He calls it ballet valet 'cause they pirouette around the cars and lift some passengers over the doors.

Phil has two martinis. I'm enjoying a Bloody Bull shot—one's my limit, ever since I had three and fell over. Bud's on his third Duvel and finally admits he's come to his senses about the stupid goat show.

"Lombardo was right again," Bud says. But Phil Froth loves the idea. He says he's been crazy about goats ever since he dated the Annapolis midshipman who was the caretaker of Bill the goat, the mascot of the U.S. Naval Academy.

Bud gives Phil the guy's number, and Phil sends off his tape. Two days later the guy's guy calls Phil to do the pilot. Phil buys a gas mask and drives to Fort Myers.

I'd Live with Goats to Be on TV never got aired—'cause of somethin' to do with concerns about goats' rights brought about by the surging popularity of Baby Goat Yoga. The producers kept rewriting and refinin' their goat concept, and the rumor is that it might have led to a program called *The Great British Baking Show*.

Phil ends up back on TV spouting weather in Fort Myers, and tells Bud he's marrying the show's goat herder, who's quitting goat management to launch Far Out, a website for gay men who're so far out of the closet, they're back in.

Lombardo's gotta find a new weatherman, and I get sucked into the search. Phil Froth was always as nervous as a border collie around Lombardo, scared of him 'cause of his tough Don Corleone style. You know, I always thought the only thing missing from that *Godfather* movie was a dog. When they went to shoot Brando at that vegetable market, if he'd had a 120-pound Italian Mastiff, instead of that wimp Fredo, things would've been different. Anyway, Phil Froth took off in the middle of the night, and when he's safely outta town, he texts Lombardo that he quit.

Lombardo doesn't yell and scream. Just says to Bud, "One door closes, another one opens. We'll get a better weatherman." Lombardo's got this look in his eye like when he catches Phil Froth he's gonna staple him to the weather map.

First night he makes the news anchor Sam Halloway stand up and do the weather. This is a big insult to Sam, who thinks he's the reincarnation of Edward R. Morrow, except he can't read the prompter, is a bad reporter, and has a lisp. He's always tellin' Bud, "I want to be a ssthar."

Bud gets a call from Lombardo at home. We've finished our jog together; Bud's had dinner and is stoned watching *Extra*, tryin' to calculate the depth of Mario Lopez's dimples, when he picks up the phone. "You and that dog are doing weather tomorrow night. Come up with something and make it work."

Bud's high as a kite, so crazy stoned ideas are rushing through his head real fast. "We'll end each forecast with the Wonder

Weather Bark," he tells me. He's been tryin' to teach me this stupid finger-bark routine where he shows one finger, I bark once; two, twice, etc. But I can't get it down. Maybe I got a learnin' disability. I can jump over a Volkswagen, but I can't count to five. "And," Bud says—now set yourself for his big idea—"I'll be The Singing Weatherman!" He tells me, "There's never been a singing weatherman on TV. I'll be a pioneer."

He's so excited that he has to switch to *PBS NewsHour* to calm down.

They might have constructed *Saturday Night Live* on pot, but The Singing Weatherman wouldn't have made the cut.

We're on. We're live. I'm standin' under a dumb cardboard sign that says, "The Wonder Weather Dog." I'm nervous and studying Bud's hands, tryin' to practice the signals. Sam Halloway lisps it over to Bud who says, "Thanks, Sam. I'm Bud your singing weatherman; as far as the weather tonight and tomorrow morning"—and he belts out—"there's no sun up in the sky. It's stormy weather." "But," he says, "starting tomorrow afternoon"—he starts singing again—"you'll have the sunshine in your life…yeah…yeah, for three days it'll be around…yeah, yeah."

Lombardo's in the studio, and he's got that 'I'm gonna nail Bud to the weather map' look on his face. "Now," Bud says, "it's time for our official Wonder Weather Bark three-day forecast."

Our graphic comes up. One bark = sun, two = clouds, three = rain, four = major storm and flooding, five = evacuate: cyclone and hurricane. We got three days of sun comin' up, so all I need to do is bark once each time Bud says a day. He flashes me a finger. I look at it like I'm tryin' to read the small print on the directions you get with any product made in China, which, unfortunately, is most products.

I'm nervous, panicked like I'm under water again. He flashes me the "one" again, and I bark a couple of times, I think four.

Bud says, "Let's try that again, Weather Dog." And I just start barking and barking and keep barking, and they have to drag me outta the studio 'cause I'm barking madly during the sports report.

Lombardo, Bud, and Buffy spend the next hour answerin' calls telling people not to evacuate. The next day Lombardo orders Bud to monitor his pot smoking and "go over to the North Carolina School of the Arts and find some beautiful girl in the TV department who could do weather."

Instead, Bud goes to an improv comedy class to find a black girl who does a perfect Oprah Winfrey impression. They rig up some padding to make her look eighty pounds heavier, and that's how our station got "The Big O's Weather Report," which Lombardo said upped our news ratings 40 percent.

"And it was all a stoned idea," Bud tells Buffy.

4

LOMBARDO

Bein' dragged out of the studio barking during Marv Herbert's sports report was not my finest hour. After the show, Marv's yellin' at me, but Lombardo comes to my defense. "The dog was nervous, Marv. Remember your first night? You called the Carolina Panthers the Black Panthers three times, and then said Brandon Stokley was Stokley Carmichael. Klan guys over in Caswell County thought you were sending a coded message." Marv slinks off to have several drinks.

And now, for whatever reason, Lombardo every so often wants me in his office with the big desk with nothin' on top of it and three giant TVs on the walls. He's asking me questions like he thinks I'm the Enigma machine of daytime television.

"Whadda you think of her?" He points at Ellen DeGeneres. Ellen loves dogs—what am I gonna do, betray her? I pant. Somehow I think he gets it. He switches to people screamin' on the Maury Povich show. Turn my head away, can't watch. Then swarms of tattooed people clawin' at each other on Springer. I head for the door. Lombardo tells me, "They got a dentist at the Springer show to give guests false teeth, 'cause they're showing up with big gaps in their mouths." They should cement their jaws shut, I think. I'm hopin' to see my favorite, Maria Bartiromo. If she could sing, I might take her over Cher.

Commercials come on.

There's a hardworking guy who takes one Aleve pain pill and who's bragging that hours later while he's still working his ass off, he's blissfully happy 'cause he doesn't have to bother to stop to take a second pill like he would with another brand. Seems to me, a thirty-second pill break might somehow be a welcome pause.

We see this Cialis commercial where they're showin' handsome, stubble-faced men with a fake confident look in their eye "for when the time is right." When the time is right with Bud, he's not actin' like these guys. These guys are trying to initiate action by givin' the woman a tiny peck on the lips like they're standing at the front door after a 1950s prom date knowing that her parents are peering at them through the window.

"Whadda you think of her?" he says. "Judge Judy." I'm nodding approval, thinkin' it's nice to see an old lady on TV, and he says he thinks she's had a facelift. Guess she'd have to have a twin sister for me to know what she really looks like. I'm confused by Family Feud. I can't figure the anatomical reason for how the host, Steve Harvey, can talk and smile while showin' all his teeth. Maybe it's some kind of special dentistry, or media training.

Bud comes to get me, and Lombardo says, "You know, Bud, I think that dog could work for Nielsen."

I can tell that Bud can't figure out what I'm doin' in the boss' office. But I think Lombardo just wants a little company beyond most of the employees who're always telling him what they think he wants to hear. Sometimes he even says nice things to me he wouldn't say around Bud. "You're not the worst dog I ever met;

you're really a strong son of a bitch. Now I know why Patton had a dog like you. My dog, Doc, is tough, but I wouldn't want him messing with you." One time he says, "You're one funny bastard, Spike. I don't know why, but you're just funny."

Thanks, Boss, but maybe that's 'cause your pal Doc is a Doberman, the breed with as much sense of humor as a fire alarm. It's true. Have you ever seen a Doberman with any expression except lookin' like he wants to rip a piece outta your leg? Have you? Huh?

A big day of the year for Lombardo is the annual lunchtime five-inning softball game against his rival, Bolster, who runs the station across the street. People at our place might've been scared of Lombardo, but Lombardo wasn't gonna screw you. Bud said everybody at Bolster's place was "scared shitless" of Bolster. Can't imagine being "scared shitless," but it's a technique Bud oughta use on me, 'cause I'm still inclined to have an "accident" in the house on the rare occasion.

"Bolster's a lying tyrant," Bud says. "Talk you out of taking a job at a bigger station one day, and fire you a month later 'cause he was gonna replace you anyway." I'm lookin' to eyeball Bolster and maybe take a little leak on his shoe to see how mad he can actually get.

We scrape together nine players and head to the playground. New on the team this year is Buffy—who ran track and played softball at college, and has hands like an iron worker from milking cows at the dairy—and Milt Moss, the art director. Lombardo puts him as catcher, figuring Milt's chronic flatulence, brought on by his obsession with cheesy garlic Brussels sprouts, is gonna throw off the batters. But after a couple of pitches, the umpire can't take any more of Milt and moves him to far right field.

I'm relaxing, havin' a good time outside on a sunny day. Some kid who's watchin' gives me half a peanut butter and jelly sandwich, which starts my lifelong addiction to peanut butter. Like Lombardo's always tellin' Bud, "Temptation is everywhere." Anyway, as usual, Lombardo's on the mound for us and Bolster for them. Bud's doin' fine at third base, and Buffy's movin' like lightning at as shortstop.

As we head into us batting at the top of the fifth, we got a 1-nothin' lead, thanks to a home run by Buffy, but trouble's ahead. Milt Moss draws a quick walk—the ump and catcher wanted him outta the batter's box as fast as possible. Lombardo pops up, which pisses him off big-time, then Marv Herbert drills one straight back at Bolster.

Two outs, and Buffy's up, and their outfield's movin' deep. She's two for two, and diggin' in at the plate. First pitch she sends a looping ball to short center. The shortstop's runnin' back tryin' to get it, but it hits the ground as Buffy's chargin' to second base. Bolster runs to cover second himself; she slides while Bolster takes the throw and on purpose plants his foot down hard on her ankle, blockin' her from the bag but worse, hurtin' her leg bad. I'm leashed up or I'd be goin' for a piece of Bolster's flat little ass.

Buffy's hobbling off the field with the help of the anchor Sam Halloway, who's lisping, "This shucks, this shucks!" Everybody's yelling and screamin' at Bolster. Lombardo shuts them up and slowly walks over, and with this freezing-cold look in his eye says, "The day will come, Bolster. The day will come."

We're all starin' at Lombardo figurin' he's about to give Bolster the "kiss of death." Bud says, "Lombardo's the kinda' guy you'd want in a foxhole with you." I've seen foxholes; not sure how that works.

Now we got no shortstop and Lombardo's worried and tryin' to figure a shift. But Bud says, "No problem, Spike can stop any ball. Put Spike in next to me."

Lombardo says, "Our goat-loving, singing weatherman has a bright idea."

"No, seriously, Boss. Watch," Bud says, and he gets balls and starts hurling hard grounders at me, which I catch with ease. Back home Bud's been throwin' a little pink ball against our wall to see how many in a row I can catch. I'm up to thirty-one.

Lombardo tells the ump, "This dog, who is an insured station employee, is now our shortstop."

I'm way more confident now than as weather dog but startin' to wonder, if we go extra innings, how do I bat?

Bolster, the Scott Pelly robot, and everybody in their dugout is laughing and pointing.

The Pelly robot yells across the field, "Goodness gracious! A dog. My, my, they must be down on their uppers!"

"Goddamn him, program some profanity!" Bolster snarls at an intern. "Pelly sounds like my grandmother."

"By jiminy, this is keen as mustard!" the robot screams.

"Shut that fuckin' thing up, you idiot!" Bolster orders.

"Crikey, this could make a stuffed bird laugh," the Pelly robot says.

The intern throws two towels over the robot's head, and play resumes.

My plan is to go for everything. First guy up, long fly to center. I chase it, but the center fielder's got it. Then this big, beefy sportscaster of theirs smashes a single to right. Lombardo gives up another single to their sales manager but easily strikes out Rudy the one-armed weatherman. Bolster's next and Lombardo's throwin' fire. He runs a full count and Bolster swings and dribbles one down the third-base line. Me and Bud get tripped up goin' for it, and Bolster's on first. Bases loaded with the winning run at second.

What happens next is gonna play forever in my little brain. At the plate is Bolster's secretary, Penny. She was a pro golfer who put on a lot of weight, got a crew cut, inked tattoos of butterflies all over her arms, and moved to a log cabin in Asheboro with a woman who looks like Sandra Bullock. She can slug the ball.

Lombardo's got a 3–1 count, pitchin' around the menacing-looking Penny. Everybody's real tense. He's gettin' set to heave but stops. He turns around and looks at me for what seems like a long time. What I'm reading in Lombardo's dark eyes is strange—like he's sending something at me, filling me up with some force. He's makin' me feel like I can do anything, like I'm Ozzie Smith with a mouth for a glove.

He turns, there's the pitch, and Penny laces it up the middle. The ball hits second base and goes straight up in the air. I'm lookin' at it like I've looked at that little pink ball in the yard a thousand times. Bolster's runnin' toward second. Up I go. High. Five feet. I got it. I start dropping down, straight down. Bolster's slidin'

headfirst into the bag, but I land on his head; Bud grabs the ball outta my jaws and tags the bag. We win.

Our whole team's screamin' happily, while I'm sitting on Bolster's face, releasing a bit of a gas from all that peanut butter.

"Give me a blowjob!" the Pelly robot yells.

My favorite times with Bud aren't when we're workin' on TV. It's Friday, when it's always just us at home. That's when I really feel most like a pet.

We start with a trip to Otto's butcher shop. A perk of my stardom is that Otto lets me in the store. He's got my photo in the window. Bud signed it, "Love your meat, thanks, Spike The Wonder Dog." Otto tells Bud, "Some people think Spike actually autographed it," which makes me want to continue my exploration into the unlimited powers of the human brain.

Friday nights we always watch the classic fights on ESPN. I study the moves of the greats and practice them in our yard. I come to realize boxing is one fighter imposing his will on another. I like Roberto "Hands of Stone" Duran, 'cause if I were fightin' I'd be "Head of Stone."

When it gets late on Friday, Bud sometimes sits in a bath talkin' to some babe on the phone. He's hot and heavy now with this tall nurse. He spotted her at a bar readin' *Raw Living* magazine. When he saw broccoli on the cover, he realized it wasn't the kind of raw living he had in mind, but chatted her up anyway.

We get in the big bed and listen to music. Whoever he's datin', he asks them, "What kind of music you like?" And whatever it is—except for that one time with Michael Bublé—he listens to it. He met a girl on a coast trip who was into show tunes, and he was probably the only straight guy in West Hollywood drivin' around blasting the original soundtrack of *Hello, Dolly* out the window.

Saturday mornings, we jog and then work on new tricks for me. Sometimes we play hide and seek, and Bud acts like he's "The Mentalist" searchin' for me in the woods out back. He finds me most times. Not all owners could do that, but Bud and me use one of those special human–animal connections. The kind they report on every couple of weeks on the nightly news when they've got nothing else to cover.

Later in the day, when the babe arrives for their "action in the afternoon," I'm in the yard sitting in my orange doghouse waiting to hear the moaning through the window, so I can start visualizin' the meat in Otto's shop. That's about as close as I'm comin' these days to an erotic experience.

One Saturday things got messed up, 'cause we had to go to Lombardo's house at lunchtime. "Come to my place at noon and bring that dog. I've got something to tell him."

Lombardo opens the door, and even though it's Saturday he's dressed same way as at the office—shiny black loafers, crisp white shirt, a sharp pants crease—he makes Anderson Cooper look like a guy who sleeps under a bench. Bud could take a lesson here, 'cause Lombardo's house is the most sparkling, neat, and clean place I've ever been, even more than the operating room where I got the distemper shot and bit the vet.

"Wife and kids and Doc are out," Lombardo says. "Let's go to the den." We trot downstairs, and even though someone's emptied a canister of Febreze in the air, I'm sniffin' evidence of a cat. There's the lingering scent of Rachael Ray chicken and brown rice cat food. You gotta figure the culinary career is really skyrocketing when a chef's serving cat food.

"Can I get you a drink?" Lombardo asks. I see this look in Bud's eye like he'd really like to belt back a few, but he says, "Ah, just ginger ale."

"How about that dog?"

He forgets that ginger ale gives me sneezing fits, and says, "Give him a ginger ale, too."

"I'm having chocolate and grappa," Lombardo says. "Want some?"

Bud once chugged a glass of grappa and ran to the men's room clutching his throat, so he says, "No, thanks."

He spots a big photo of Lombardo and Frank Sinatra. Bud's starin' at it like Frank's about to start singin' right to him.

"Wow," he says. "You knew Frank?"

"Great-grandparents had a house near the Sinatras in Hoboken."

I'm hopin' that Lombardo's not gonna ask Bud what kind of music he's listenin' to now, 'cause the current babe's into Tame Impala, some Australian psychedelic rock group, and I don't see Lombardo goin' to San Francisco with anything resembling a flower in his crisply parted hair.

"Love Sinatra," Bud says.

Lombardo goes to this giant black thing by the wall and says, "I'll play one for you." And blastin' out of speakers from every direction comes Sinatra snarling "That's life…." It's like we're sitting in an audio showroom. The music gives Lombardo that mysterious look in his eye like at the softball game.

Song's over; Lombardo says, "That's my theme song. You get knocked down, you pick yourself up and fight back." Bud and Lombardo are lookin' at that Sinatra picture like they're about to drop to their knees and pray to Frank for masculine guidance, when Lombardo says, "OK, so do you think that dog can carry a Pizza Pouch?"

"You mean that thing where you can walk around with a piece of pizza around your neck?"

"Yeah," Lombardo says. "As if this country isn't fucking fat enough, now you can have hot pizza inches from your mouth at all times—even while you're sleeping. You can get up in the middle of the night and have a nice warm slice of pizza while you take a piss. Their ad agency wants a regional commercial explaining why it's apparently now mandatory to have pizza with you at all times. And they called about you and that dog running across a field wearing Pizza Pouches in the commercial."

"This is really stupid, Boss."

"Five thousand dollars."

"How soon can we shoot?" Bud asks.

I'm happy 'cause one of my favorite pastimes is spending an afternoon eating cheese that somehow defied gravity to stick to the lid of a cardboard pizza box.

Lombardo walks us to the door and tells Bud to wait outside 'cause he's got a special message for me. I'm figurin' it's gonna be a kind of "Keep up the good work, Spike" for what I contribute on the show.

He gives me that Lombardo look, like his eyes are sending a bolt straight through me, hitting the doormat I'm standing on and bouncing up and jabbing me in the ass.

All he says is, "You're pissing on my car's tires in the parking lot."

A week later we're at the field for the Pizza Pouch commercial. Personally, I don't think anyone who's got a Pizza Pouch hangin' on their neck's gonna have a desire to run across a golden, sun-drenched wheatfield, unless maybe they're sprinting for their life bein' chased by hungry people who just went off the keto diet and need real food.

Louis, the director, is parading around like he's the Martin Scorsese of commercials for dim-witted products. He's got lenses jammed in his safari jacket even though it looks like they're shooting the whole thing with an iPhone.

"Let's try a run across with no pouches, and just look happy and relaxed," he tells us. Afterward, it's, "Oh my, much more happy needed. The dog's tongue should be hanging way out, and you, Bud, what are you thinking about out there? What's your motivation?"

"That I'm making five thousand dollars and I like pizza," Bud says.

"Well obviously, not enough, Bud. Perhaps I could suggest some direction. As you run, imagine you've been granted eternal youth and you'll never, never, never have a care in the world, and you are just rich, rich, rich, and happy, happy, happy."

Bud says, "Oh, I know the look you want, like the couple in the bank commercial who come out of the bank with new credit cards and their eyes are sparkling with joy about all the stuff they can buy, and they're not even worried how in three months they'll be twenty thousand dollars in debt and their house is being repossessed?"

"Exactly," Louis says.

We get fitted with the Pizza Pouches. Louis is gazin' at them like they're nude photos of Kate Upton.

"This is our new transparent pouch where you can see the slice bubbling against the ultranonstick filament. What do you think?"

"I can understand why you're dedicating your life to this," Bud says. "I really can."

I get the "pant" command from Bud, and my tongue's hangin' out as they slide in the hot pizza. I try to lick it, as intense pizza vapors go straight up my nose.

"OK one, two, three…happy run, happy run!" Louis says.

As I'm runnin', the pouch is swingin' up close to my mouth. Even more pizza smell is tempting me, so I try to grab the pouch. I'm runnin' and snapping for the pouch, runnin' and snappin'. When I catch it, I chew all the way through, swallowing a tasty combo of pizza and toxic nonstick filament. Sun's pounding down on me on a beautiful day. I'm eating double-cheese-with-bacon pizza lying on my back in the middle of the field. Life is good.

If you ever see the Pizza Pouch spot that we did that day, and Bud says it's on YouTube, look careful at my pouch as I'm runnin', 'cause after four more delicious attempts with smoldering pizza around my neck, Bud finally said the only way I could do it was with an empty pouch.

5

The Visit

Bud's in his office workin' on an investigative report for the six o'clock news that Lombardo's makin' him do.

"I want to see you reporting and making some headlines," Lombardo told him, "so go out, investigate, and bring in something."

Bud's idea is to expose what is "really going on at Edna's Foot and Rub on Guilford Pike." Half the guys in town call it The Geyser, for what they're sayin' is the "release that gives you peace" in the Happy Ending Room. Bud's plan is to have a tiny camera he's callin' the "groin cam" strapped to himself so the video will show the "therapist at work."

I got no idea what he's talking about.

The research reveals that Edna's Foot and Rub is part of a nationally franchised massage parlor operation that offers franchise buyers higher returns than Subway, Dunkin, or McDonald's and "a lot more fun for you with your employees in the back room."

Bud's planning to go to Edna's disguised in a Fareed Zakaria Halloween costume he ordered online, but for some ABC legal reason, Lombardo won't let any station employee do the under-cover work. So Bud needs to find a "civilian."

This Edna's thing is way too complicated. A simple investigative report uncovering hidden additives in organic dog food's a way better idea. There's gotta be some reason it makes my dumps look like bright green candy bars.

Buffy comes racin' into his office. She gives Bud a message that some woman in Pennsylvania called sayin' she's the owner of my brother Billy. Bud checks it out and tells me the people are driving through High Point on Saturday and coming to our place with Billy. I'm feelin' high 'cause like I said, I never figured I'd see any of my litter again, and Billy was my favorite. He was our leader who kept order in the pen and made sure there was no nipple confusion when Mom was feedin' us.

Me and Billy'd work together when people came in to buy us. You can tell real fast if you want someone to be your owner. It's just somethin' you have as a puppy that protects you from evil forces. Like the day the buyers we called "The Blob Family" came squeezin' through the door. Suddenly we got these giant ten-year-old twins, who look like they're pumped full of air, staring down at all five of us in the pen and pokin' us hard with porky fingers. I'm stretched out on my side, and Billy's lyin' on top of me. We both got glazed-over eyes, trying to appear as deranged and developmentally challenged as possible. The kid's mother picks up Billy, who's smart enough to hang his head down with his tongue flapping outta the side of his mouth like he just got a lethal injection.

"Is this one OK?" the lady says, and our breeder, Mrs. Erdrick, says, "Oh, Billy just must be tired." So the twins are poking him and pulling his ears, but old Billy's so smart. He keeps that tongue out, doesn't move, and drools half-chewed puppy chow on the kid's hand and shirt. We're safe.

On the day of the visit, Billy comes chargin' through the door in front of his owners, and we're nose to nose and our tails are flyin' back and forth. Everybody's lookin' at us going, "Ahh…ahh… ahh…. It's so cute. Ah…ah…ah, oh…ah…oh…. Look at them…. It's like they know each other. Ahh, ahh…ahh…ahh…oh…oh… ahh." So we stop waggin' to get them to shut the hell up.

Billy goes sniffing around my living room, while I let his owners pet me. Kinda nice people.

The dad, Calvin, is small; smallest man I've seen 'cept for busboys in Mexican restaurants. Turns out he's a jockey, and Billy says he's tough as nails and always gives Billy part of his dinner 'cause he's gotta stay skinny. The mom, Bee, is real tall and teaches Latin and history at a community college. She just got suspended from her job for using the phrase "chinks in the armor" to describe flaws in German defenses at Normandy. Students staged a two-day protest saying she'd offended Asians, which actually pissed off the Asians 'cause they didn't want to miss classes.

They got two kids—boy twelve and girl ten. Billy nods that the kids are cool, so I start lickin' them as they're petting and studying me.

"Spike looks just like Billy!" the girl screams in amazement.

"Mom, Dad, he looks like Billy, except for a different face spot!" the boy yells.

Kids, I love you. Billy's your dog, so you're like family to me. But what were you expecting? Maybe that Billy's brother was gonna look like an English sheepdog?

All we want to do is get out in the yard, but both of us have to stand there listenin' to how our owners got us, what the drive here was like, how bad the food was on the road, the five-day weather forecast. Pure human small-talk crap. Not like the stimulating discourse I know I'll be havin' out back with Billy, 'cause Billy's a deep thinker.

I'm givin' Bud my "Let me outta here now, 'cause I gotta take a dump" look, which involves crossing my eyes and hopping up and down. But he's distracted 'cause the mom's asking him for advice.

The little girl's gonna audition for a school production of *Annie*, and because Bud's on TV, Mom figures he'll know exactly what to tell the kid to do to get the part.

When she starts singing about how the sun is gonna be out tomorrow, I feel like crashin' my head through the screen door. Billy's givin' me this look like, "I hear this eighteen times a day," and considering how loud she's blasting, he's probably experiencing early-onset hearing loss.

After two of the longest minutes of my life, it's finally over, and the father, who's acting like the kid is a horse that just won the Kentucky Derby, asks, "Hey, Bud, how about that? We think she's quickly developing into a dramatic soprano. But honestly, what do you think?"

"Honestly? Well first," Bud says, "in terms of performance, don't wave your arms like you're a school crossing guard."

"Good point," the mother agrees. "Honey, only throw your hands straight up in the air each time you sing the word 'tomorrow.' OK?"

"Anything else, Bud?"

"Ah, she's belting it like those contestants on *The Voice* who never heard a soft note they wanna hit, so I'd say when she starts, maybe tell her to leave someplace to go."

"What does that mean, Mommy?" the girl asks.

"I think he means not to sing as loud as humanly possible from the first word."

Finally, Billy and I head out to the yard, and as I'm followin' him I notice he's missing some crucial equipment. I feel bad and gotta make him aware I'm sorry. He tells me he didn't know it was gonna happen. Just thought he was headin' to the vet for routine puppy shots, and next thing he wakes up with a plastic cone around his neck and "phantom balls syndrome."

What's it like, I want to know, as we hear the girl singing that now her end is near. Billy says 'cause of being neutered he'll never be able to jump as high as me, but maybe it's made him even more cerebral. He's so cool that he seems more embarrassed by a ten-year-old girl blaring "My Way" like it's the National Anthem for fifth graders than about the loss of his manhood.

His life's good, happy, and has lots of music—whole family sings a lot, and in spite of the fact that the kids are not the next Bruno Mars and Cardi B, or even Siegfried and Brunhilde, he loves them. He goes runnin' mornings at the track next to Calvin on a horse. He's got an orderly schedule, watches a lot of the National Geographic channel, where he saw part of a Vegas show with trained elephants, so now he's against the exploitation of animals as entertainment. Main thing is, he feels he's deserving of what he says is the highest accolade an English Bull Terrier can get—professional pet. And I'm feelin' a little envious.

When I tell him what I'm doin', he's surprised to hear I'm way more of a TV clown than a professional pet. I let him know how much I love Bud and how good he is to me, and I'm just hoping we stay here forever, 'cause my yard is big fun, and I'm building muscles tossing tires, leapin' hurdles, bouncing around in a big circle, and sleepin' in my orange doghouse.

But bein' with Billy, seein' his life, I'm startin' to feel paranoid like after the time I ate the baggie of Bud's pot gummies and thought demons were outside in the dark peering at me through the windows. I think I'm dumb 'cause I'm not as smart as Billy and I'll never be a pro pet. And I'm embarrassed show business life is so nuts, and worrying maybe Billy thinks I'm bein' exploited, and thinkin' Bud's probably too scared to make a commitment so he's never gonna settle down and have kids that I'd be able to protect and play with. Plus, he wants to go to New York, and I'm scared of that, and I'm suddenly wonderin' if maybe Billy's jealous of my balls. I'm havin' a panic attack so I run into my house.

Billy's barking for me to come outside, but I'm not budgin', so in he comes and lies next to me on the cedar-chip floor. He looks around and is wondering who that woman in the big picture on my wall is, and I let him know about Cher, who he's never heard of. I'm figurin' he's probably got shots of Nobel Prize winners and scientists in his doghouse, and I got Cher.

We're on different paths, he tells me. When you get picked out of a litter, you never know what awaits you. You just gotta be the best Spike you can be for Bud. Don't live a fear-based life, he's advising. As I listen to him, I'm realizing my brother, a dog, is makin' far more sense than Doctor Phil did on Bud's show last week.

In the house, Bud's stopped the kids from damaging any more songs by getting his karaoke system workin' and singin' a few himself. As we listen, it feels so good lyin' there with Billy, who's telling me, "Just be here now, Spike; be here now. We may never see each other again."

And Bud's doin' this song "The Pilgrim" that he picked off the album Kristofferson gave him. He's been singin' it to himself for days. It's a real confusing song to me, all about questions like: Is the going up worth the coming down? Is believing a blessing or a curse?

I figure goin' up, comin' down has something to do with jumpin', but I'm looking to Billy for maybe more insight than that, and Billy thinks Bud's singin' it to himself 'cause he doesn't really know what he's searching for, what kinda shine he never found. As I'm struggling to grasp poetic deconstruction from a two-year-old dog, suddenly everything changes and I have to snap into action.

Bud gets a call from Buffy about The Geyser investigation. A friend of her cousin is workin' the legit foot and neck massage operation in the front room and hates the owners, who're harassing her for sex all the time.

She tells Buffy that they try to grab her crotch with what they call the "presidential handshake."

She's quittin' her job and wants to help us. Buffy gives Bud the big news—Edna's is having some special "blowout" sale, and Bolster himself has scheduled an appointment for "tightness in the thighs," which is code for "Get me in the back room for a release."

Bee Googles "Edna's Foot and Rub."

"They're nuts!" she screams, laughing. "The website must be copying reviews from *Wine Spectator*; listen to this: 'Our hand-krafted massages'…. Ha, 'crafted' with a 'k'"—Bee laughs—"'offer a lush, brilliant, yet youthful mouth-feel with a hint of natural acidity,'" she reads. "'The finish is long and elegant with an explosion of minerality that shows great finesse and focus.'"

Calvin and Bud are suddenly lookin' a little thirsty, but Bud's got to get someone in there fast to catch Bolster for the investigative report. He tells Bee and Calvin what a hypocrite Bolster is because of his daily "family values" TV editorials that simultaneously condemn abortion, sex education, birth control, and masturbation.

"I'm game to go in; sounds like fun," Calvin offers, and tells his wife, "Don't worry, honey. We won't get to the hand job part with me." She shoots him a look like, "It'd have to be a pretty small hand, honey."

He calls for an immediate "tightness in the thighs" appointment. Instead of the groin cam, which Bud figures is too big for Calvin's groin, he gives him the spy cam watch that Lombardo bought for investigations.

At Edna's Foot and Rub, we park in the lot. Calvin heads up a long flight of stairs. He gets to the back room and tells the therapist he has to meditate before the massage, and tips her ten bucks to go outside. We see her on the back deck furiously texting, eating a banana, and smokin' a crack pipe.

Bud's nervous 'cause the WGHP camera guy's late. Calvin texts Bud that Bolster's on the other side of the curtain. We hear live audio of what's going on. It sounds like Bolster's coaching a limbo dancer—"Lower, lower, lower, lower, lower…"

The WGHP van pulls into the lot, and the girl on the deck freaks out, throws her crack pipe into the woods, and is yelling, "A TV station's here!" Bolster looks out the window and starts madly pulling on his clothes.

"He's gonna head down the back stairs," Calvin tells Bud over the watch.

The crew guy's getting out of the van and slowly walking to get the camera out the back, and Bud says, "Shit, he's gonna get away, Spike…"

Bud starts shooting video with his phone, and points at the bottom of the stairs and says, "Spike—detain position, detain position," which we've been working on from the Army guard dog manual.

I charge toward the bottom of the steps to stop Bolster. Billy leaps out the car window and is running next to me.

Bolster's comin' down the staircase with something inside his pants that looks like it might be life-threatening and last longer than four hours. At the bottom of the steps, I snap into the detain stance. Billy copies me—legs apart, head up, fangs out, growling low.

Unless he uses that thing in his pants to pole-vault over us, Bolster's trapped. I'm feelin' good 'cause Billy's looking at me like, "Don't worry, brother; you *are* a professional pet."

The next morning our picture's in the paper. Headline: "Wonder Dog and Brother Foil TV Executive's Escape From 'Happy Ending' Parlor."

I was sad as Billy stared at me out the back of their Cherokee as his family drove away. The windows were up, so the sound of the little girl trying to be a dramatic soprano singing "Under the Boardwalk" was partially muffled.

Before Billy hopped into the jeep, we had an eerie farewell.

"You will be tested, Spike," he told me softly. Then he looked at me for a long time before he said something in Latin. "*Horam expecta veniet*—await the hour, Spike; it shall come."

Like he was seein' my future.

6

VEGAS

You probably thought when we left *The Tonight Show* we'd never see Ike "I Got Money" Piles again. But no!

When the phone rang, Bud was still basking in the glory of his exposé on both Bolster and Edna's. High Point was swirling with rumors that Bolster left town for a long vacation in Thailand, and that Edna's Foot and Rub was closed, but relocated to the back of a health food store disguised as a "Fresh, Hot, Organic, Bone Broth Bar." Anyway....

"I one of Money Piles' people," the guy on the phone says. "I James Three. Money call all his men James so not strain brain, and I be James Three."

"What can I do for you, Mister Three?" Bud asks.

"Money Piles want rent that monster beast dog of yours for Max-Ex Laxative Drone delivery ring entry at MGM Grand Garden when Money fight Karl 'The Kitty' Williams for WBC belt. You get five thousand dollars, ringside seat, first-class transportation, high-roller suite, and Triple-Dollar-Sign Money Piles All-Access 3-D Hologram Boxing Glove Total Access Pass. No James even get that pass. You even wander around money counting room with that thing round your neck. Nobody stop you nowhere."

"Well this sounds intriguing, Mister Three, but what does my monster beast dog have to do exactly? And what, by the way, is the Max-Ex Laxative Drone?" Bud asks.

"Max-Ex Laxative Drone be new airborne system get world's most highly powerful fast-acting laxative to brothers and sisters in wilderness of Midwest who home all bound up with unsightly constipation 'cause they havin' too much fun with opioid use," James Three says. "Drone motto be 'When you stop, we drop.'"

"Impressive and much-needed use of drones," Bud says.

"Yeah, you subscribe to Max-Ex Laxative Drone, you automatically in Frequent Flusher Program. All kinds rewards."

"Of course," Bud says, "but my dog evacuates his bowels with the accuracy of a Norden bombsight. Why would he be endorsing a laxative delivered by a drone?"

"He no endorse. He be delivered to ring by new Max-Ex Laxative Drone. Max-Ex pay Money Piles million dollars. They want drone promotion. Drone hover over boxing ring, and Max-Ex box flaps open, your beast have giant ugly stuff cat toy in jaws. Drone land and he be leaping around ring chewing on cat toy. Drop toy at feet of Karl 'The Kitty' Williams. You take dog to seat, and Money Piles start usual entrance sitting in money-covered fur chair carried by four naked gold-painted California girls, while we hear Jay-Z sing 'Money, Cash, Hoes.'"

"And my dog will be up in the air in a box carried by a drone?"

"OK, Money Piles pay you ten thousand dollars. What else you want? Lifetime escort service coupons? How 'bout case of Money Shot Pleasure Cream? Research show it turn sandpaper rough hand of Kentucky coal miner to love glove in five seconds. Pleasure

Cream sponsor Money's Massage Madness Tournament. We get you ringside seats at finals."

"Er…massage tournament?"

"Girls-on-guys tug of war. They down to final-four bracket when you be in Vegas. Ringside include free buffet."

"I always eat too much at buffets," Bud says. "I'll pass."

"OK, sweeten deal…want Chevy Malibu? Money buy ten bright green Malibu for his James, he have four left. What you want?"

"I want to make sure Spike, my dog, is safe."

"Then you talk James Six," James Three says. "James Six now flyin' Max-Ex Drone over Karl 'The Kitty' Williams headquarters blastin' combo Norah Jones and James Taylor ballads, sending training camp into deep trance. You try skippin' rope to Norah Jones. So Six know drone. You interested?"

"Yeah, sure, tell Money Piles I'm interested. But I gotta talk to Mister Six."

"Anything else?"

"Yeah," Bud says, "did he ever buy Willie Nelson's guitar, 'Trigger,' like he was trying to do back at Fallon?"

"No, man," James Three says, "but Ike 'I Got Money' Piles buy Willie tour bus, paint it red and yellow. It now Vegas only hop-on-hop-off sex bus. Sign on side say, 'You Come While We Go.'"

"Remarkable attraction," Bud deadpans. "Have Six call."

Bud tells me he has to make sure I'm not gonna plummet from the drone headfirst onto Mike Tyson ringside. Plus, as usual, he's got to run the caper by Lombardo.

"How do you know that dog's gonna be OK carried by a drone?" Lombardo asks, as he's spit-shining a shoe.

"I'm going find out all of that from Six," Bud says.

"I'm assuming Six is a person," Lombardo says. "So what kind of deal are they offering?"

"Ten thousand, first class all the way, high-roller suite, special backstage pass, even an escort-service credit."

"For God's sake, don't do that. You could get drugged, robbed, videotaped, arrested, or even worse," Lombardo says.

"Worse?" Bud asks.

"E.D. 'cause of guilt."

Bud laughs. "I'll steer clear; not my style anyway."

"OK, keep me posted," Lombardo says.

Next day, James Six calls.

"Your dog be safe as long as he stand still for ten seconds after flaps drop 'fore we land 'im, and we practice that," James Six says. "If dog not able, Money Piles still pay you. There nothing to lose."

"OK, good, so whom do I talk to for all the arrangements?"

"Whom James One; here he be."

"Mister One," Bud says.

"Hey, Mister Bud, you call me James, 'cause I original James. I got list to check off. Ready?"

"Yes."

"OK, so Mister Bud, you here for only few days; so let's get your essentials. What you need? Here list: coke, uppers, downers, pain-killers, hookers, alcohol, VR porn, gambling, pot, Viagra, fetish gear, ASMR, oxygen, growth supplement, club drugs, Ketamine, piercing, tattoos, jewelry, and smoothies."

"Ah…" Bud says.

"You want get laid? You go free to Money's Indoor Sky Diving Sex Club. It be like havin' intercourse in outer space. Business also boomin' at Money's new Guys and Sex Dolls House, but you no wait; you just walk right in and get custom fitted for doll."

"Custom fitted?"

"Money have only sex doll brothel, employ team of grandmothers to custom fit dicks to dolls."

"Grandmothers?"

"Yeah," James One says. "Money hire three old hippie babes from Carmel that was Sixties plaster-castin' groupies. Nobody in world know ins and outs of dick-molding process like them."

"Back out of retirement like The Spice Girls," Bud says.

"And Money tell me, he want you mention on TV that all Money Piles' facilities be one hundred percent sex slave free. Money only employ U.S.D.A. approved Midwest farmers' daughters who make you feel all right while they livin' the American Dream."

"God bless Money Piles, but I'm fine," Bud says.

"Yeah, maybe you fine now, but at drunken' moment at four in morning you need emergency airlift of you to Bunny Ranch in Carson City? Then James need twenty-minute notice; we short on sober copter pilots that time a night. You want dog get laid? Easy round up horny strays on Strip."

"I think we'll be OK," Bud says. "I just like to go swimming, and the dog eats raw ground steak. Oh wait, maybe a little sativa pot."

"How many pounds pot?"

"No, just enough for a couple of joints."

"I give you five pounds of Haze Wreck. Take rest home; you flyin' private jet."

"Actually," Bud says, "forget it. Just the raw meat, and another one of those special passes for my dog and swimming for me."

"Your Triple Dollar Sign Money Piles All-Access 3-D Hologram Boxing Glove Total Access Pass let you in all pools anywhere in state of Nevada, even pools at every private high-roller townhouse on strip, even if you not stay in one. Suppose A-Rod and J-Lo are co-po-lating madly in their private pool over at MGM? You just jump in that pool, flash your pass, and yell, 'Lo-Rod, you two get the fuck outta your pool. I here now!' But at The Grotto Have It Your Way Topless Pool—guaranteed fifty percent natural, fifty percent enhanced breasts—there be five-dollar surcharge to get in."

"Five dollars?"

"Yeah, support breast implant research, but Money say it tax deductible."

Two weeks later, we're on a jet to Las Vegas. People on board don't have that self-satisfied look like I saw in the Fallon audience. They have a "This is where I belong; good for me" expression that's covering up a "Holy shit, I'm on a private plane" face that they don't want to show.

The pilot is this big tough military-looking guy who probably wishes he had a tail gunner to shoot down some small planes for target practice on the way. He's givin' Bud trouble about me, says he doesn't want "that big white dog up here." He points to a guy at a table in the back whose hair's gone prematurely orange and says, "He might disturb Sumner, because this is still his plane."

"We gotta crate him," he growls, with a voice that sounds like he's been smoking Camels since his mother carried him home from the hospital.

"Hold on a minute," Bud says, as he starts fumbling around in his small leather Coach bag that's covered with bites, 'cause I thought it was an inflatable chew toy when he got it for Christmas. He pulls out my Triple Dollar Sign Money Piles All-Access 3-D Hologram Boxing Glove Total Access Pass and shows it to the captain, who starts bowing to us with his hands together like he's a Hindu holy man who flies jets. A woman who Bud says is Wendy Rhodes from *Billions* gets moved so Bud and me can sit together.

"Anything I can get for you?" the captain asks.

"Champagne for me and a Bloody Bull shot with ice for my dog."

After the first hour, everybody's had a couple of drinks, so most of 'em spend the rest of the flight sleepin' or starin' glassy-eyed at their phones. Bud posts a shot of him and me and Wendy Rhodes on Facebook. Ray Donovan, who seems way more relaxed than on television, comes over and wants Bud to tell him about my breed. He tells Bud he just got a beagle puppy, and I'm thinkin', "I hope you're prepared for a life with nonstop yapping and barking, Ray."

Next morning, we go to practice with the Max-Ex Laxative Drone. We're in a big, sparkling-clean gym with a boxing ring in the middle of the basketball court.

Ike "I Got Money" Piles is in a corner pounding on the heavy bag listening to the confidence-building lyrics of Sho' Um BigWood, a rapper he manages.

He spots us.

"Who dat?" he yells, running over, pointing at me. "Who dat here for drone delivery that makin' Money's money piles more money piles?"

"Hey, Ike," Bud says. "Thanks, this will be fun, and…"

"You no sell me beast for last fight, so I rent for now," Money says.

"Yeah, thanks, I love these passes, and…" Bud stops. He's staring at the three women tattooed on Money's sweating chest.

"Money, I'm sorry, and correct me if I'm wrong here," Bud says, "but is that a Ruth Bader Ginsberg, Sandra Day O'Connor, and Sonia Sotomayor tattoo?"

"Bullshit bad tattoo from fucked-up, bow-tie-wearin', cracka law student who work part time at Flying Ink tattoo shop at Dallas airport. And it all be 'cause Money love Motown music."

"Me too," Bud says.

"Money love Motown so much, he have brilliant idea to put big Supremes tattoo cover left pec to remind him you can't hurry love, to give him more pleasure time when he playin' with Money's Butter Girls."

"Well, yes," Bud says, "that makes perfect sense. But—"

"Money tell cracker boy, 'Tattoo me The Supremes,' and dumb kid ask, 'Which ones?' Money say, 'The three fuckin' chicks, you dumb bastard!'"

"Oh, and—" Bud says.

"Two hours later while Money jet still on runway burnin' valuable high-octane fuel, Money get off table and see three wrinkled old babes in robes starin' at him over top of his nipple! Cost Money two inches off his money pile to get assault charges dropped."

"Wow," Bud says. "You gonna leave it there?"

"After fight, Money adding big Aretha Franklin head to top of three bodies, so then just look like it be Aretha wearin' extra-wide church robe."

A tall guy, who's got that peas-and-gardenias Money cologne smell and a big "2" tattooed on his forehead, comes racin' up and says, "James Two need rehearse now with little crane holding drone with dog in. Then, when dog ready, James Six fly drone up in air with dog and land in ring."

I have to give the Money Piles people credit, or maybe it's the laxative people; they had it set up great. All I have to do is get in this box about twice as big as me, sides fly up, and inside I hear Bud's voice comin' over a little Bose speaker commandin' me: "Still Spike, still."

The plan is, as I'm flyin' around, I just gotta be steady and wait for the next step.

Then: "Ready, Spike; count five, four, three, two, one, flaps."

The flaps go down, so I grab the giant cat toy filled with meat juices and start chompin' away on it. Drone lowers me into the boxing ring. I leap out and run around. Bud's in the practice ring flashin' me directions. After two times I got it down.

I'm having a big drink of water, 'cause I'm feelin' more heat in Vegas than I ever felt before, when this squat, muscular guy with seven gold chains around his neck and a big "6" tattooed on his forehead comes over to Bud.

"James Six ready to fly dog in Max-Ex Laxative Drone. First we weigh dog after James Four put on costume."

"Costume? What costume?" Bud asks.

A bleached-blond with a "4" tattooed on his forehead, who looks like he should be working in a Linens 'n Things in Palm Beach, prances over. He fits me with a red cape covered with pictures of Max-Ex Laxative bottles with "Explosive Relief" in bright blue letters in the center. James Four puts a big gold-colored cardboard Money Piles logo around my neck and says, "He's divine, just divine."

"Just shut the fuck up, Four," Six says. "Let's weigh 'im."

I weigh in at sixty-two pounds, which is heavy for me. Maybe I'm bloated from the flight?

I'm in the box, and up I go bein' carried by the drone. I'm seeing my great-grandfather Brick in the Glider Squadron and I'm thinkin', "I'm carrying on a great family tradition of bravery in the sky," except I throw up. Why? Try hovering sixty feet off the ground, jammed in a giant flying laxative bottle box that's covered with pictures of people holding plungers and smiling like they just took the biggest dump of their lives.

We run through it ten times, and finally Bud says, "He's had enough."

A guy named Tony who's standin' with the Jameses says, "Anyone want go to The Grotto? I hear they got a bunch of extra girls in working as mer'mams 'cause of fight weekend."

Bud doesn't have to worry about a bathing suit 'cause the Triple Dollar Sign Money Piles All-Access 3-D Hologram Boxing Glove

Total Access Pass lets him have a free wardrobe anytime he walks into a store.

Tony, Bud, and me climb into a big white limo that Bud says looks like a pimpmobile and probably is. The James driving has a big "5+" on the back of his neck. "Tattoo be there so Money Piles know who James I be when Money Piles in back seat. All he do is look at my neck and he know."

"What's the plus sign for?" Bud asks.

"Call me Five Plus," he says, "'cause Five Plus drive, plus Five Plus do extra. Five Plus handle Money's dogs—Money have lotta dogs—and two big parrots. I train parrots to say, 'I got money piles; do you?' That's how I get to be the only James who a James Plus."

Bud launches into telling Five Plus about a parrot he knows named Henry. I'm staring out the window at the wonders of the Vegas Strip, but it's hurtin' my neck straining to see the tops of big hotels. One flashing sign says "Urinetown"—a welcoming note for any dog on a Vegas visit.

Tony's the manager of a fighter named Gail "One Climax" Greeley, who's a big deal in female mixed martial arts. Bud's not a big fan of those fights, so I'm wonderin' what he's gonna say to Tony, but in Bud's usual way, he's right up front about it.

"It's sometimes hard for me to watch MMA," he says. "You know, the head kicks, and then hitting repeatedly when the woman's down."

"Really? But with the women, I think it's kind of sexy, actually very sexy. And, hey, the girls want to do it, and, ah, they make big money, they train like mad, and they got a lot of guys who want to meet them," Tony says.

Bud nods his "Just not my scene, pal" nod.

Waiting for us at the VIP entrance at The Grotto Have It Your Way Topless Pool, guaranteed fifty percent natural breasts, fifty percent enhanced breasts, is a woman dressed in an electric blue, skintight jumpsuit who Bud says is of "gargantuan proportions."

"Greetings, gentlemen, I'm Mindy Mounds, The Grotto resort director. Hello, Tony, Bud, and this must be Spike The Wonder Dog. What a charming, virile animal. Come with me; I always like to tell our VIP guests a little about our concept."

We go into her office, which is a lot like Lombardo's office except no *Judge Judy* on the monitors, just live shots of topless women swimming around and floating men leering at them.

"First, I want to state that this is a wholly female-owned and operated enterprise. Our motto is 'Make money to infinity from toxic masculinity.' Right now, you'll have to pardon our construction. We're expanding to become the world's first gentlemen's water park, with, of course, fine dining and the highly anticipated Cialis Smoothie Bar.

"Our architectural firm is Brian, Gumble, and Pompus, designers of the Sand Universe Park in Dubai, but their influences here are the grotto at Hugh Hefner's mansion, Sea World, and a club in New York called Plato's Retreat, which sadly closed because of a herpes epidemic many years ago.

"We're excited about our first additions—this is the mock-up for the Hooker Encounter Lake, and the BGB logo there is for Bitches Got Back, which is our Large-Rears-Only Wading Pool. TMZ is calling it a 'posterior petting zoo.'"

I'm really not following this, and personally would like to go for a swim right now with or without hookers in a lake. Tony's looking at the pictures on the walls and seems kind of annoyed. Bud gives me a "How sleazy is this?" glance, but I can tell he's still gonna try to be polite and ask questions.

"Well," he says, "these women, they must all have to swim pretty well and fit, ah, certain anatomical requirements. How do you find them?"

"Brilliant question, Bud, and yes, it's a challenge," Mindy Mounds explains. "Many of our best swimmers were once of the unusually flat-chested Olympic competitor variety, who've been retrofitted with a minimum E-cup enhancement. They have the option to go much larger, of course, and each cup size fortunately increases their buoyancy, so many can float and read a hardback book at the same time."

Tony's squirmin' around in his chair makin' little grunts; I'm settlin' in for a nap 'cause I feel like Bud's on a track where he's gonna interview Mindy Mounds like she's a Peabody Award–winning medical correspondent.

"And the Hooker Encounter," he asks, "these women also swim?"

"Oh yes, and they must swim very well; just think of a more intimate version of the Dolphin Encounter in Atlantis, except with a different species of warm-blooded mammal. We have, shall we say, ladies of the night secretly training to become ladies of the lake right now at the Swimming Hall of Fame in Fort Lauderdale under the direction of a man who claims to be a former coach of Michael Phelps."

I get the feeling Bud's heard enough. He stands up.

"Oh, well, OK, well, gentlemen," Mindy Mounds says, "let's go outside…. Oh, but first, your mandatory donation of five dollars. And, oh yes, we have the thousand-dollar Tie a Pink Ribbon Round the Old Oak Tree special today."

"What might that be?" Bud asks.

"You get to tie a pink ribbon around your private part…with a guaranteed hands-free ribbon removal by one of our mer'mams in your own surveillance-camera-free cabana."

"I'm outta here!" Tony blurts, jumping out of his chair. "This is all about the objectification and exploitation of women. I can't stand it."

Mindy calls after him, "But these girls want to do this, and they train very hard and they make good money."

We finally go in the pool, which has glass walls and a glass bottom and guys underneath armed with something like laser pistols. I'm standin' in the shallow end, and Bud's keeping one eye on me and one eye on about forty topless women, but after about ten minutes we have to get out of the pool, 'cause they're starting the laser competition.

"This is everything you've ever wanted in a topless laser tag game," Mindy boasts. "First man to identify and laser tag all twenty of the nonenhanced-breasts mer'mams wins an oak tree pink ribbon. Enjoy," she says, walking away.

"All right, I've had enough of this. I'm starting to feel dirty in clean water," Bud tells me. "Let's get back to the hotel and go for a real swim, Spike."

Next day we run through the drone thing again. All's great; Bud's comin' in loud and clear over the little speaker, and I'm OK looking down from sixty feet up—no more of that dizziness that made me throw up.

Bud wants to take a stroll on the Strip, which is gonna be hot as hell, but he's got this special water bottle for me with a nipple that's way longer than any I spotted at The Grotto topless pool. I'm just hopin' that somewhere on the way I'll find a patch of earth to—as humans say—"do my business," because they set up a fake plastic-grass rug in our hotel room that smells like coal fumes and nail polish remover. Attention, party planners: Just 'cause something looks like grass doesn't mean dogs can hardly wait to finish dinner to take a dump on it.

My keen nose is not a benefit on the Strip, 'cause I smell the BO pouring off everybody. They claim, "It's a dry heat, so you don't sweat." OK, so you just stink. You been to Vegas? You smell when you're there; take it from a dog.

Over by the Bellagio fountains Bud spots a TV crew shooting something, so we use our Triple Dollar Sign Money Piles All-Access 3-D Hologram Boxing Glove Total Access Pass to get up front and watch. Turns out we're next to a reporter named Richard Johnson who was on the plane and is coverin' some gossip angles of the big fight.

"They're shooting *The Former Housewives of the Vegas Strip*," he tells us. "Marianne and Maria were both married to Tony, and they're fighting with him over who gets to live in their double-wide trailer, but they can't get their lines right. This is like their seventh take; Maria's about to explode."

"Seventh take?" Bud says. "Isn't this supposed to be a reality show?"

"Yeah," Johnson says. "It is, don't you just yearn for the pre-Kardashian era of TV?"

We see these two women in skintight dresses. They look like they're goin' to the inauguration of a Mafia boss. The sun's beating down, but they're wearin' mink stoles in the 105-degree heat.

"Cut," the director says. "Maria, again, you've got to pull Tony's sleeve while you call him a skinny, greasy Wop sleazeball. You need to rip that sleeve off so we see he's changed the tattoo on his arm from Maria to Marianne."

"Wait a minute," Maria screams, suddenly pointing at me. "Get that goddamn dog outta here; he's so ugly, he's throwin' me off."

"Ah, sorry, Maria," the security guard says sternly, "that dog has a Triple Dollar Sign Money Piles All-Access 3-D Hologram Boxing Glove Total Access Pass. He doesn't have to move."

Realizin' that I'm igniting controversy, and hating mink stoles like I do, I start snarling at Maria, who throws a water bottle at me that bounces off my head. She yells, "I don't care if he's got Money Piles' boxing glove shoved up his ass. Get that fuckin' dog off my set!"

"We're outta here, Richard," Bud says. "See you at the fight. Come on, Spike."

As Bud is yankin' at me to leave, I'm lookin' at Maria thinkin', "The day will come, Maria. The day will come."

We're back in our hotel suite that night. Bud's soaking in one of our three hot tubs, and I'm relaxin', lickin' my feet, tryin' to sooth the burn from hot pavement. He gets a call from Mindy Mounds.

"Bud, how are you?"

"Fine, Mindy. What's going on over there at the Jurassic jiggle world?"

"Well, that's why I called. We're having our all-nude sensory deprivation total darkness swimming party tonight, ten-to-one ratio women to men, never know what you might grab."

"I have enough problems grabbing things when my senses aren't deprived, Mindy, but thanks anyway," Bud says. "I think we're in for the night."

"Sure," she says, "but if you're in the mood, bring your pass and come over the morning after the fight for our Wake and Bake Breakfast."

"What's that?"

"All the marijuana pancakes you can eat," Mindy says.

"I'm hungry already, thanks. See you at the fight."

Another call, this time Richard Johnson.

"Bud, got anything for me that Money's doing or saying that I can put in the column?"

"Well, he's been spouting poetry today, like, 'They be no defeat, because of da feet,' bragging about his defensive skills. He's saying that over and over."

"That's good," Richard says. "Thanks. Hey, you going to the Dead Celebrities party at the Bellagio? It's the hottest ticket in town, but you can get in easily with that pass."

"What is it?"

"A company in Silicon Valley's perfected interactive holograms of dead celebrities, and you're supposed to be able to talk to them like they're alive right in front of you. They got Sinatra, Elvis, Marilyn, Reagan, Robin Williams, major names. This is the premiere before they launch as a major Vegas attraction. They hired Larry King to host it, 'cause he looks sorta dead."

"You know, I missed seeing Siegfried and Roy's *Secret Garden*, so this'll have to do. Plus, I'd like to talk to Reagan and Frank for sure. See you there, thanks."

There's a huge crowd at the door, so Bud hikes me on his shoulder. Our pass gets us around hundreds of people tryin' to get in. Very orderly inside; waiters walking around with champagne, and there are different rooms and stages and sections for the hologram stars.

Showing us around is a little guy named Jules with bright white teeth. He's wearin' a shiny gray suit and a polyester thing on his head that looks like he took advantage of the recent Rug Event of the Year Sale at the Hair Club for Men.

"I can guide you around a little bit," Jules announces. "You get ultra-VIP treatment with the Triple Dollar Sign Money Piles All-Access 3-D Hologram Boxing Glove Total Access Pass."

"Terrific," Bud says. "I'd like to talk to President Reagan."

Ronald Reagan is next to a cardboard model of Nancy Reagan, and smiling and waving. I'm lookin' at Nancy's shoes figurin' she's wearin' Manolos, and I notice that she's got kinda thick ankles that seem to go all the way up to her knees.

Bud says, "Mister President, I've always admired your Berlin Wall speech."

"I once climbed a wall in an RKO movie," Reagan says. "And I hurt my knee."

"Did you write that yourself?" Bud asks. "The wall speech?"

"Heh, well…er…you know, yes, I once climbed a wall in an RKO movie," Reagan says. "And boy, did the Gipper hurt the old knee."

Bud looks at Jules. "Is the hologram stuck?"

Jules whispers, "No, no, the team's not crazy about Reagan, so they programmed him in the early Alzheimer's phase. I know it's mean, but he's getting the biggest laughs in the show, and he likes it."

"OK, goodbye, Mister President," Bud says.

"Say hello to Margaret Thatcher here," Reagan says, pointing to Nancy.

Jules ushers us into the "Elvis Weight Gain Experience." We watch Elvis starting to sing "Hound Dog" at 160 pounds and ending up at 240 pounds when the song's over.

"A couple of the exhibits aren't complete," Jules explains. He takes us to "They Died in the Closet," where Liberace and Roy Cohn are just kind of looking at each other not knowing what to say.

"And this will soon be a spectacular music show—*Plane Crash Stars*—but right now we only have Glenn Miller, Ricky Nelson, and Patsy Cline, and they can't get a song working right."

Jules stops and points. "That's going to be our biggest hit: "The Rat Pack Dinner Party." You've got Frank, Sammy Davis, Dean Martin, Joey Bishop, with Marilyn Monroe as special guest, and see President Kennedy with her? He snuck out of "The Dead Kennedys Compound" to sit with Marilyn. The pissed-off guy serving them is Joe DiMaggio. The producers think he was a prick for punching out Marilyn after that blowing-up skirt shot in the movie, so they made him the waiter."

"Oh, God, this is great," Bud says, really excited. "Walk around for a while, Spike. I want to talk to Sinatra, but a couple people with the pass are ahead of me."

I'm happy to be on my own, and just watch things, 'cause as my brother Billy says, "I may never be this way again."

I'm sitting in a corner looking around. After a while, this guy comes up to me—kinda lonely, oddball guy; about sixty or so; bald, puffy face—and he says softly, "I saw you on *The Tonight Show*. You were great. I did that show a long time ago."

"Here," he says. "Have some milk and cookies." And he takes out a bunch of cookies and puts them on the floor and empties a couple of little creamers into a cup and holds it so I can drink. "I used to give people milk and cookies after my shows."

"Isn't this swell?" I'm thinkin', and I can tell he's gonna pour his heart out to me, 'cause sometimes certain people do that to dogs. We got a great talent to listen, particularly while someone's feeding us.

"You'll be the only one I'll tell."

I'm so curious, I stop chewing.

"See that guy over there at the "Dead Comedians Who Killed" exhibit? He's doing the lip-synch pretending to be Mighty Mouse singing? That's me. I'm Andy Kaufman.

"I found a homeless vagrant who looked a lot like me and had a horrible disease, and paid his sister a hundred thousand dollars to switch our identities. He died; they thought it was me. I fooled them. Moved to Amish country outside Lancaster, Pennsylvania, and when I actually die, I'm going to be cloned and come back to performing at age thirty-five, same age as when people think I died. All I do right now is write the Not So Gorgeous George wrestling blog and watch TV. But I came here to see myself."

I'm looking at him tryin' to let him know that I think he's the Albert Einstein of practical jokers. Robin Williams comes on after Andy, and then in the middle of Freddie Prinze, Bud finds me.

"There you are," he says, and he looks at Andy and says, "Hi."

"Hi, Bud," Andy says. "I'm George Wagner. I saw you both on Fallon. How's your back? Did you really hurt it?"

"Oh, God, yes, that was awful. I'm still trying to forget it."

"I thought it was performance art; I loved it," Andy says.

Bud's looking at Andy. "Anyone ever tell you kind of look like Andy Kaufman, George?"

"Who?"

"No, never mind. Excuse us; we gotta go now. Spike's got a big day tomorrow."

"I like your dog. Bye."

"He sounds like Andy, too," Bud says on the way out, then stops and glances back. "What's that stuff on the floor, Spike? Did he give you milk and cookies?"

I give Bud my "I'm just a stupid dog" look, and we head to the hotel.

The next night it's time for me to deliver the goods to Karl "The Kitty" Williams. We're in the drone-launching area by a ring entrance in the MGM Grand Garden Arena. It's roasting hot in the flying laxative box. I'm draining my big-nipple bottle. I got my cape and crown on, and I'm set to go into action with the meat-soaked cat toy.

I can hear James Six bein' interviewed by Al Bernstein next to the drone.

Six is telling Al that this'll be the greatest entrance in ring history, and Al's asking him what's in the Max-Ex Laxative Drone box, but Six won't tell 'im. Al says there are rumors that Money Piles took steroids, 'cause it looks like he gained about twelve pounds since the weigh-in.

James One jumps in sayin', "No steroids. Money just eat a pizza from Money Piles' Solid-Cheese-Crust Pizza restaurant, intersection Flamingo and Paradise Roads; for franchise opportunity, dial 'you my money.'"

One says, "Here, Al," and shoves a slice of pizza halfway down his throat. Al's choking and gasping madly for air, while James One's yelling the phone number over and over. Finally, Al screams, "I broke a tooth on your goddamn solid-cheese-crust pizza! Back to you, Steve."

On the little speaker I hear Bud: "OK, Spike, here we go."

The plan is the drone goes up just as Karl "The Kitty" Williams starts his ring walk. "All be watching drone; no one be watching 'The Kitty,'" James Six said.

I'm slowly flyin' up and tryin' to listen to Bud, but the crowd's screaming louder and louder and I can't hear him anymore. He's yelling something at me, but I don't know what it is.

The sides drop. The crowd goes completely nuts, standing, shrieking, yelling, roaring. They're taking so many pictures, it's blinding me. I'm up about sixty feet and chewing on the cat toy. I start descending to the center of the ring, and I spot what Bud musta been tryin' to tell me—a shiny black panther on a thick leash is in the corner with "The Kitty." He's looking up at the drone like he wants to break loose and pounce on me the instant I land.

I finally hear Bud say, "His fight camp knows our plan; they've got a panther. Run, Spike; run and jump outta the ring."

What would you do? Drop into the ring, and then with your tail between your legs run for your life? Or would you think it through?

I'm thinking.... I see the white knuckles on the guy holding the panther leash; he's got a grip that's telling me he's not about to let go. Is "The Kitty" ready to damage his fan base by attacking me with his pet panther in front of twenty million television viewers who've already overpaid to watch his fight? No...they're just trying to scare me and make Money look bad. I got no problem making Money Piles look bad. He's already doin' a pretty good job of that on his own. But I'm not about to embarrass my breed, so...

I land and charge straight at the panther, who's straining to attack, as I do a leaping spin to my left. The panther snaps at me.

He gets my cape between his jaws and rips it off, just as I flip the cat toy backward over my head. The toy hits Karl Williams in the chest, bounces to the floor, and the panther turns and starts chewing on the kitty toy himself. Panthermonium!

I'm takin' a victory lap and winkin' at Andy Kaufman, when I spot Maria, from *Former Housewives of the Vegas Strip*, sitting in the front row. I lift my leg way higher than usual to hit her with a nice warm stream of you know what. The crowd gives me a standing ovation. I'm thinking, "I hope Lombardo's watching, 'cause he's gonna love it when Bud tells him why I sprayed her."

Money Piles won on a controversial unanimous decision, which of course had nothing to do with the three new bright green Chevy Malibus parked in judges' spots out back.

7

"The Hebe Named Zebe"

Not many people back home coughed up ninety-five dollars to watch a fight that started at twelve thirty in the morning. But social media is spreadin' all kinds of phone videos of me in the drone and my trick with the panther. The little number I did on the Vegas housewife seems to be a particular hit.

We land at the Greater Greensboro airport, and I imagine I'll be greeted by a huge throng—like the good old days of Brad and Angie when they were arriving in any African country. I'm visualizin' people thrusting handfuls of raw meat at me the way they'd hold out their babies for Brad and Angie to adopt—but no! The only person waving at us is Buffy, who's gonna drive us back to the station.

Lombardo's happy.

"Well, Bud, you and that dog seemed to be a big hit in Vegas, and someone finally embarrassed that bitch Maria, who gives us Italians a bad name on that moronic show, even if it was only your canine under my employ who did it," he says.

"Her ex, Tony, told me it probably wasn't the first golden shower she had that week," Bud tells Lombardo.

"Revolting!" Lombardo says. "Now, Bud, I got a call from a guy I know, a FOX talent executive in New York who was impressed with you in that interview you did with Al Bernstein about his broken tooth after the fight, and he liked that thing you shot with Deborah Norville, too. Thought you were very funny."

"I don't know how that could have happened," Bud says.

"Well, anyway you may hear something from them, but don't call, just wait.

Meantime, Joel Isaac Israelson wants you to contact him. Probably about his annual do-it-yourself Nativity scene."

"The crazy former rabbi who calls himself 'the Hebe named Zebe' now? Right?" Bud asks. "The guy who took his barnstorming pro volleyball team 'The Hopping Hebrews' to Israel and got thrown outta the country?"

"Yep."

"Hey, why did they get thrown out, anyway?" Bud asks.

"None of the players was Jewish. They were all retired NBA guys," Lombardo explains.

The Hebe named Zebe is a big character in town. He has a commercial claiming Lloyds of London insures his bris, but there's a two-inch deductible. Never could figure that out, or why he wears a Frank Sinatra hat with a way- too-wide brim.

Bud asks, "What's the story with him? All I know is he stages religious stunts, grows Christmas trees shaped like menorahs that don't sell, and has those billboards saying, 'The Hebe named Zebe—pick a god, I do the job!'"

"He came here about ten years ago," Lombardo explains, "and was running Synagogue Beth Shalom, and doing OK. Then the new Beth Israel Synagogue opened across town. The place looked fabulous, like Ralph Lauren decorated it, with little touches like boxes of designer Kleenex in each row.

"You know Jewish people and guilt, right? So what happened is, the new place has a female rabbi who sings, and sounds like Streisand, and their cantor's a dead ringer for Barry Gibb. Each week when they sang 'Guilty,' the congregation went nuts."

"Ha," Bud laughs, "that's great."

"Yeah, who ever heard of encores in a Shabbat service, right? People were fleeing his place over to Beth Israel like the Pharaoh was chasing them down Main Street with a stun gun. Only ones left in his congregation were old timers—purists who just liked the early Streisand and never saw *Saturday Night Fever*, but there weren't enough of them."

"That's sad," Bud says, "that they never saw *Saturday Night Fever*."

"True…so suddenly he's got no money, and panics and screws up big-time by selling the naming rights to the synagogue to the Rodney Dangerfield estate. Beth Shalom becomes Temple Rodney Dangerfield, but now he can't get a single Bar Mitzvah 'cause parents don't want Rodney Dangerfield's name embossed in gold on the copy of the Torah that the kid reads at the ceremony."

"So what happens?"

"Bud," Lombardo says, "the guy quits being a rabbi and totally reinvents himself by going rogue to serve all religions as the Hebe named Zebe, and he patterns himself after his favorite deejay, Jerry Blavat, from Philadelphia."

"My father knew Jerry Blavat!" Bud says. "'The Geator with the Heater,' 'The Big Boss with the Hot Sauce.'"

"Who? Yeah, well anyway, go over there and talk to him, but remember, he's an irredeemable con man now, so watch your wallet, too."

A couple of days later we drive over to meet the guy. Bud's got the soundtrack from *Fiddler on the Roof* playing to get us in the mood. His eyes are misting up listening to "Sunrise, Sunset," thinking about a marriage he hasn't had, children he hasn't had, and the marriage those children he hasn't had aren't having. I'm not sure if he wants to go the "Sunrise, Sunset" route, but he's having a peak experience thinking about it. I'm with him either way.

We park in front of The Dangerfield Syna-Church, Mini-Mosque, and Part-Time Funeral Home. There are handwritten signs plastered all over the front door.

"Welcome All!"

"Our Fasts—Gluten-Free"

"Drive-Thru Gay Weddings"

"It's Never Too Late for Circumcision!"

"Atone by Phone"

"Grab-n-Go Communion"

"Jesus Christ Superstore Now Open"

Bursting through the front door, snappin' his fingers, lookin' at Bud and barkin' out, "My man!"…snap, snap. "My man!" is the Hebe named Zebe. He's got a long gray and white beard dotted with breadcrumbs and a couple of tomato soup stains, and he's wearin' an all-black suit with the big hat. Actually, he's not really an old guy, but the beard makes him look way older. I'm imaginin' Justin Timberlake in this same outfit with a beard confined to an assisted living residence in Boca.

"Great to see you, my man, my dog." Snap, snap. "You're talkin' to the Hebe named Zebe"…snap, snap. "The Jew who's new"…snap, snap. "Jesus your boss? We've got the cross"… snap. "Muhammad your man? Stand in our sand"…snap, snap. "Religious alt-right? We'll keep you uptight"…snap. "The Jewish tribe? You'll dig our vibe"…snap. "No god at all? Your own private stall!"…snap, snap. "Need to confess, use the email address."

"My man, Bud—Bud, bo bub, banana fanna, mo mud, me my, po-pub, Bud…. You're cool and that dog's no fool; let's go inside."

He gives me a couple of towels to lie on, which is good 'cause I'm gleamin' from getting washed, and the rug hasn't been vacuumed since Golda Meir went to her senior prom. We're in his basement office with no windows or signs of ventilation. He's got images and slogans from every religion all over.

Behind him are two freshly painted signs promoting new ventures:

"Burial? Cremation?

Torn Apart Deciding?

…Try our 'half and half special!'"

"Son's Law School Rejection?

…Custom made high-quality pre-recorded wailing, crying, and moaning at reasonable rates."

THE ADVENTURES OF SPIKE THE WONDER DOG

On his desk there's a picture of his daughters—Faith, Hope, and Mindy—plus dusty bobblehead dolls of Jesus, Sandy Koufax, and Muhammad.

"Let me get right to the point; oh, wait, want a joint?" he asks.

"No, actually, no thanks. It's a little hard to breathe in here as it is," Bud says. "Oh, ah, what do I call you, Hebe? Zebe Rabbi? Holy One? Joel?"

"My man! Call me Zebe. Remember, I'm not a rabbi anymore. Ha! I just play one on TV. Now here's the deal, it's real—I gotta use the head to make college bread, which I dread. I got a wife—she's strife. Guilford Community's no cost, but Sheila's the boss. Harvard, Penn, Yale, that's millions for bail."

"At least," Bud says.

"She spends and spends with no end. Twice a week she's got a team of migrant workers cleaning the house at two hundred a pop, cash off the top. All kids go to astronaut camp, their space suits—twelve hundred, plus boots. Who cares if they're the first Jews on Mars? Not me, unless it's free."

The Zebe looks at the ceiling, shaking his head. "She's now demanding I work as an accountant for her father. Can you see me on the corporate ladder?"

"No, and it sure doesn't sound like fun," Bud says. "But where do we come in?"

"My man! Wait"…snap, snap, snap. "Let me break through to the other side. So first I thought, you know—just start a new religion…. I'm not kiddin'! Sheila's grandmother was a friend of Isaac Asimov, and you know what L. Ron Hubbard told Asimov when they were poor struggling sci-fi writers?"

"Become an accountant?" Bud says.

"My man! Ha, ho, but no! He says to Asimov, 'If you want to make money, Isaac, start a religion.' Can I invent a religion? Not forbidden! Easy to do. Big bucks from a lotta schmucks. But look what could happen while you're nappin'? Jamestown is renowned. Scientology? Where's the apology?"

As intently as I'm listening to his rap, I can't help being distracted by the moldy rug smell making me dizzy, so I climb up on a chair.

"My dog!" he says. "A big greeting, and welcome to the meeting, 'cause here's where you come in, big guy, or is it goy? Bud, my man, remember Christmas when you were a boy?"…snap, snap. "Pretty bright, toys in sight, right?"

"Indeed," Bud says, "we always had great Christmases."

"But let's start hissing at all that's now missing! I'm gonna drop my rhyme, that's no crime—fanatics like Mayor Gordon and groups all over the country who're against the Christmas-ing of Christmas? They want you to say 'merry federal holiday,' and they're makin' Santa Claus in the mall just wear a big red bow tie—kids are lucky if maybe he's got a white goatee. He's surrounded by spray-tanned elves who look like they should be working in Sephora, not making toys in the North Pole."

I'm feelin' sorry for Bud, 'cause I can see by the look in his eye he's recallin' happy times from the past, some childhood memories, like mine with me and Billy rolling around on the rug the first time we got out of the big box.

"Well," the Zebe says, "my man, I'm planning to get rich by doing something new for a Jew—saving Christmas. And your Wonder Dog here, whom I'm extoling, is gonna get the Yule log rolling."

The Zebe is about to explain how I'm personally gonna save the beloved national holiday of Christmas when his cell phone rings. Before it's at his ear, he's in a screaming fit with his wife about a fur coat she just bought. Judgin' by the volume of the Zebe's barking, and his fist pounding on the desk, it's likely several innocent fur-bearing creatures paid an even higher price for that coat than Mrs. Zebe did.

He slams down the phone, throws up his hands, and is running around the office yelling, "No more! No more! Why didn't I marry Christine Edmundson?"

Bud's got that look on his face people get when someone two feet away is makin' a fool of themselves. I'm figurin' maybe the Zebe should save up, buy a razor blade, shave that beard, and go marry Christine.

He's panting hard like I do after a three-mile run in the sun: "My man...my dog...my life is strife 'cause a the wife."

"Couldn't help but notice," Bud says, "and you think that we can actually help you?"

He falls back into his chair, and dust and pollen and spores come shooting out of the cushion.

Bud's having a coughing fit, like the time he swallowed the lit microroach.

"Here's the deal, it's real—the CIC is paying..."

"CIC?" Bud asks.

"The Christmas Industrial Complex."

"Ah, that's a new one." Bud nods.

"Right, and outta sight. The CIC is paying big bucks to fight the de-Christmasing of Christmas. Think a bit, each year should be a hit—but are the tree growers happy with warning signs marching around the Rockefeller Center Christmas tree? Are the Hallmark people having orgasms that you can get fired for sending the wrong kind of card to someone at work? Are the inflatable Rudolph people pumped up about not selling enough Rudolphs? No! So! My man, my dog, I'm one of hundreds across the country this year who're being paid big to set forth rigs."

"What rigs?" Bud's askin'.

"Each one's different"…snap, snap. "Mine's a giant flatbed with a good old-fashioned politically incorrect Christmas display—music, the works, and here's the hit, there's no mystery…. It'll be history. Santa and Jesus—arm in arm for the first time—singing duets of all your holiday favorites. But it's not over without a closer, right? So how about a dwarf who's no stranger to a manger popping out of it as baby Jesus and leadin' the crowd in 'Holly Jolly Christmas' while we pass out virus-free made-in-China gingerbread houses…and I'm launching the gig that's my rig at the High Point Square Park."

"Do you want Spike, like, to dress as a sheep in the Nativity scene? What's up here really, man?" Bud asks. "What are you asking for?"

Snap, snap, snap. "There's no show without promo…. We can't get permits for public displays with Jesus, let alone my big stars, transgender Mary and Joseph. There has got to be a crowd, then, boom, we appear without fear…"

"So…?" Bud asks.

Snap, snap. "My dog! Every kid in the Piedmont Triad wants to meet you after Vegas."

Who's counting? But I'm nodding in agreement. My fan mail's currently thirteen-to-one to Bud's.

"Note how I'll promote—a 'special appearance by Spike The Wonder Dog,' no mention of Christmas, and all he's got to do is stand in the light so the crowd gathers in the night."

"So technically the show is illegal, 'cause you don't have a permit, right?"

Bud asks, using his talk-show-interviewer voice.

Snap, snap, snap. "My man!"…snap. "But only Mayor Gordon in person can shut us down, and from what I hear, he won't be near, 'cause he's not movin' much, not even with a crutch."

"What's wrong with him?" Bud asks, which is a dumb question, 'cause I know what's wrong with him—he's married to that woman who's still campaigning to have me neutered.

"I'll keep the rumor mill still"…snap, snap, snap. "So are you into sayin' Christmas is no sin?"

"I love Christmas," Bud says, "but Spike is technically an employee of WGHP, so I have to talk to Lombardo, 'cause this is not actually legal."

I always like a meeting with Lombardo. He's got a soft, clean rug, and I can stare endlessly at my reflection in those spit-shined black shoes.

He's standing behind that big clear desk lecturing Bud and watching three TV monitors at the same time.

"I'm all for kids watching Christmas action," Lombard says. "I'm all for Santa not being seen as a microaggressive terrorist. But you're dealing with this suspect semi-holy man where everything he touches goes down the tube, and his sworn enemies, who are two PC anti-Christmas fanatics. Mayor Gordon actually had a sidewalk Santa arrested last year and kept the money from the red pot. And then there's his wife, Doris, who's consumed with rage that I've still got your increasingly famous…What do I say? Oh yeah, reproductively unrearranged dog working for me. Why risk putting that dog in the show?"

"Well, I tell you," Bud says. "He's nuts, but I kinda' like the rabbi, although he says he's not a rabbi anymore, but beyond anything else, I'd like to help put one over on the crooked mayor and his neutering-obsessed wife."

Lombardo's nodding and starting to enjoy Bud's pitch.

"You tell me how a guy who was literally the dog catcher, and his wife, who ran an animal shelter out of her one-car garage, now have a beachfront villa in Cabo, a Cadillac Escalade, a mansion in

Rosedale Park, and a full-time live-in servant, all just three years after he becomes mayor?" Bud asks.

"Total graft," Lombardo says, "straight out of the Paul Manafort playbook…and the soup kitchen can't even afford to buy soup. You're right, goddamn it, screw 'em both. Put that dog up there and shine a light on his balls, and let Santa and Jesus take selfies with every kid in the state."

"Anyway," Bud says, "I think we're safe 'cause the rabbi told me only Mayor Gordon in person could shut down the show and order arrests, but he said that Gordon isn't leaving his house."

"Right, that's what I hear; he's not moving much, and I'm sure Police Chief Mulrooney, who's a devout father of nine children who love Christmas, won't stop you."

"But what's up with Gordon?" Bud asks.

Lombardo sits down to explain, and starts scratching my head with nails way smoother than Bud's.

"According to what Tim the cable guy accidentally saw at his house, and some Google research he did, the mayor's now so obese, he might not even be able to get out of bed. Theory is he and Doris are in some kind of kinky 'feeder-gainer' fetish relationship."

"What?" Bud asks, leaning forward, 'cause I think the word "kinky" has some appeal.

"It's two crazed people who get off on one making the other as fat as possible.

Tim says he accidentally opened a door looking for the Wi-Fi router and spotted Doris pouring an industrial-sized container of hollandaise sauce into a big green funnel with a tube going into the mayor's mouth. Doris was cackling, 'No pain, no gain, Herb,' while the mayor was making gasping noises and swallowing and swallowing.

"Tim said it looked like Gordon was being waterboarded with salad dressing. He says the mayor's probably weighing over four hundred pounds, and that's why he's running the city by phone from his mansion. He's probably too heavy to move much."

Bud's mouth is hanging open as he's staring at Lombardo blinking. "Gainer-feeder relationship, what the fuck?"

"Yeah, that's what we think. Go ahead, on with the show," Lombardo orders.

For the next two weeks the Zebe is promoting my special appearance as: "Meet Spike The Wonder Dog and Friends."

It's real windy and cold for High Point the evening of the show. Bud and me are on a flatbed truck with the sides up. I'm peering out at a crowd of kids and their freezing, bored parents, who are frustrated trying to type on iPhones with gloves. Everybody's waiting to see me and whatever special guests they're fantasizing I'm going to produce.

"Trust me, kids," I'm thinkin', "there's a big shortage of superstar talent on this truck."

The Zebe is snap, snap, snapping away while puttin' people in place for the Nativity scene. The Three Wise Men are teenagers from the Greensboro Special Needs Center; each one's holding a leash attached to an old wrinkled man in a Joe Camel headdress. They're furiously puffing on Camels, which Zebe got as a sponsor.

Jesus is the guy who performs Ethel Merman sing-alongs at nursing homes, and Santa's his boyfriend, who does Judy Garland tributes. Mary and Joseph started the year as Joseph and Mary, but they've been discharged from gender reassignment surgery just in time to gingerly walk up the steps to get on the truck as Mary and Joseph.

Danny the dwarf, who's playin' baby Jesus, is running around in a Depends diaper with a green and red peace sign drawn on it, handing out red cherry gummies and telling everybody, "Have fun; they're gummies!" I lick several off the floor just before I hear the Zebe snapping and telling Danny not to give the pot edibles away until after the show.

I'm not happy about what I consumed, 'cause right after I swallowed them, I started to feel strange. I realize I'm contemplating one of the sheep by the manger like she's a long-lost relative. The sheep's staring back at me like I'm some teenage kid in Scotland trying to pick her up for a Saturday-night date.

Ten minutes later, I'm wobbly as Bud leads me out of the truck and up to the ledge. All I'm supposed to do is stand still in the spotlight.

"You OK?" Bud asks me. "No reason to be nervous, Spike."

I suddenly think I can talk, but all that comes out is barking. The crowd hears it, and the kids are screaming and pointing at me. I'm on display standing on a pedestal in the spotlight, paranoid that I might not have a clean rear end. Just as I'm thinking things couldn't get worse, I spot one of the animal control's mobile "Mr. Fix-It" neutering vans pull up with the mayor's wife, Doris Gordon, at the wheel blasting the horn.

The wind is howling, the Nativity scene's on display, and suddenly it's like Jesus and Santa are belting out "Winter Wonderland," and it's the best music I've heard since....

The mayor's wife starts screaming through a bullhorn, "Stop the show!" Police Chief Mulrooney is waving her off. The Zebe jacks the volume way up. Everything I see is spinning around. I just want to be home in my orange doghouse eating as much as I can—a gainer-feeder relationship with any dog in North Carolina would make me happy right now.

Everybody's gleefully singing along with Jesus and Santa. I'm staring straight ahead pretending to pay attention to people gaping at me, but I feel like I'm falling backward through outer space. I hear the mayor's wife yelling, "That dog's not licensed or leashed; if we capture him, he'll be neutered!" Bud's looking at me like "Don't worry, pal, it'll be OK." At the same time, he's got an anxious expression, 'cause he just realized he never bothered to get me a dog license. Actually, I prefer not havin' one—it's like "going commando."

Santa and Jesus are singing "Toyland." I gotta ask, why did no one think of teaming Jesus and Santa musically before? Zebe's three little kids in astronaut suits are piling gifts in the manger, and Danny the dwarf is frantically tearing them open, when I smell cheeseburgers, and the scent's comin' from a large flatbed truck roaring toward us. It pulls up right under my pedestal, and my tongue's hanging out.

In the back of the truck I see the head of Mayor Gordon sticking out of a giant blue nylon tarp. There might be a baby elephant under the tarp, but I'm guessing it's all mayor.

Outta a bullhorn, he's yelling, "Officer Mulrooney, I order you to close this show. There's no permit for use; arrest that rabbi. Animal control, apprehend that ugly dog. Bring Mary and Joseph, I mean Joseph and Mary, or whatever the hell they are now, bring them in for questioning, and for God's sake, keep them out of all restrooms."

A wind gust lifts a corner of the mayor's covering, and I see piles of McDonald's Triple Cheeseburgers. It's not easy, but I steady myself and leap down to the truck and crawl under the cover. As I stand up with a cheeseburger box clamped in my jaws, the wind catches the tarp and blows it way up in the air. It flips over the mayor's head, mufflin' the sound of the orders he's screaming about capturing Danny the dwarf for tax evasion.

The crowd lets out a loud "Oh my God" as they see a body that's a mountainous blob of rolls and rolls of pink-white flabby fat. The blob seems to be quivering and alive, like a giant jellyfish I saw on *Animal Planet*. I'm volunteering to help him reduce by swallowing what I hope are dozens of his burgers, but a guy with a mean smile and bad nicotine-stained teeth is tryin' to snare me with a wire loop on a stick. Bud's running to stop him but gets blocked by two animal control men.

My heart's poundin'. I dodge the wire and jump off the truck. I'm shaky, stoned, scared. Not good. Need Bud, who's yelling, "Run, Spike." I'm movin' down the street way slower than normal, but people are cheering me as the guy with the wire stick is losing the chase.

I feel this sharp pain in the back of my right leg, and someone yells, "They shot The Wonder Dog with a dart." I'm breathing harder and harder, legs gettin' floppy and heavy.

At the red light, there's a dusty old Nissan pickup with the bay flap down. I stop. I'm weak, but I gotta jump up. I hear the stick guy's boots. He's closing in. I feel the strength of my ancestors in my legs. I leap and manage to crawl on. A couple of darts bounce off the truck as the light changes. The Nissan chugs off into the night.

8

On the Lam

The next morning as I'm coming to, I'm dreaming that CBS medical correspondent Doctor Jon LaPook and me are doing an investigative report on the dangers of edibles for pets. I'm interviewing Snoop Dogg's dog about a couple of bad trips he's had.

I'm lyin' there with a full-body hangover that's a ten on the widely recognized Keith Richards International Hangover Scale. None of my vital dog senses work—can't smell, got blurry vision and no sense of direction. I could be in China except I'm right where I passed out last night, and a dirty little kid with freckles is pointing at me yellin', "Mister Smith, a pig got into Mister Kelper's truck!"

Mr. Smith slowly shuffles over puffing a cigarette. He's old and creaky, but he manages to lift me outta the truck and lead me into his smoky-smellin' little trailer. Mrs. Smith gives me a warm greeting. She's got a faded red cotton dress hangin' on her. She's real skinny, with a wrinkled face that looks like she saved a lot of money over the years not buying sunblock.

She's mighty happy to have a canine visitor, and puts down three slices of bologna and a bowl of water. I'm eating so fast, I bite my tongue while frantically chewing. It's the worst pain I've had since Bud accidentally hit me in the nuts doing swings with a Big Bertha driver on the show. That hurt, but this time, I'm thinkin' I'll pass out from tongue pain.

Mrs. Smith pulls the dart outta my leg, and sticks it in a cork bulletin board next to a certificate from PBS sayin' "Emma Smith was on the 'Trailer Trash Treasures Edition' of *Antiques Roadshow*."

The Smiths look like people who dedicated a big part of life to inhaling thousands of cartons of cigarettes, which they're now likely regretting, judging by the oxygen tank Mrs. Smith is dragging around, and the one in the corner for him. They've given a place of honor to three things that are hangin' a little crooked on the wall over their little yellow '50s dinette set—an autographed picture of Andy Griffith, a soldier with a light blue ribbon and medal hangin' on the picture frame, and an Employee of the Month certificate from Walmart.

They're grillin' me like a Senate subcommittee investigation on missing pets:

"What's your name, big fellow?"

"Are you from the trailer park?"

"We never seen you before?"

"Where's your dog tag?"

"Wanna stay with us?"

"Our dog Marty just died. He was sixteen."

"How'd you get shot with a dart?"

I like the Smiths, and that's a shame about Marty, but my head hurts so bad that I close my eyes and drop off to sleep.

Nobody's around when I wake up, but they left the TV on and there's a report on what happened last night at the park. It's the story of the mayor's appearance and my disappearance.

They got video of the Zebe bein' led off to jail surrounded by little astronauts. His wife's twirling around for the cameras in the new fur coat. I see Bud tackling the guy who shot the dart rifle.

Police Chief Mulrooney says no charges have been made against Bud, but the animal control officer's accused of public endangerment for firing tranquilizer darts on a crowded street.

The tarp flappin' up over the mayor is being played over and over with a medical expert sayin' the mayor is in the superobese weight category.

The city council's president is calling for his resignation unless the mayor can show up at City Hall and conduct business in "a normal fashion." But his wife, Doris Gordon, is lying saying that the mayor is heavy because he went on a low carbohydrate diet that somehow went terribly wrong. "He's now taking laxatives," she announces, "and the condition will clear up soon."

There's video of me runnin' down the street. I'm relieved to see my rear end is clean, but it hurts to watch the dart hit me as I disappear into the dark.

Doris Gordon has all her "Mr. Fix-It" vans on the lookout for me. "We will find him, and like any unregistered stray, we will neuter him. Based on information on the license plate from video surveillance, we have a strong idea as to the whereabouts of the so-called Wonder Dog."

Bud's on next with a thousand-dollar reward for me, and news that Lombardo's tryin' to get a court order for the information on the surveillance tape. At the end of the report, they flash headlines from the *High Point Enterprise*:

"Former Rabbi Arrested for Illegal Christmas Show
Says, 'Wait Until Next Year'"
"Mayor Displays Eating Disorder
 Children Frightened"
"Tranquilizer Dart Hits Baby Jesus
Hospital Sets Up Manger"
"Wonder Dog on the Lam
Animal Control in Pursuit"

I go outside through the door port Marty musta used and take a leak, but stop fast when I realize I'm pissing on Marty's grave. Not good. I'm making a New Year's resolution: "Look first, piss second."

The dog senses are returning. I sniff around a chewed-up doghouse, and it seems like Marty was a good dog. I'm smelling the air, looking at the sky, tuning in on the ancient animal powers of magnetic direction I'll use to get home to Bud. I'm figuring I'll head west, but not bein' real enthusiastic about capture by a neutering van, I'll travel by night. Or maybe the Smiths see what's going on and call Bud. Hope so.

The Smiths return with two pounds of delicious bologna and a small rawhide chew toy. Figurin' their limited income based on the condition of their trailer, their missing teeth, and the pile of unopened medical bills on the counter, that was a mighty generous purchase.

Doctor Oz is now on TV. He's asking, "Are we ready for the countdown to my high colonic?" Mrs. Smith says, "I can never figure what that guy's talking about," so she switches to *The Price Is Right* to yell price guesses at Drew Carey.

I rest all day, bulking up on bologna for the journey. I'm feeling sad leaving the Smiths, who think I'm their new pet. They're calling me a "Christmas miracle" and naming me Frosty. But that night, after they brush me for a half hour, say goodnight, and go to sleep, their Frosty crawls through the door port.

Nothing's going to stop me from getting home. It's a simple escape—all I have to do is dig under the chain-link fence to get out of the yard. After fifteen minutes of very hard digging, my paws hit the underground concrete the fence is stuck in. No way outta the yard.

The next morning I'm planning to bolt out the door the first time someone opens it. That'll be painful for the Smiths to witness, but a dog's gotta do what a dog's gotta do. I'm watching Mr. Smith gumming away on Fruit Loops while Mrs. Smith is fiddling with the gift iPhone her sister just sent her, for FaceTime calls together.

A pounding on the door shakes the little trailer.

"Anybody home? Animal Control, open up now!"

I'm under the table fast. Mr. Smith peeks out the door, and the guy who had the stick and wire pushes in. Behind him is Doris Gordon, who should be home force-feedin' the mayor, not out hunting for me.

"Can you give us any information about the whereabouts of a large white English Bull Terrier with a black patch on his eye, who goes by the name of Spike The Wonder Dog?" Doris Gordon asks, like she's auditioning for *CSI: Stray Dogs*.

"No, you better go to the next trailer," Mr. Smith says. "They always know what's goin' on around here."

"There he is under the table!" the wire guy yells. "I'll get him."

"Leave him alone; that's our dog Frosty," Mrs. Smith says.

Furniture and stuff is flying in all directions as he's chasing me. Doris Gordon's yelling, "Dart him! Gus, dart now!"

As Gus fumbles for his dart pistol, Mrs. Smith throws a bottle of stool softener that hits him in the face. Pills scatter all over the floor. They're gleaming and kinda' tasty looking, but not a snack I see aiding me in this moment of crisis.

A dart stings as it sinks into my shoulder. I charge straight at the front door, hoping to use "Head of Stone" to ram it open, and figure Bud'll pay for the damage, but it's metal and I bounce off. Gus is whacking me over the head with the stick, and I break the rules and bite him on the calf. He falls over screaming. Doris Gordon grabs the stick and is kicking me and tryin' to get that wire around my neck. I'm snarling and snapping at her foot.

She's yelling, "We'll euthanize you. You just bit Gus; you're trying to bite me. You're dead, Spike, dead, and then I'll sell that asshole Bud a puppy from our puppy mill."

I got a lightheaded "Oh my, I've been darted again" feeling. I'm dizzy as the wire slides around my neck.

Mr. Smith is pleading, "Please let us have this dog. He didn't mean to hurt you. We love him; we'll pay a fine." Mr. Smith reaches under the sink for a small jar of dollar bills they got saved.

Doris Gordon spits out, "Look at you people; evolution passed you by. You live in a shithole. You don't need a dog—you're already in a kennel. If my husband were the mayor around here, we'd wipe this filthy trailer park off the face of the earth and build condos and make money, just like we did with that dump Mobile Manor in High Point."

I'm being dragged toward the door, but wiry old Mr. Smith won't let go of the animal control guy's arm. "I'm not used to feeling like a lucky man," he says, "but this is our lucky dog. Please, please, just leave him here!" Doris Gordon shoves him, and Mr. Smith topples backwards.

"You'll do a lethal injection on Spike, Gus, then cut off his balls for the usual exchange. Let's get to the clinic," Doris Gordon says.

My tongue's goin' dry, head pounding as I'm snapping at them. They harness me in the back of an SUV. My dreams of a long life, fatherhood, and seein' Bud settle down are all disappearing as things are gettin' foggy and weird. Just before I pass out, I imagine I hear Bud yelling, "Spike, Spike, Spike…. Are you here?"

Bud actually wasn't too far away when I was captured. Buffy dropped him at the Level Cross Mobile Residence Retirement Gardens to follow the lead from the license plate. He was going trailer to trailer and spotted two old people sitting on their front steps crying. When he learned what happened, he told the Smiths he wanted to borrow their car, but all they had was a golf cart to go to the store.

Mr. Smith called Mac Leahy, who lives in the next row of trailers. In a couple of minutes Mac pulled up in a 1956 Plymouth Fury. "How fast you willin' to go?" he asked Bud.

Bud told him, "As fast as it takes to get to the High Point Animal Control clinic before them."

"That'll be fast," Mac said. "Get in."

In the *Animal Planet* re-creation show that they did about what happened to me and the exposé on Doris Gordon's neutering crusade and the kickbacks she was getting from North Carolina puppy mills for each neutered dog, Mac "Buzz" Leahy's Fury plays a starring role. It's gleaming white with gold lightning bolts on the sides; the engine's rigged with three four-barrel carburetors.

"Not a cop in North Carolina can catch me," "Buzz" says. They hit speeds up to 140 miles an hour and by the time they got to the clinic they had four police chasing them. On the way, Bud called WGHP to get a cameraman to meet him. When Doris drove up in the SUV, tape was rolling.

Doris Gordon wasn't happy to hand me over to Bud.

She wasn't happy when Bud told her he'd be showing the iPhone video Mrs. Smith shot of her and Gus beating me with the stick, and insulting the Smiths, whose dead son, Donald, is North Carolina's most famous Medal of Honor winner. She wasn't happy that Bud told the *High Point Enterprise* to investigate what she said about making money from closing Mobile Manor.

"You and Mayor Gordon are going down," Bud said.

Then he walked into the clinic to get a dog for the Smiths. He gave a donation and got them a year-old stray pug that was headed for the needle.

I woke up on Bud's lap in the Smiths' little trailer, watching 'em play with Frosty Two, their new dog. They sure were happy with the thousand dollars from Bud they spread out on the table. The WGHP news was on with the story of my rescue and my stay with the Smiths, who were already kinda famous in North Carolina as the parents of a war hero.

As the news goes to commercial, the phone rings. It's Zebe calling from jail.

"I want you and your husband as Mary and Joseph in my Christmas show next year," he tells Mrs. Smith.

"We'll do it for ten cartons of Camels," she rasps.

9

The Phone Call

I'm lyin' on the floor of Bud's office happy to be alive, but worried that I'll never eat bologna again. I love it. I could live on it, even if it turns my face slightly pink. Problem is, Bud never buys the stuff. Unless I'm magically able to bark "May I please have a pound of bologna, thank you" to the deli guy—no more bologna.

Bud's producing extra shows to get time off for Christmas to head home to see his mother in Philadelphia, so it was twice as busy in the office when Buffy's big surprise arrived.

She'd been tellin' Bud for months that she was gonna get a female English Bull Terrier and name her Daisy. The Budster secretly waved his magic wand and arranged for my breeder, Mrs. Erdrick, to ship a twelve-week-old puppy to WGHP as Buffy's Christmas gift.

When little Daisy walks outta that crate, a room full of people are lookin' at her like a baby dinosaur just broke outta its egg. Buffy lets out a shrieking sound and is kissin' Bud full on the mouth like she wants him as much as the dog. I lose control and wet the rug.

Lombardo, thinking maybe the screaming might be an impromptu orgy in the workplace, comes to check and says, "You people are nuts about these dogs. What we need around here is a health and science reporter, not another dog getting shot up like a dartboard…. Bud, come down. I had a phone call; I need to talk to you."

I never saw a more beautiful creature in my life. All thoughts of the bologna famine are gone. I'm hit by a lightning bolt of love at first sight, like the first time Bruce Jenner got dressed as a woman and looked in the mirror. I'm playin' with this little white angel by showin' her some basic bull terrier head fakes. She's lovin' me. I pin her on her back and let her lick my nose. Buffy's laughing watching us. I'm happy in a new way…in love.

Bud comes back. Our world changes. He tells us Lombardo OKed a deal for Bud to go to New York City and take over as host of a ninety-minute afternoon talk show.

I'm thinkin', "Hell no, I won't go."

Buffy's got a happy look and a sad one at the same time.

Bud's gleaming with joy.

I'm not feelin' the licks on my nose anymore, or enjoying her little needle teeth biting my face. I'm sayin' goodbye to this beautiful puppy. I'm seein' my orange doghouse on the side of the road in the trash, and feelin' like I'm being shipped to active duty in Yemen.

A couple of days later, Lombardo has everybody into his office for a farewell drink for Bud. There's champagne and a big white cake that says, "If you can make it there…"

Lombardo's askin' Bud if he's really so sure about taking the job.

"We got some syndication, great ratings; that dog thing is workin' well. No telling how far we might be able to push *Southern Exposure* if you stay. *Oprah* started the same way."

But Bud's firm on what he sees as the big time in New York.

Lombardo says, "Well, Bud, whatever it is you're searchin' for up there, I hope you find it."

He drops a giant rawhide bone on the floor for me and tells me to take care of Bud. Then shakes Bud's hand real hard and tells him he's done a great job. As we're leavin' he says, "You gotta be careful that New York doesn't suck you up and spit you out," as if Bud hasn't experienced that before….

Hold it…. You know what? Forget it—I'm not makin' any "Ha, ha, paw in your ribs" jokes tellin' this part of the story. I got no funny memories of getting ripped away from a perfect life and my first-ever love interest, except for that crush on Cher, which I gradually realized was never gonna work out.

This change is suckin' the energy out of *me*! I give myself a failing score as a pet. I'm purposely ignoring Bud, drinkin' extra water so I can do more anger pissing. I'm overeating, not exercising. I'm wasting time watching TV infomercials featuring over-the-hill celebrities posing as investment authorities to convince homeowners to risk their only asset—and maybe explore the colorful possibilities of bankruptcy and living on the street—by getting a reverse mortgage.

I'm so upset as we're driving away from our perfect life in Thomasville that I throw up in the car. Bud stops at Clem's gas station to clean it up. I jump out the window and run back to the house. Bud finds me shaking and hiding behind my orange doghouse. This is when it finally dawns on him that maybe I'm not so thrilled about leaving.

"It's gonna be good, Spike," he says. "We're gonna have a great time. We've always had a great time; we'll have big fun." He picks up all sixty pounds of me and is hugging me and gently stroking my head.

"Why? Why?" I'm asking myself. That's when I hear Billy's voice reminding me of my duty, and I snap back into focus, figurin' that as long as I'm serving my master, everything will be OK.

"We got two days. Let's go home to Philadelphia for Christmas and see my mother. You haven't been there since you were eight weeks old, and you can play with Pip," Bud says.

I get back in the car. Bud turns on the radio. I'm on the front seat, slowly realizing that maybe I'm cynical, but Christmas music doesn't make me happy. I'm hearing too much of Frank singing about having a so-called merry little Christmas, and how through the years we're all gonna be together, if the fates allow us, and maybe in the meantime we'll just muddle through life somehow. I can't help thinkin' the song's a complete load of holiday bullshit.

I didn't know it then, but I was gonna need all the cynicism a dog could summon where I was headed.

Bud's mother lives alone in northeast Philadelphia in the place the family had since he was really little. I walk in; she gives me a look like "What's this prehistoric thing doing in my house?" I think I scare her with my massive physical presence, 'cause I only weighed fourteen pounds the last time she saw me, and now I'm takin' up half her little living room.

Immediately running out to defend her is her dog, Pip, who she's got dressed in a ridiculous reindeer outfit. He's barking furiously—thankfully drowning out agonizing Christmas music. He's flashing fangs, so I just roll over, signaling all's OK with me and I'm not planning to take a chunk outta Bud's mother's leg.

Bud lights a fire in the little brick fireplace. He puts down a couple of gifts for his mom. There's one "from Spike," which makes it look like I went shopping at the mall to buy her a sweater set.

Pip and me stretch out under the old dining room table to get to know each other. Pip's a black and tan wire-haired dachshund.

As I help him rip off the green felt antlers, he starts to explain himself. "I'm a hunter," he tells me, with a deranged twinkle in his eye. "I've bagged the big three—your rats, your mice, your badgers, but I give chipmunks a pass. Can't do it; they're too cute."

I nod in agreement, even though three annoying chipmunks are singing about Christmas on the radio.

Pip's eight now and starting to have little pains in his back, so he's worrying he's slowin' down and running out of time.

"We're all running out of time," I'm thinkin'. But Pip looks like he's still in great shape; he's joggin' five days a week with the kid next door. He's mainly just hoping Bud has time for their annual Christmas squirrel hunt in the morning before we rush off to New York.

"The one thing I never got as a hunter: I never caught a squirrel," Pip's complaining. "My whole life I've been chasing them, and I never caught one.

I'll be buried out back, and my little tombstone will be like a tweet: "Pip, good dog. Never caught a squirrel. Sad."

I'm thinkin' a fine fellow like Pip shouldn't be so obsessed with hunting. Find a better outlet. Mine's hurling tires around the back-yard—then I remember, no backyard anymore.

Bud's home is warm and cozy, a far cry from his love grotto in Thomasville. It's decorated with Christmas ornaments from over the years; there's even a Pip ball hangin' on the tree. His mother sits in a little rocking chair and settles into petting me. She's nice, with a wise way about her that older people have, as long as they're not worried about bladder leakage in their underwear.

That night we open gifts. I get a blue and red sweater with a big "W" on it; Pip gets a yellow rubber raincoat. The last thing Bud opens is a gift that got delivered to WGHP. It's a blow-up, life-size female doll from Mindy Mounds. While he's stammering away with a long story, tryin' to explain the thing to his mother, I go up to bed, figurin' maybe the doll's my new roommate.

Early the next morning, Bud's yelling, "Squirrel hunt!"

Pip's leapin' with joy at the prospect of chasin' squirrels around a frozen golf course. Me, I admire squirrels, have great respect for them, the way they leap from a roof to a branch, make high-speed climbs up trees, and walk upside down on phone lines. I think if there'd been a squirrel up there with Philippe Petit when he walked on the wire between the Twin Towers, the lowly squirrel would get the respect it deserves.

Bud and Pip can have their tradition. I'm happy staying and watching his mother cook, hoping for food droppings, but Bud hauls me along. As soon as we get there, Pip leaps out the car and charges three squirrels that are innocently gathering nuts. Even though they got legs like an eighth of an inch long, they make it back to a tree real easy. Pip turns around, embarrassed.

He's runnin' this way, runnin' that way, and not even getting close to a nip at a tail. He's got no technique, no plan. I'm watchin' and feelin' more and more sorry for him, so, against my no-hunting principle but out of loyalty to my species, I slip into Wonder Dog gear to help him.

Unless you've ever been attacked by a scurry of squirrels, you can't know the horror I'm about to face.

There's eight or so scattered in a big open space in front of their headquarters—a giant oak tree about twenty yards away. I eyeball Pip to let him know I'm in on the game and to hold back till I get in position. I circle around behind the tree and crawl down in a freezing-cold sand trap and signal Pip to go. He's madly runnin' at the squirrels. They start for the tree. I leap out of the trap to force them back at Pip. Except the squirrels don't turn around, or go up the tree, or run sideways. They head for me, with a reserve squad dropping out of the tree like airborne Rangers.

Pip's got no concern for my safety—he keeps chasing them, driving rabid rodents straight at me.

THE ADVENTURES OF SPIKE THE WONDER DOG

A different kind of dog—like Lombardo's macho Doberman, or a dim-witted coonhound—would've stood his ground and made internet headlines about being ripped to shreds by a pack of angry squirrels on Christmas morning. Not me. I turn and start running for my life. I'm galloping straight down the middle of the course, flyin' along like the kind of golf ball Phil Mickelson wishes he could still hit.

Fifty yards later, I check if I'm in the clear and see Bud's helped me by throwing honey-roasted nuts all over. The squirrels are scattered around gathering them.

That night, under the dining room table, Pip's considering admitting defeat and retiring from squirrel hunting. Bud's mother googles "squirrel attacks" and finds the headline "Rampaging Squirrels Protect Nests and Kill Large Dog in Germany."

For their bravery and teamwork, I'm now appreciating squirrels even more. But I'm also thinkin': Angry squirrels, illegal Christmas shows, Animal Control swindlers, tranquilizer darts, panthers in boxing rings.... Danger's lurking everywhere—what's next?

Oh yeah, New York.

Part Two

10
The Trailer

Before we left North Carolina, Bud went online and picked out a furnished rental apartment at Sixty-Third and Madison. It costs him ten times more than the house in Thomasville with the pool. "This is turnkey!" he proclaims. "And Spike," he says with great pride, "there's a pup park for you on the roof."

Yeah, small footnote here: The "park" turned out to be a patch of plastic grass about the size of a Little League pitcher's mound with a ten-foot-high chain-link fence around it and a sign sayin', "Fifty cents a minute, maximum capacity eighteen dogs."

The building has a fancy, phony name, The Cheshire Gardens Mews. It's missing any evidence of the gardens part, but at least it's a couple of blocks from his new station—channel five. The internet pictures look like King Abdul from Saudi Arabia would live there, but they don't show that the apartment is actually long and narrow—shaped like a mobile home. I'm feelin' like I'm back in the Smiths' trailer, except there's no bologna and I'm on the eleventh floor with the bedroom window facin' Madison Avenue, so we can have the comforting sounds of traffic, sirens, and blasting horns day and night.

The first morning, there's about a quarter inch of snow on the sidewalk as Bud and me start for a walk in the park. The doorman's throwin' heaps of salt on the pavement. He looks like he's got nothing to do in his spare time but pump himself up at the gym, but he still must be too weak to lift a broom and simply sweep the sidewalk; that's why he's tossin' salt with one hand and checkin' Facebook with the other.

So we gotta go back up to the trailer and wash my paws, which are stinging like I've been doing the Lindy hop in a vat of plutonium. We never make it outside, 'cause Bud gets involved in a long phone call with his new boss. I end up having to take a dump in the kitchen. Nice start to the new life.

Next day he's off to work to meet everybody. He rushes back at lunch to walk me, sayin', "I'll take you in tomorrow." He tosses me a couple of biscuits and runs back out. Didn't seem to care that my brain's melting watching *The Maury Povich Show* with some kid screamin', "You had sex with me and my dad, so who's your baby's father?"

I set a personal record for daytime sleepin'. I wake up. Bud's still not back. To comfort myself, I spend a half hour barking, till I hear someone pounding on the wall. I go over to investigate. They pound three times, so I bark three times. They pound once, I bark once. They pound five times, I bark five times. Then I hear screaming and the pounding stops. First fun I had all day. I'm feelin' like I'm Clint Eastwood in a prison movie plotting an escape, which I wish I were.

When he's finally back, Bud's Skypin' with Buffy, tellin' her about work.

"I was a total stranger to these people; they had no idea what we've done. They just heard some new guy from the South was coming in. The story is, their host quit because management set up an appointment for him to have a facelift. He wouldn't do it, so he walked out and he's gonna sue. That makes me the fresh face in town till I'm the one with bags under my eyes."

"So what's it like there?" Buffy's asking, while I'm glued to the screen hopin' to catch a glimpse of Daisy.

"I got my own office with a door, which is good, but the show has weird problems. They constantly have to replace student interns from these fancy Eastern colleges, 'cause the kids take sick days if something they have to research offends them, and a lot of them won't even preinterview guests they don't agree with politically. So they get rid of them. The three interns who stayed are from a cheap community college where the only trigger warning they ever heard was that the kid at the next desk has a loaded gun."

"Oh, boy," Buffy says. "What's Skrill like—the GM Lombardo said to watch out for?"

"He's nuts…. Ready for this?" Bud asks. "His big claim to fame is that he created a moronic program they put on before awards shows called *The Countdown to the Countdown to the Countdown to the Red Carpet*. It starts so early, the carpet's not even laid when they come on the air."

"That's a challenging visual," Buffy says. "Just empty space and wires all over the place, I guess. Hey, how's Spike? Let me see 'im. I'll show you guys Daisy."

Daisy and I are pressing our noses to the screen; I'm tryin' to play it like I could take her or leave her. Meanwhile my heart's pounding.

Bud's sayin', "I'm gonna take in Spike at some point. I gotta pick the right time; these people are all on edge. Everybody's protecting their own turf; Erica the producer seems like a control freak. I don't think she's gonna win any awards for flexibility when she meets

119

Spike. It's early, but I'd say they seem more interested in keepin' things as they are rather than making changes."

I'm pressin' my nose so hard against the screen, I start drooling all over Bud's keyboard, and he's gotta power down to clean it.

"I'll talk to you soon, Buffy. They're still in reruns up here. How's the show?"

"We're in reruns, too. I'll be in your chair sometime next week. We miss you guys," she says.

"Me too," Bud says, and I'm thinkin', "Me three."

We leave to go for a walk, and in the little elevator going down is a beautiful tall blonde. Naturally, Bud intros us. She says she just read in the paper that he's the new guy who'll be taking over the noon show at channel five.

"I'm Donna Hanover," she says," not the one who was married to Mayor Giuliani; I'm the one who was with CBS Sports." There's a connection between them 'cause of TV, and it's real likely Bud's gonna see if she might want another kind of connection later that night, so he says, "Let's get a drink."

"Oh good, I love to drink," she says, smiling with teeth that are way whiter than normal really white teeth.

"Let's go to Nello," Donna says. "It's right down the street, and it's one of my favorites in the neighborhood, 'cause they got the biggest pour, plus I never cook anyway; I'm always going out to eat. I call it 'meals on heels.'"

I figure Bud's getting an eyeful of an authentic single New York woman with this one.

"But I don't know if they'll let the dog in," she says.

This is the first time Bud gets to use the fake ID he got for me before we left High Point. After we get back from Vegas, Bud wants to find something that'd work anywhere for me, like the Ike "I Got Money" Piles Triple Dollar Sign All-Access 3-D Hologram Boxing

Glove Total Access Pass did during fight week. So he goes to Gertie at City Hall to get her to make fake government documents that'll get me in anywhere.

All she wants from Bud for committing dog ID fraud is a pair of tickets to the Radio City Music Hall Christmas show. Bud's always saying, "People will do anything for tickets to that show." So he's figured ways to get them.

They take a headshot of me for the ID that makes me look too heavy—bad lighting.

A week later, Bud gets a bunch of different plastic cards saying I'm a therapy dog, a Homeland Security agent, a robot dog you get free when you buy a Tesla, and a food and wine taster for *Dog Food* magazine.

"If none of those badges work, which is not going to happen," Gertie says, "use this." She gives Bud a little red vest thing for me to wear that says, "Service Dog in Training."

"This could work for the rest of his life," Bud says. "I'll just tell them he's a slow learner."

He hands her the tickets. She looks at them and bursts into tears. She's sobbing so loud clutching those second-balcony, ninth-row tickets that I hear her all the way to the parking lot as we're leavin' City Hall.

The food and wine ID works at Nello. I guess they figured they'd score a review in *Dog Food World*.

Walkin' to a table in the back of the place, I'm feelin' sad seeing a lot of fur coats hangin' off the backs of chairs and dragging on the floor. I can't help but notice that a lot of people are pointing, going, "A dog! A dog!" Like sailors yelling, "Land ho!" after four years at sea.

The place is real noisy. People are talking loud and eating fast. I recognize an investigative reporter for NBC News, can't remember her name. She's shovin' food into her mouth and starting a long sentence at the same time. Not a pretty sight. You won't see your dog doin' that. We're smart enough not to bark while eating. We take one, maybe two bites, then swallow stuff, mostly whole. Our digestive systems are like shredders—large chunks of meat, bones, gravel, wool, aluminum siding—in it goes, and it all comes out, well, you know how it comes out.

After about ten seconds Donna starts squirming around. "Don't you hate it when you have to wait like this to order your first drink?"

Bud's tryin' to calm her, sayin', "We just sat down," but she asks him if he'll go to the bar and get her a Grey Goose martini, "dry, dry, dry and straight up with a twist, please, and bring the shaker, too."

We settle in as Donna starts work on what will be a river of elegant, large, glistening martinis. Bud's a little self-conscious. He's got a woman getting drunk and sloppy on one side, and a big white dog sittin' on the other. Normally I like the floor, but I jumped on a chair, figurin' I'll review the meal while watchin' Bud watch her get loaded.

"They fired me," she's moanin'. "Fired me from my sideline reporting job."

"What happened?" Bud's asking, while he quietly signals the waiter to stay away, 'cause she's draining another glass.

"Waiter!" she yells, waving both hands, "Come back!"

"Is that why you're drinking like this?" Bud asks. "Because of CBS?"

She's explainin' that she didn't know much about football when she got hired, but turns out she couldn't fake it like she thought she could. Bud says that he likes a woman who's not good at faking it, and there's a massive laugh from her, when all of a sudden Erica, who's gonna be the producer of Bud's show, is standin' by our table looming over us.

"Bud? Bud?" she's yelling over the din. "What are you doing here? Why are you here? I don't understand."

The sound of her voice is about as calming as a leaf blower blasting outside your window at seven thirty in the morning.

The Budster, who's not a big fan of stupid questions, says, "Well, everybody's got to be someplace, Erica, and I just happen to be here."

"What's *that*?" Erica yells, pointing at me with a finger that's never seen the inside of a nail salon.

"That would be a dog, Erica. My dog, Spike. Say hello, Spike."

I look her up and down. She's one of those fifty-year-old women who dress like a teenager in ripped jeans and a camisole to try to look young and seductive, and end up seeming about as sexy as the hostess at pie night in a Shaker village. I bark at her, and it's not my warm and friendly bark that gets people to pet me and go, "Ahhh."

"How come he's sitting on a chair at Nello with a napkin around his neck and a twenty-five-dollar bowl of chicken noodle soup in front of him?"

"They didn't have the meatloaf, but the rest…that's a long story. I was planning to tell you about him tomorrow, but for a preview of who he is, just google 'Spike The Wonder Dog' when you get home.

"Say hello to Donna Hangover…er, I mean Hanover. Donna Hanover, sorry," Bud says.

"Your son Andrew's a professional golfer. My brother's a professional golfer," she yells.

"No, I'm not the Donna Hanover who was married to Mayor Giuliani."

"Oh, you're right!" Erica blasts. "You're right, you're not!"

Donna shoots her a look like "Of course I'm right, you idiot. I may be drunk, but I can still remember I wasn't married to Rudy Giuliani."

"Oh, oh, yes, I know who you are. You're the one who got fired yesterday from CBS Sports," Erica says. "So what are you doing now?"

"Waiter! Waiter!" Donna yells. "Come back."

Bud's staring at his steaming bowl of pasta, I'm yawning, and Donna's looking at her veal chop like she'd like to club Erica senseless with the thing. Erica gets the clue and makes a U-turn back to her table.

During most of dinner, Donna's face is on the table and she's moaning, "I just want to be Erin Andrews, I just want to be Erin Andrews."

The bill's around five hundred dollars. I see Bud's jaw clenching over the price, so to get more value, I take a big roll out of the basket. As we're leavin', there's a chorus of, "That's the dog." "That's the dog." Wish they knew I was a canine human food authority at work.

It's snowing. Bud's half carrying, half dragging Donna. Her shoe comes off, so I got both it and the roll in my mouth, as I'm blinkin' back wet snowflakes walkin' up Madison Avenue.

I see a guy under a couple of smelly, snow-covered blankets, just lyin' on the pavement sleepin' right there by a window full of big blue handbags. For the first time, I'm seein' and smelling the homeless people they're reporting about on local news. I wonder what the five hundred dollars Bud just spent would do for this poor guy. All I can do is put the roll in his dirty, frozen hand and hope that it'll be there when he wakes up.

"Good boy, Spike," Bud tells me.

Can't quite explain it, but that night we sleep closer than usual in the king-sized bed that's part of his turnkey deal.

The next morning, I smell a dog outside the apartment, and Donna's knocking at our door.

"I *am* Donna Hangover," she says, walkin' in and looking cute but worn, and older than she did last night in the dim lights at Nello.

"Sorry, Bud, three martinis should absolutely be my limit, unless they're small ones like over there at the Atlantic Grill."

Bounding over to me is an old chihuahua—gray muzzle, gray legs, back going gray, but he's hopping around like he's on springs. "Very spry dog," I'm thinking, and then wonderin', "How old you gotta be to get called spry?"

"Benny, be nice; say hi to Spike and Bud."

Donna's got some flowers for Bud and askin' if he knows anything about her shoe. Benny's sniffing me all over and I'm enjoying the attention from a breed I greatly admire, 'cause chihuahuas always want to be the boss, but I let Benny know that's not the deal with me by batting him around the floor with flicks of my paw. He loves it! Here's a pal.

Donna's tellin' Bud that's she's got lots of time and is happy to walk me when she takes out Benny—who, judging by his age, is getting his "frequent urinator" card stamped so much, Donna's running low on ink. Anything that gets me out of this trailer is good news, and I figure I can probably learn a few big-city tricks from a New York veteran like Benny.

All that day, I'm pushin' furniture around with my head to relieve boredom, and celebrating that I figured how to work the channel button on the TV remote by clicking it with the middle nail of my right paw. For better or worse, the world of daytime TV is now opened for me. I'm switching back and forth between FOX News, CNN, and New York 1.

They're all blastin' warnings about the potential dangers lurking in Times Square on New Year's Eve—ISIS, the Taliban, homegrown terrorists, crazy people buying guns and ammo from vending machines at Walmart, skinheads, angry postal workers. The news is scaring me so much, I'm planning to sleep under the bed that night and hope for the best.

Donna has to run some errands with Benny, so she gets me and grabs my bomb-sniffing ID. Bud figures it's pretty much good anywhere—unless, of course, you meet an actual bomb-sniffing K9-unit dog and cop like we did that day waiting for the number-six train.

The cop asks Donna why such a big dog like me is in the subway. He starts studying the ID and notices the word "freelance" in real small letters under "Bomb Detection." He sees what looks like a government logo, but it's just something Gertie invented to look official—a firecracker, a fish, and a parakeet twisted together in front of the Las Vegas Pyramid Hotel with puffs of smoke coming out the top.

The German shepherd with the cop is lookin' at me like he's the bartender and I'm a twelve-year-old trying to enter a Jägermeister drinking contest. Fortunately, he's got no bark signal for that.

"OK, let's just stroll the platform as a little test of your dog," he tells Donna, with his hand stroking his gun, makin' her feel like she'd better drop on all fours and sniff around, too.

The shepherd's patrolling next to me and I'm copying his every move, knowing that if there is an actual bomb, he'll bark and my superior reflexes will get me to it first. I'm smellin' the subway stench as carefully as I can: the heavy headline smells—vomit, urine, BO—then the lighter smells—hairspray, deodorant, breath mints, then the intriguing tang of people who had morning sex.

I'm inhaling big blasts of a Starbucks Venti Mocha Cookie Frappuccino somebody spilled when I smell something else and run behind a garbage can with my tail on speed wag.

"He hasn't barked," the cop says, "but let's see what it is."

I'm swallowing a pizza slice when the cop says, "This is no bomb-sniffing dog," and asks Donna if he can see her identification.

"How is Rudy Giuliani?" the cop asks. "He was good to the cops, a great mayor."

"I'm not the Donna Hanover who was married to the mayor."

"You're right," he says. "You're the one who just got fired by CBS Sports; that's a shame. I know football, and I thought you really had a handle on the game, except for that time you called the field goal a punt. So what are you doing now?"

Donna shrieks and charges upstairs out of the station. It's freezing, and even though he's wearing a blue knit sweater, Benny's so cold he's vibrating. We're walking around heaps of sad-looking Christmas trees—a couple of days ago they were glowing in somebody's living room, and now people are pissed off 'cause they're blockin' the sidewalk.

We end up in some Irish bar, where Donna gets greeted like she's Lady Gaga getting out of a helicopter in Provincetown. Benny and me are on the floor under her bar stool eating the whole peanuts that Donna's droppin' to us, while she's downing pints of Guinness with whiskey shots.

Benny's goin' on about the arthritis in his left leg and how he knows he's losing his sense of smell 'cause the Lauren perfume Donna splashes on every morning's not stinging his eyes anymore. He also lets me know that life for dogs in the city isn't as good as dogs pretend it is to their owners. Mostly, he's upset 'cause it's been ninety-three days since he had grass under his paws.

On the way home, Donna's drunk and singing—makin' some Van Morrison song, that never had a melody in the first place, sound even worse. She's staggerin' along, barely stopping to let little Benny take the several leaks he needs to take each block.

Next day's not good—I'm in the trailer alone. Donna's off somewhere. Bud doesn't make it back to walk me, so I gotta use the kitchen floor again. Only redeeming value is that Bud puts down the *New York Daily News* for me to use, and you can figure whose orange face I'm dumping on most days.

Barking and playing the wall-banging game's my only relief. I get the person pounding the wall again, except this time I keep barking after they scream, hoping they'll keep pounding, but instead I hear big band music being played real loud.

The worst is the CNN news. They got a great rating ploy.

It's a guest who's a "danger imagination engineer." He's calmly listing threats he's dreamed up that could theoretically happen in Manhattan on New Year's Eve.

I'm watching animation of paralyzing electric shock waves, gas attacks out of windows, poison water spraying from sewers while people are running in horror from exploding confetti and dodging death rays shot at them from drones. He's warning that missiles could theoretically be launched from rooftops in Jersey strip malls, and he's talking about how a certain sound blast could deafen half the population of Manhattan.

For extra fun, the guy shows what would happen if the ball they drop at midnight was actually one of Kim Jong-un's small nuclear bombs. My heart's pounding. If I had the pistol, I'd tranquilizer-dart myself and pass out till New Year's Eve's over.

To try to calm down, I switch to MSNBC, where *Hardball* host Chris Matthews is vibrating with optimism for the year ahead because recently discovered DNA may lead to the cloning of Tip O'Neill.

Bud's at home next morning for New Year's Eve day. He's not noticing I'm trembling with fear at the prospect of our annihilation that night.

The chief of police is now on TV sayin' thousands of cops will be protecting us. He's got a chart of all the different security spots the people will have to go through to be able to stand in seven-degree weather for five hours to see a ball drop. To keep everybody tuned in, the producers make sure the next guest is the comforting "threat expert." He's spent the last twenty-four hours dreaming up even more scary ways that the city could be turned into heaps of smoldering rubble that survivors will be hurrying around on their way to work after the holidays.

Based on the warnings, Bud's plan for the night is dangerous. He wants to walk over to Fifty-Ninth and Seventh to watch the crowds and "experience my first New Year's in New York." In the unlikely event we survive, the reporter Richard Johnson's having a party at some fancy restaurant.

Bud spends almost ten minutes tugging and twisting, trying to pull my Christmas sweater on me 'cause I'm squirming around, tryin' to leap out the window and end it all.

We're passing the checkpoints, and they're waving us through 'cause he's using my "Homeland Security" badge. One threat the guy didn't imagine: "exploding dog with fake ID."

Way down at the end of the street we can see the ball that's gonna drop so a million people can sing and scream and kiss and then stampede to Ruby Tuesday's for the only available bathroom.

Of all the places to stand and watch, Bud's got us by two Arab women wearing those little tents with eye slits that look like gun turrets. But I'm gettin' good whiffs of these two, and even in the frigid air I can smell a couple sets of warm testicles under all that burlap. I give three short barks, the same short barks I'd give for a man when Bud had me blindfolded on TV playing my famous Man, Woman, Child, or Dwarf? identification game on the old show.

After about ten sets of "It's a man" barks, Bud finally gets my message and goes to a cop sayin' that he's pretty sure his Homeland Security dog thinks the two Muslim women in the crowd are men. The cops question them. I'm figurin' I've pretty much saved Western civilization, until we find out they're just two guys who put burqas over the doorman uniforms they wear at the Fifth Avenue building where they work. We're safe! They're just Muslim drag queens. I guess if you're a Muslim cross-dresser, you don't have a lot of wardrobe options.

Bud tells the cops they should have been suspicious when the women weren't carrying designer handbags. He gets a picture of me with them to send to Buffy and Danny to show that the Man, Woman, Child or Dwarf? game was a hit on New Year's Eve.

Richard Johnson's party upstairs at Le Cirque restaurant is roaring when we get there. Men in tuxedos and beautiful women who make the girls in High Point dressed up for a big Saturday night at Pierre's look like haggard cashiers at Costco.

There's even Cloudy, a small white dog with Richard Belzer. I get the cold shoulder from her. Cloudy's actin' like she's the big star 'cause she's with Belzer. She's got no idea she's dissing The Wonder Dog from North Carolina. Same with Bud—in High Point at a party, people would be flockin' around him like he's handing out wads of cash. Here, he's getting about as much attention as a flight attendant showing how the oxygen mask works.

A little kid in a tuxedo and wearin' a black superhero cape comes walking by, and Bud says, "Hi, who are you, pal?"

"I'm Carlos Danger Jr.," he says. "Protecting the world from evil."

He's petting me while his dad's telling Bud that the kid calls himself Carlos Danger Jr. 'cause he heard the name Carlos Danger on TV and thought it was an action hero.

"My son's named himself after one of the sleaziest politicians in history," the guy tells Bud.

"Our civil servants continue to set such fine examples," Bud says, "but try to steer him more toward Batman, before he finds out he's actually pretending to be Anthony Weiner."

They're laughin' together when Richard Johnson comes over and welcomes Bud and me to New York. This is when I hear what Bud's been keepin' secret from me. He's tells Richard that the producer doesn't want me on the show.

"Well, that's stupid; your dog's probably had more YouTube hits just from that drone thing than their show's had in two years," Richard says.

Bud, as usual, is confident and determined. He tells Richard that one way or the other, "Spike is gonna be on my show."

"Let me know if I can help. They're gluttons for publicity over there," Richard Johnson says.

Bud tells Richard about what just happened with me bein' able to identify the Muslim cross-dressers in the park.

"Send over the picture. That's hysterical; maybe I can use it. I'm gonna circulate and be host. If you want to meet anybody, let me know."

Bud's movin' around a little, striking up some conversations, but everybody seems to be lookin' over his shoulder trying to spot somebody they think is more important.

"They got 'cocktail party eyes,'" Bud tells me.

Back at the apartment, Bud calls his mother like he always does on New Year's Eve.

"Have a happy, healthy year, Mother, and I hope you'll come up to New York and see the show."

"We'll see, Bud, but I want you to stay well, be a good boy, and be yourself. Remember, whatever got you this far is going to work for you."

"Thanks," Bud says. "You know, I miss Dad more than usual tonight. We always had such a great time on New Year's. I remember when I was a boy walking down the street at midnight, and he was ringing that loud bell."

"He had great faith in you, Bud. Be true to that. Happy New Year, and tell Spike I said hello," his mother says.

On TV, they're screaming real loud and counting down for the ball to drop.

"We're gonna have a great year, Spike, a great year," Bud says, scratching my head and digging his fingers into my neck.

I'm hopin' he's right, but I'm not lookin' much into the New Year. I'm just missing little Daisy and thinkin' about my orange doghouse sittin' there empty in the yard. I'm worried it's gonna end up somewhere like a piece of trash.

I gotta fight off this negative thinking, so I remember the nine little meatballs I just ate at the party and drift off to sleep tryin' to recall that Latin thing Billy told me.

11
The Show

"Well, Spike," Bud says, "let's see how these New Yorkers react to a little livestock grazing around their office today. You're going in, and going in on a crazy day. First guest is a guy on with a device to convert sound waves from uncontrollable snoring into a renewable source of home energy. He just got investors from *Shark Tank*."

I'm glad to get out of the trailer. Donna Hanover's disappeared. Bud's hoping maybe she's in rehab, and I'm havin' boring days alone. My only activity's improvising some kind of workout to keep me the big bruiser I am, 'cause in New York I'm seein' a lot of people who're in way better shape than their dogs. Maybe the mayor oughta announce that walkin' your dog down the block a couple of times a day is not building muscle tone.

I'm hearin' some dogs are being fat-shamed by friends of their owners, so they're sent to Doggie Weight Control, where they get the stimulating experience of walking on a treadmill all day while staring at a wall. My new fitness routine isn't as good as bouncing around the yard pretending to be Muhammad Ali, but at least I'm makin' an effort.

I got a version of a spinning class where I stand in the middle of the living room whirling around in a circle for ten minutes. First time I do it, I get kinda dizzy and crash into the end table by the TV and bust its legs, and the crystal vase on top smashes me in the head, but I'm only dazed.

Step aerobics is simple. All I do is jump on and off the sofa a hundred times for leg strength and cardio. This might be a little tough on the leather, 'cause it's scratching up real fast from my nails. Sofa's also developing a big worn spot on the side from where I'm pushing it around with my head.

I'm also working on slow-movement walking. I started doin' it to cheer myself up from the plight of living in a peewee space in New York with my only company bein' a crazy wall-bangin' neighbor.

I got the slow-walking idea from watchin' people in TV commercials who seem to be at the height of human happiness when they're in slow motion. They could be curing a spastic colon or contemplating the prospects of life-threatening spinal surgery—whatever it is, if they're doing it in slo-mo, they're beamin' wide-eyed and grinning with moronic joy.

And check this out—even food looks happier being piled on a plate in slow motion. I'm still waitin' for the desired cheery effect to kick in. I tried slow walking on the street but had to stop 'cause Bud thought I was havin' a stroke.

On the way to the station that chilly morning, I'm seein' more homeless people. They're shaking little cups of coins while everybody's rushing by, pretending not to see them. I get a sadness I never felt before. Back in High Point, everybody just seemed okay.

There's another thing that's been makin' me glum. It's a store on Madison Avenue with a window full of beautiful clothes for little kids. Every time I look in that window, I'm thinkin' about the lucky boys and girls who're gonna wear all that expensive stuff, but then I get these pictures flashin' in my head of the scared little faces of refugee kids wearin' rags. How do you figure it? Lucky kids? Unlucky kids? Lottery of birth, I guess.

I'm sighing sadly, and I never sighed before. Thinking all this, by the time we get to channel five I'm ready for a dog psychiatrist, which is another stupid thing available for dogs in New York—that and other crap, like the Happy Paws Canine Nail Salon. Save your money, folks. Your dog would rather be home chewin' on a table leg than getting his nails filed to an unusable stub by some Korean woman wearing a mask.

When I walk through that door at channel five, I gotta be seen like the star I am, so I go into my command-posture mode to look as tough and macho as possible. I march into the lobby like a four-star general, but the first thing I hear is the voice of Cher. Cher! She's coming toward me with a classic "show it and hide it" walk.

"OK, Cher, here we go!"

I flip on my back, waggin' my tail, being as submissive as possible. I'm gazing straight up at her, hoping I can lure her to the floor to roll around with me. But no! She just points and says, "What the hell is that?" Then it's out the door and into a limo.

"Spike, get up. Here comes Mort, one of the associate producers," Bud says.

I'm upset that I missed the chance to lick Cher's thigh, and Mort's now lookin' at me sayin', "What? Is your dog OK?"

"I think he may have fainted briefly," Bud says.

You never get a second chance to make a first impression. And to make it worse, when I first saw her, I wet the lobby rug.

The office is big with a lot of little enclosed pens. I smell tension—the people here aren't boiling over with glee.

Mort's really quiet and repressed. He looks like the kind of kid who's likely to masturbate to the point of injury. He's the youngest of 'em all, and he got the job 'cause his mother knew the host guy who just quit.

There's a loud, burly, bald guy named Goldfarb. He's wearing a half-open Hawaiian shirt showing tufts of fuzzy gray chest hair. He's got his baggy pants pulled up over his stomach like he's a banker in a '30s movie. I figure he's the person voted Most Likely to Wear Black Socks on the Beach by his high school class.

Susan is smart, well-dressed, and really pretty, a Candice Bergen type who might end up foolin' around with Bud, except for the minor fact that she's already foolin' around with the married news director. Susan's afraid of the executive producer, Erica, who talks to everybody with a big smile on her face but a dead look in her eyes.

"Wag with your eyes," brother Billy told me, "not your tail."

The nicest of the bunch is a young producer named Andy, from Chicago. He's a happy kid. He treats Bud as a guy to look up to and maybe learn from. He's also one of my fans, and he's seen everything on our YouTube channel. He's the only one all day who spends time with me. He even gives me a little piece of his salad-bar tilapia, which unfortunately tastes like the oil slick where they probably raised it.

I don't feel good for Bud. He's not castin' out that free-and-easy personality like at WGHP, when he was in charge. He's only been in the place for thirty minutes, and he's tellin' Erica she's being too rigid against his ideas.

We're all in her office. She's got greasy bags of food from a Red Robin restaurant on the desk. Unfortunately it looks like Red Robin's bottomless-fries policy has gone straight to her bottom.

"Bud, you have to understand, *we're* producing you!" she tells him.

"That's interesting," Bud says. "So far only my parents were able to do that."

"We're not using the dog," she says, lookin' at me like I'm a mound of dirty laundry. "I'm producing a talk show, not the World Dog Awards."

Just then a good thing happens. Lillian, one of the interns, pops up with, "I thought you oughta see this."

She hands the *New York Post* to Erica. The picture of me and Bud and the cross-dressing Muslims is in Richard Johnson's column. It announces that I'm Spike The Wonder Dog, who'll be part of the *Noonday with Bud* show debuting soon. The headline is "Barked Outta Burqas."

Erica looks wide-eyed at Bud. "Wow! How'd you do this? Johnson's never mentioned the show in his column, ever."

Bud says, "Things happen with Spike. Did you Google his YouTube hits from Vegas, or with Fallon, or any of his other stuff?"

Erica doesn't say anything. Then Andy pops in: "I did. He set a one-hour record on YouTube for the month with his drone thing in Vegas. On Bud's old show, the dog had a higher TVQ rating than a Scott Pelly robot, at the rival station, in spite of the robot's popularity because of its bursts of profanity from behind the anchor desk during the High Point morning traffic report.

"This isn't High Point," Erica says.

"Yeah," Bud says, "but it is still daytime TV, and hard as it may be for you to believe, Erica, people actually like dogs up here in New York just like they do in North Carolina. This is my plan for Spike."

He's tellin' them he wants to go out on the street a couple of times a week in the middle of the show and do a segment called "Spike at Noon." He's listing all kinds of ideas, cross-promotion stuff. He says there might be a possibility of a dog-food-sponsor tie-in. Andy and Susan are nodding, loving his concept, and Andy says he'll work on promoting me on the web. Goldfarb's playin' politics by waitin' to see what Erica's gonna say. She's got a threatened expression, and her hand's clawing deep in the bottomless-fries bag.

"I'll have to think about it," she says. "That's it for today, everybody. Back to work."

It takes Bud two more weeks to finally give it a try, after straining through daily arguments about ideas for "Spike at Noon." During those weeks I'm mostly alone, bored, workin' out, and listening to Bud complaining to Buffy or his friends or his mother about the crap he's dealing with at work.

The next couple of times I go to the office, everybody's nice to me except Erica—we're givin' each other the evil eye. Best thing I do is get up on her desk when no one's around and empty her bottomless-fries bag. Bud's calling what happened "The Canine Mutiny," 'cause Erica's blaming one after another for eating her fries. I'm innocently under Bud's desk slowly releasing French fry gas while lookin' at Susan's red Diane B. shoes across the way.

The first "Spike at Noon" segment has a clown on a moped, a guy dressed in black with a painted white face calling himself a mime. There's also Mario, a gnarly old Italian man wearing a bebop beret. He's got a monkey gunfight act. They're from a little one-ring circus that's opening that night in Larchmont.

The mime is having problems, 'cause he's not able to get through the air that's right in front of him. He thinks there's a wall and he's pressing his hands against it, and I keep running up jumping through it letting him know nothing's there. Stupid guy, dumb act. Next time I see him, he'll be sitting on the street shaking an imaginary cup of coins.

I never been with monkeys, just saw 'em on the nature shows— up close the things stink. These two are wearin' little cowboy outfits and have tiny cap guns in holsters. They're on the street, standing back-to-back. They pace off, and when I bark, they whirl around and quick-draw shoot at each other. It works great, and Bud's interviewing Mario when one of the monkeys jumps on my back and is screeching and waving his tiny cowboy hat like he's on some big rodeo bull.

His ugly, smelly feet are clawin' into my sides, so I start hoppin' around, jumpin' straight up in the air to shake him off, but his hairy little hands are clenched on my ears. I don't get pissed off much, but I am now.

"OK, you little ape, cry 'havoc' and let slip the dogs of war," I think. I start a full-speed run down Sixty-Seventh Street toward Second Avenue.

The mime gets through the wall and is chasin' us. The clown takes off on the moped, and Mario's screamin' at Bud, "Your-a fuckin' a-dog, he steal-a my monkey!"

Bud calmly looks into the camera. "It's 'Spike at Noon' live, folks. I have a feeling The Wonder Dog is enjoying a little trip around the block with his new little friend."

I make a wide left turn and dodge a couple of cars zooming at me down Second Avenue. The monkey's having a screeching fit and pulling my ears to stop, but I'm sprinting up to Sixty-Eighth Street. People walking along transfixed on their phones actually look up. Kids in school uniforms are pointing, yelling, "A monkey's riding a dog!"

I swing a hard left at the corner and hope he'll fly off. No luck. I'm charging up the pavement on Sixty-Eighth Street headed to Third. People are scattering like a ballistic missile is locked in on them. I gotta hurdle a garbage container so I don't knock down two little kids, whose mother's not watching them 'cause she's yelling at the maid over the phone.

Thirty feet straight ahead, there's a cluster of terrified old people on walkers who are lookin' at me like I'm a bowling ball. It takes deft paw work, but I weave through 'em. This is when I realize New York needs a special "really old people lane"—an ROP. They could totter along as slow as they want and not hold everybody up. Maybe all the slow-walkin', mouth-breathin', picture-takin' tourists could pay a toll in that lane, too.

As I'm racing along considering a new career in city planning, the monkey stops screeching and puts his hands on my neck, and crouches down to ride me like a jockey would. All of a sudden, we're in a rhythm together. I feel like he's a tiny, dirty, hairy, smelly version of the Lone Ranger, and I'm his gleaming-white great horse, Silver—so I settle into a comfortable gallop.

This is cool! We make a left at the corner. We're cruising along, but the monkey pulls on my ears to stop. The Lone Ranger's voice in my head is sayin', "Whoa, easy steady, big fella." I let out a whinny as we pull up in front of Mariella Pizza. The monkey hops up, grabs two slices from the sidewalk counter. He puts one in my mouth, jumps back on, and we trot around the corner with him holding pizza in one hand and waving his hat at the cheering crowd with the other. I slip into the slow-motion walk, and I hear people say, "He looks like one of those Lipizzaner stallions."

Bud's announcing, "They're coming back, and it looks like they stopped for pizza. Where's my slice, Spike?"

The clown's ridin' right behind us, but the mime stopped to do his act for a crossing guard and two kindergarten children.

After the show, we're all in Erica's office and she's yelling because Spike upset the monkey trainer. Bud's lookin' at her like she's nuts, and even Goldfarb, who always agrees with her, is admitting, "That was pretty good TV."

Bud knows exactly what to do, 'cause the clown on the moped got the whole thing on the GoPro camera on his bike. Andy puts it on our YouTube channel that night, giving "Spike at Noon" the worldwide attention it richly deserves. The next day I learn we had the highest-rated segment of the show all week.

The old Italian man offers me a job as a horse in his monkey cowboy act, but Bud says no. They send Erica a huge bunch of flowers thanking her for the PR, saying their entire New York state tour is sold out.

All she says is, "Bud, every detail of this stuff at noon with the dog will have to be cleared through me." He just wants to blow things out of the water like he did in High Point, but he's wasting a lot a time fightin' to try to make it happen.

Right off, she won't let us do one of our hits from the old show. She puts a veto on "Barked out of the Closet"—where I pick the gay person out of a lineup. Even though Bud's somehow got dozens of gay people dyin' to be outed on TV by a dog, she won't let us do it.

"Not politically correct," she says.

"I guess that's why Amy Schumer and Sarah Silverman aren't working much these days," Bud shoots back.

But by using all his powers of charm and creativity, he wins a lot of arguments, and we do some pretty good TV a couple of times a week. He works with Teller, from Penn & Teller, who creates a hood to go over my head for a new bit called "Psychic Spike." I can see through a slit, so I bark answers to all kinds of challenges and gain recognition for having mystical canine powers.

I'm doin' my old hopping-around routine from WGHP but now with Alvin Ailey dancers, playin' "To Tell the Toupe" usin' my uncanny rug-guessing ability, running around the block with a camera on my head, meeting every animal who's got a role in a Broadway show, and getting placed in a driverless car for a ride up Third Avenue with my paws on the wheel. This is my favorite bit, 'cause every time I do it, I freak out drivers by swerving around them while barking and honking with delight.

We have a judge from the Westminster Kennel Club show who's putting me in competition against every breed in the terrier group, and a Yorkie beats me, which is like losing to a hair dryer. Bud gets a sponsor for "Spike at Noon"—The Little Lassies Learning Center, so every once in a while I get to fool around with some puppies who are the future leaders of our species.

Not everything works. One day they bring over a van of very old dogs whose owners are paying a fortune for them to live out their lives at Silver Tails Manor, a canine nursing home. The dogs thought they might be lucking out, hoping maybe the van was taking them somewhere to put them outta their misery. Instead, they're huddled together on TV—trembling and drooling—with the audience going, "So sad, really sad, oh my, very sorry."

A week later, Bud takes me to visit them at the center. I'm glad to see a few gray tails half wagging while I prance around. But they're an unhappy, miserable sight. I'm pondering, "Before I end up like them, I'll finish myself off by swallowing ten Viagra pills and exploding." Yet, maybe I wouldn't? You only got one life, and ya never know what you might be thinkin' at the end.

Soon, I'd learn.

12

Our Life

Even though I'm on TV twice a week and people on the street are waving at me and stopping Bud to talk about the show, Bud and me are not spending much time together. Don't know why it takes way more people way more time up here to turn out the same-length show as in High Point, but it does.

Donna Hanover, who was hangin' all over him drinkin' martinis, turned out to be gay, which was OK with Bud, 'cause he didn't want to go out with somebody he'd have to drag home every night as part of the deal. She tries to fix him up with dates a couple of times, but her idea of beauty is a woman who looks like she works in the logging industry.

Donna's back from a secret seminar for football-sideline reporters where she picked up a lot of the cogent lingo men invented to describe the game.

Donna tells Bud she learned that as often as possible, it's vitally important to offer shrewd insights like, "This is a football game!" or "This team came to play!" or, "They have to take care of the ball!"

"But my big breakthrough," she explains, "was when they told me never bother speaking with adjectives, just use the word 'some' instead. I learned that 'some' can describe absolutely anything going on in sports."

"That's some kind of discovery," Bud says.

Most days Donna walks me with Benny. Other times, Bud's gotta figure out what to do with me in the daytime, 'cause the old neighbor on the other side of the wall's complaining about me. The guy's slidin' messages under our door sayin', "Stop your dogs from barking."

Yeah, he thinks there's more than one of me. I always say, "One dog, in his life, has many barks," so by shifting my barking style, I confuse him into thinking I'm three dogs. To block me out, he starts blasting songs from some ninety-year-old singer named Marilyn Maye, but he's got no idea how much I'm actually enjoying her swingin' tunes and sultry ballads.

So, Bud decides to send me to a fancy free-range care center, where I figure I'll be runnin' around with chickens. But it's just for dogs, so I get to frolic with my peers. All they do is complain about not spending time with their owners. I'm offering my sympathies until a worker spots that I'm not neutered, and he locks me in a cage for the day. On the street, I'm like the Coke Classic of dogs, "The Real Thing." Here, I'm a prisoner of my own nuts.

Bud's goin' to a lot of parties, and sometimes he takes me. He doesn't get it that at a cocktail party all I do is stand around. I enjoy lookin' at the shoes and knees and all, but I get self-conscious when plates and drinks get piled on me when people think I'm an end table.

Bud hauls me to a President's Day bash at Joy Behar's apartment. By now, the New York people are letting Bud talk to them, 'cause they figure he qualifies as worthy by bein' on TV and also, maybe he can do something for them. I'm facing the door hoping Cher's gonna walk in so I can apologize, but no luck.

People are standing around, talkin' loud while shovin' food in their mouths from the trays bein' passed. They use a different food-in-mouth technique than the NBC reporter did at Nello. She jammed a huge forkful of steak in her mouth midsentence. These people got the common decency to keep a big lump of food out of sight in one cheek, so they can talk and chew at same time. If I tried eating and barking like that, I'd choke to death.

There's a guy playin' the piano over in the corner. Must be a real inspiring job pounding those keys all night with nobody paying attention. I lie down for a couple of minutes to listen and see why—the guy stinks.

I get to sit on Whoopi Goldberg's lap, and I'm enjoyin' a slight contact high from licking whatever oil she rubbed on her arm. I bark to get her attention, 'cause she's lookin' the other way when the waiter's offering a tray of food, and she gives me the compliment of sayin' I'm smarter than Ted Cruz.

Regis Philbin's making fun of Bud 'cause he's got me as a date. "Bud, bad enough you didn't take the goat show, but where's the supermodel? You're a TV star, not a ranch hand. People think you're walking around with Babe the pig." For that body shaming, Reege, I'll chew the smallest of holes in the cuff of your pants.

We meet Drew Carey, who's enjoyin' a big beer, and Bud gets him to do a FaceTime call to his big fan Mrs. Smith in North Carolina. I see her beamin' with joy, waving her wrinkled hand and Camel cigarette at Drew. She's flashing two sparkling new front teeth that she bought with the money Bud gave her. Frosty Two is curled up with Mr. Smith watchin' TV. Frosty's probably gonna die young, 'cause of secondhand smoke, but right now, he's experiencin' domestic bliss in their little trailer.

There's a woman who's "had some work done" that makes her look like she might or might not be Barbara Walters. Joy says to her, "I'd like you to meet Bud and Spike; they're on the noon show now."

"Hello." Long pause. "Spike…so you…must be Bud," she says, looking at him like he's ten feet away and not in front of her. "Someone in the Watergate break-in was named Bud."

"Did I interview you on my show in High Point?" Bud asks.

"No, but have you interviewed Bud Abbott, Bud Wilkinson, or Bud Selig?"

"Er, n-n-not yet," Bud stammers.

"I must go, Spike," she tells him. "I haven't seen Hugh Downs for days. Maybe he's here."

Bill Maher gets in a talk with Bud about good pot and bad politics. "President's Day used to be, 'I cannot tell a lie,'" he says. "Now it's, 'I can't tell if I'm lying.'"

"Good one," Bud says.

"If you ever write a book trashing Republicans, you're welcome on my show," Bill tells him.

"I'm sorry I never finished my term paper on William McKinley."

"Well then, bring on the dog," Bill Maher tells him. "I'll sit him next to Mary Matalin; he looks like her husband."

"That'll be quite a beauty contest, but I gotta tell you, Bill, Spike's a fan of Tucker Carlson. He likes the bow ties."

"Forget it; I should kick him," Bill says.

"But," Bud says, "he growls big time at Hannity."

"OK, he's back on. See you guys later; I'll be out on the terrace if you want to join me," he says, winking at Bud.

I spot a good-looking guy with a great smile, and I'm thinkin' he might be wearin' a toupee and give Bud the "potential rug alert" bark. Bud shakes his head no and charges across the room to talk to him. I'm still studying the hair when Bud brings him over and says, "Spike, this is Seth. I think he has a message for you."

And out of this guy's mouth I'm hearing my all-time favorite TV star, Stewie from *Family Guy*, sayin', "Hello, Spike, aren't you bright and clean tonight. Have you been rolling around in a tub of Clorox, or perhaps using Gary Busey–sized Crest Whitestrips on your body?"

Then Peter Griffin says, "Oh, Stewie, you can't talk to a pig like that. Save it for your sister, Meg."

I'm freaked, so I jog to the terrace hearing Brian, the *Family Guy* dog, yellin', "Come back, Spike, I got a couple of hot dogs here for you—and I think you know what I mean."

Outside, Bill Maher's havin' a toke lookin' at the sky. "Full moon, tonight, Spike. Weird things can happen."

Four days later, they're painting me green, because…

Bud meets a tall, handsome guy with a big shiny brown head named Alexis de Shoven. He's wearin' a long green robe covered with green and yellow stars.

"At first I thought you were gay," he tells Bud with a beautiful booming voice. "You're wearing black AG jeans, a cashmere purple-label Ralph Lauren blazer, an Eredi Pisano shirt, a suede Balmain belt, and Bruno Magli loafers."

"Is this a gay costume?" Bud asks him.

"In New York, on a single man with a good haircut, potentially—but then I saw the way you were looking at Brooke Shields' ass over there."

"Sorry to disappoint," Bud says.

"Don't be insulted just because I'm not trying to pick you up, but I do need a tiny favor, darling, just the smallest of favors."

"What's that?"

"I want to paint your Spike The Wonder Dog green."

He explains that his latest fashion collection's theme is "Green Is the New Orange, Which Used to Be the New Black." During his runway show, all of the models will be wearin' his new green designs and walkin' on the green runway with green parrots on their shoulders.

All he has to do is sell Bud on my paint job, but I can tell Bud's hoping to get away from this guy and go over to mingle with Uma Thurman and Brooke.

"It'll be such fun. I'll come out for my bows walking your macho, muscle-bound dog, who'll be bright green. Standing ovation for me, brilliant PR for that always funny noon thing on your show, which I love, love, love, and you'll be in the front row with Jaden and Willow, Barry and Diane, Jennifer Lopez, David Beckham—the biggest stars. Afterward, at the party, you'll meet all the top models in the business. Straight men like you would donate an organ to get in," Alexis says.

"Depends on the organ," Bud says.

Beautiful women throwin' themselves at him, more video for Wonder Dog TV on YouTube, press coverage, minglin' with the A-list crowd, so Bud—'scuse the expression—green-lights the deal. Of course, there's not one word of consultation with his loyal dog about undergoing a potentially life-altering experience.

All I hear is, "Hey, Spike, great news. You're gonna be in a fashion show on a runway with beautiful models and parrots…. And oh yeah, by the way, even more great news, you get to be painted green for a day. Cool, huh?"

The morning of the fashion show they send a limo for us, but Bud, of course, is dealin' with the small matter of bein' on live TV, so Donna takes me. By the time we get to Bryant Park, she's finished the bottle of champagne she managed to pry out of the limo's back-seat bucket before she sat down.

Generally, if I'm gonna be painted, I like to have someone—maybe Bud, a close friend or, even better, a world-class expert on coloring dogs—supervising the ordeal. Donna's supposed to ask the colorist a couple of crucial questions from Bud, but she wanders off to—'scuse the expression—the green room, searchin' for more booze. I'm left alone with a cute little Cuban guy, who's tellin' everybody he's worried that 'cause I got such short hair, the dye's gonna seep into my skin.

Since no one with a brain's around to ask him to test it—say, on the back of my leg—he dyes me the color of a Saint Patrick's Day greeting card. I take one look at myself and head-ram the mirror five times, tryin' to break it.

Late that night, after the fashion show and party, Bud and me are headed home. It's pitch black in the giant limo, and I go nuts barking at myself, 'cause I'm glowin' in the dark.

Bud makes a call. "Hey, Alexis, we're sitting in the back of the car and Spike's glowing like a neon sign. Illuminating him was not part of the deal. Your people just told me he'd be green, but now he's so bright, he's casting a shadow."

"He needed that extra luminous pop for when the little monster and I first appeared on the runway, so the colorist used fluorescent green."

"Oh really," Bud says. "Well now he looks like a sixty-pound lightning bug."

"Please, darling, don't worry. You saw it; we were a big hit, and my boy Ryan will be picking him up tomorrow, and by the end of the day he'll be whiter than country music."

The next day, Ryan takes me to Mel's Organic Grooming Spa and Canine Meditation Center on Amsterdam Avenue. I'm observin' counters of cold-pressed fruitarian dog food, free-range vegan bison smoothies, and artisanal kale-infused antelope mini snacks, thinkin', "Spike, get the Alpo, the Milk-Bones, and let's get the hell outta here." Feed me a can of anything with 100 percent real artificial flavors and I'll be happy.

Some dogs are exhausted with blurry vision, 'cause their owners have 'em on the pegan diet. Others are watchin' videos of the wonders of the Appalachian Trail while bein' massaged and havin' their teeth whitened, or enduring the tortures of belly waxing.

Ryan takes me to the private VID grooming suite, where every organic trick Mel's got to clean a dog does nothing. By the end of the day they got a muzzle on me to stop me from biting Mel, who's scrubbing my skin raw with Ajax-soaked Brillo pads.

I get home and I'm still glowing bright green. They tell Bud they'll work on me every day till I'm white again, and that'll be around eight days.

I never saw Bud so mad as when he's yelling at Alexis on the phone.

Alexis starts sending Bud flowers and champagne and pictures of models he could date, sayin', "You're getting only their head-shots without makeup, so you'll know what they'll look like in the morning."

Life's a nightmare. I'm a walking sight gag. Everywhere I go, people are pointing and laughing at me. Children scream and run away. I have trouble sleepin' at night, 'cause my own glow keeps me awake.

The only comfort I'm getting is from little Benny, who feels like he's a mad scientist in a movie with a radioactive monster.

And it's under these dire circumstances that I get called up to active duty for the first time as a stud. Here we go…

13

Tryin' to Get Laid

When Bud bought me from my breeder, Mrs. Erdrick, she told him she'd only sell me if Bud promised to do her a favor someday and breed me when she asked.

She said that I had a perfect head for an English Bull Terrier, and there would be clients who'd want me to "stand at stud."

Anyway, all my life I've been waitin' to unleash the power of my manhood to send forth into the world my so-called perfect head…. Expect me to make clever there with "perfect head," "manhood," and "Bud"? Forget it. I'm too pissed off being green to make up jokes.

Mrs. Erdrick calls Bud, frantically informin' him that her lead stud dog, McFee, has an ear infection and can't go to Secaucus, New Jersey, to pass on his own perfect head to some totally ready "in season" lady bull terrier named Edie. She's tellin' Bud this is the favor he promised. It's not like she's Carmela Corleone callin' one in for the don, but the Budster takes his promises seriously and, completely overlookin' that I'm green and my confidence is at an all-time-low, says yes.

Drivin' to Secaucus I'm askin' myself, "If I'm one of those drunk green-painted guys at a Jets game, what's the chance of my gettin' laid with a sober virgin in a luxury box?"

I'm feelin' so insecure, I'd like to jump through a TV screen and get the E.D. pills the guy in the commercial needs as he's hang gliding with a woman and suddenly feels the time is gonna be right for sex soon.

I was hopin' the inflatable sex toy doll Bud got for Christmas from Mindy Mounds mighta come with a Viagra dispenser in its hand—but no, just a tag in Chinese and what looks like a faded Anna Nicole Smith trademark.

It's a freezin'-cold night when we get to this big house in Secaucus.

The people who own Edie are Tom and Jane Rundowski. They can't have kids, so to satisfy their urge to raise something other than plants, they go the dog owner route. They could've taken the path of petless peace and harmony. That way, they'd have no responsibility except to make each other happy and travel a lot. Instead, they're homebound with a dog. It's naive couples like this that keep the global market for canine companionship strong. Thank you.

Bud told them about the "green problem," and they didn't care. They're just dyin' for their "little girl" to be mated with a TV star dog, and they're also clamoring to meet Bud from *Noonday with Bud*.

We walk into the place, and before Bud takes off his coat, they're clickin' photos of him and me and posting the shots on Instagram. What's really freakin' me is that they got a live feed arranged on this video stream called Periscope. They want to show the breeding to millions of people. For the sake of my reputation and in the interest of public decency, Bud makes them turn it off.

They invited a lot of other "dog parents" in to watch. They're sitting in folding chairs in a circle—Edie and me will be in the middle as the featured attraction. I realize I'm at a breeding party. If this is what it's gonna be like having sex, let me die a virgin.

They open a door, and Edie comes chargin' out—good-lookin' female: nice muscle tone, small waist, one black ear on a pretty head. Wow! She's givin' off a scent, and a couple of licks and I'm feelin' a little tingle down south, suddenly thinkin', "Hey there, paly, you just might be getting in the mood."

The dog parents are sipping white wine and eating popcorn like they're in premium seats at the Secaucus multiplex eager for the dog porn to start.

"Oh, boy, here we go!" someone says, chugging a glass of buttery-smelling chardonnay.

But it's not so fast, 'cause after about thirty seconds of stimulating nose-to-nose licking, Edie backs up and is staring at me. I figure she's thinkin', "What the fuck? You're bright green; you think I want a litter of lime-colored puppies?"

But since I got more of the tingles, I nuzzle up to her and lick her soft black ear. She nuzzles me back but lets me know, "It's not gonna happen, my new green friend." She thinks the color's kinda kinky, but she's madly in love with Angus, the schnauzer next door—she likes a dog with whiskers.

For two days, Angus has been outside freezing his paws off, tryin' to get to her by clawin' at the sealed dog port in the downstairs rec room. Edie is strong, but not strong enough to pry the inside handle open. She lets me know she thinks I got the jaw power to do it, so Angus can get in.

I don't know if I can pry the damn thing open, and this scent of hers is like nature's way of telling me I don't need the same medicine as the guy in the commercial who's hang gliding and gets a sudden urge for sex. So I got a more immediate challenge—being mad with desire and accepting sexual refusal. Take it from what the old Wonder Dog learned that night, guys, you need to know how to be a gentleman and slam on the brakes.

"On with the show; get moving," someone yells. "Let's go, let's go!"

"You have consent, Spike. Please advance," Mr. Rundowski says reassuringly.

While a fervid lust to see dogs going at it is sweeping through our audience, Edie has a plan. She'll do a shy-dog routine, and I'll signal Bud like we need a little time alone.

"Oh," Mrs. Rundowski observes. "I think our little girl's embarrassed. She's shy."

"Not like *you* the first time," her husband says, which gets the kind of roaring laugh that men's friends make when one of them cracks a feeble sex joke about his wife.

I've stopped the stimulation down below by picturing the E.D. commercial, and imagining the horny guy in the glider falling into the ocean and being circled by sharks.

We trot downstairs to a wood-paneled room with large posters of Elvis and Jimi Hendrix on the walls. There's a sign sayin', "Keep Calm and Carry On," which is helpful 'cause I'm racing against time tryin' to pop the latch on the dog port. Outside, in ten-degree weather, the force of nature and love has Angus scratchin' and whining to get in.

When the port flies open, Edie looks at me like I just dropped a bridge over a moat and her knight in shining armor is charging into the castle. Unfortunately, the knight bites me in gratitude. It's the first time any dog ever attacked me. I feel a bolt of anger and want to grab Angus by the throat and shove him back out the door. But out of consideration for his bride, I know it's no time for confrontation. I let it pass.

157

Angus and Edie are circling each other, getting set for a little intimacy, as Bud calls it. I tiptoe off to the ping-pong room to study a shelf of Hummels over a soundtrack of dog yelps and groans.

Edie's glassy-eyed when she comes to get me. Angus is gone. She's closed the port. To signal Bud, I start barking with joy, and then lie on my back looking like all I need is a cigarette. Edie's in the corner all cute and happy and shy, as everyone rushes downstairs, growling pissed-off obscenities because they missed the action.

As we're leavin' the house, Angus is barking a friendly bark at me from his front yard, and Bud says, "Nice dog. German schnauzer, right?"

In the car, I'm doing my strong silent act, while Bud's quizzing me. "Wow, she bit your neck, but what went on down there, Spike? I heard noises, but it didn't sound like you. Plus you got that 'I pulled one over on you' look, like when you'd hide my shoes in the clothes dryer."

Eight weeks later, the Rundowskis call Bud mad as hell, claimin' the green paint musta damaged my sperm, 'cause all of Edie's puppies were born with whiskers.

Bud gives me his "You did pull something" wink and says, "You really are Spike The Wonder Dog,"

I'm actually glad it didn't happen. Distance and time are probably slowly tearing us apart, but I'm still dreamin' hopelessly of saving myself for Daisy.

14

Disco Fever

I'm mostly seein' life like a black and white movie with a soundtrack of nonstop blasting horns. Hey, New York, you wanna make money? Give out tickets every time some driver's layin' all over his horn 'cause the car in front's not movin' a fraction of a second faster after the light changes.

Sad people are pushin' shopping carts piled with everything they own. If the wind's blowin' in my direction, I catch their scent from two blocks away—crummy bodies, dirty hair, pants stinkin' of urine, stale food stuffed in their pockets. Every once in a while I get lucky and run into one who's sprayed himself with Aramis samples he probably fished out of the trash at Bloomingdale's.

Bud gives them money. In High Point, it was the topless. Here's it's the homeless. Best I can do is carry bread or a roll for the bum on the corner, who unfortunately is not an Aramis man.

Then you got the crazy men on the street. You can spot 'em 'cause they wear the same heavy coat and scarf on real hot days or real cold days—must be something about being nuts that gives your body the same ventilation system as a reptile.

They devote their daylight hours to walkin' around hollering about God or money or some woman who dumped them—can't figure why any woman would want to dump a guy whose career is screaming in public.

The crazy men are yelling just a little louder than some Chinese people, who scream into their phones like their voice has gotta be loud enough to carry through a little wire under the ocean to the person who's yelling back at them in Beijing.

Are the best years of my life behind me, even though I'm just goin' on three? And don't start calculating my age in that stupid dog years crap. Humans invented dog years to feel better 'cause their cute little puppy's gonna be dead before the kids are in college. Last time I checked, one equals one, unless *Sesame Street* got it wrong the day I watched.

The saddest is watching Bud in the morning. Too many nights he's out like some gladiator in glitter land. He's got disco fever for parties and downtown clubs. He's doin' all this crap to be happy? Can't figure how it's worth the moanin' he's doing most mornings in the shower. He's partying, but like I heard in some song, "every form of refuge has its price."

Once he's out all night. About sunrise, he comes staggering through the door. "Late night, Spike," he says, like I couldn't figure that out.

On the show that day, he's doin' a good job but he's lookin' tired—like his old Sunday-morning face back home. Maybe he wouldn't have stayed out all night if he'd remembered that on the "Spike at Noon" segment we got a chef from Eat It Live, the latest trendy restaurant—'cause it only serves live food.

There's stuff squirming around on the table. They got live shrimp crawling with ants. There's a plate of cedar plank partially roasted termites, a cut-up octopus that can't figure out it's dead, and a big, sad fish whose body is fried but his head is still on, and he's gasping for air like a goldfish that jumped outta his bowl.

The fish is staring at me with the kind of intimacy that only a half-fried fish and a dog can have. He's beggin' me to stop the torture and bite off his head.

Bud's burping bad, likely from some meal he had at four in the morning.

The Norwegian chef's beaming like he's got a display of the most wholesome treats any average American would leave for Santa on Christmas Eve. He's offerin' Bud an ant-covered shrimp, but Bud's got his hands jammed in his pockets. He gives me his "Help me out, little pal" look.

The chef tries to get me to eat a squirming octopus leg, and we have a moment of decent TV together, 'cause I just give him the stare. I keep my mouth shut and lock eyes with him as the piece of octopus he's holdin' keeps flipping back and forth, flicking grease on his chef jacket. He has to do something with it, so he puts the thing in his mouth and starts proclaiming how good it tastes, while the leg's pounding up against the side of his cheek trying to escape.

Bud throws up. I run away barking, so Mort the outside producer walks on camera and starts sampling everything like he's gobbling desserts by Daniel Boulud. I hide under a parked car till they clear the stuff.

That night Bud has a "health night," which is the best for me, 'cause he's able to get up in time for us to take a morning run together in the park.

The air's fresh and nice, the grass feels good, but I got questions about the big-city stuff I see. I'm lookin' at the buildings on Central Park South and seein' cranes and construction and the giant Time Warner Center, and I can't stop wondering what happens with all the millions of dumps the humans take every day.

Dog dumps are easy to spot—people walking along carrying a Gristedes bag of groceries in one hand and a swinging baggie of "dog dirt" in the other. You think somebody'd invent a baggie you can't see through. But where the human dumps are going is a big mystery to me, so I try to block the question outta my head, and I'm hoping you can do the same now that I planted it in yours.

Bud is saying yes to every invitation. He's the emcee at events in fancy hotels, goin' to red carpet premieres, doing charity auctions, and speaking at black-tie fundraisers, like The Rita Hayworth Gala for Alzheimer's, where he "just has to get up and say a few words." So Bud, who can be partly truth and partly fiction when he needs to, gives a rousing speech about the tragic and pathetic end of his war hero uncle's life because of Alzheimer's.

People have tears runnin' down their faces. They're writing big checks and waving them in the air. I gotta admire Bud, 'cause he made up the whole thing. His war hero uncle actually died only because he couldn't slow down eating and choked on six buffalo chicken wings—which is something I always gotta be careful of not doin' while speed-chewin' wings.

One day, we rush from the show to a big fundraiser lunch for the ASPCA. I'm proud to be going. As soon as we get there, Bud runs off to circulate, meet some stars, and say hello to Chuck Scarborough, the WNBC guy who's the host. He parks me with a bunch of dogs that are hoping to be adopted. I get my attitude whacked—yeah, I'm lonely, but at least I got an owner. I'm not desperately showing my cutest possible face to everybody, beggin' to be taken home, like these orphans.

It's good to be with normal dogs—and not those pampered weirdos at Mel's Organic Grooming Spa and Canine Meditation Center. I'm enjoyin' myself, but after hanging out with them for fifteen minutes, a woman slips a leash on my collar and is walkin' me over to her table, 'cause she's paid to adopt me. Oh yeah, gave a huge contribution. Claims she owns me.

People are politely inquiring, "Isn't that the dog from TV?" but she's got no idea what they mean. She's telling me that we're going to my new home at her estate in East Hampton. The neighbor's even got a female bull terrier he might want to breed.

For a minute, I'm actually fantasizing about sneaking off with her. Simple. I revoke my Wonder Dog identity and go into a celebrity-dog protection program. Maybe I emerge as, say, Warren, a former junkyard dog who lost his job because he wasn't mean enough.

Hey, why not? She's very nice, gives me half the food off her plate, and pets me during the speeches, including a real passionate one by Bud about "never leaving your dog alone in public." When the event's over, she's tryin' to take me with her, but I won't move. My jaws are clamped on a chair. If I go, she gets a new chair, too.

It's an emergency situation, and as much as I hate to do it around all these well-dressed dog lovers, I give Bud my MIA bark. He finds me, and there's a major argument about my name, which she says is now Floyd, and who owns me. Bud's gotta use the service dog ID with that bad picture. She makes him fork over a donation to get me back.

Why is Bud runnin' around at a party like that and leavin' me alone? Why is he out late so many nights? I keep feelin' he's looking for something he thought was gonna happen in New York that's not happening. Why is he so tense, even when sleepin'? Is it 'cause he's smoking less pot, or 'cause he's not makin' the effort to get laid much? Some days it looks like he's got the weight of the world between his legs.

I'm figurin' the reason is because he hates his own show and won't admit it.

When I watch, it looks like a bloated TV talk show with too many guests and bad camera angles. I see Bud struggling with topics like "transit-cop law reform" or whole shows like the revolting one on overcoming laxative addiction, where the guests kept running out to the bathroom, or on modern medical advances, where he was tryin' to stay awake during segments on "you and your spleen," understanding eczema, and new pronouncements on podiatry.

They book celebrities, which Bud loves, but Erica's always worrying about some guests being too old. He's gotta fight for interviews with stars he had on *Southern Exposure*, like Michael Douglas or Robert Klein. When she thinks they're too old, they put a soft filter on the camera and cut down on their airtime. They put so many filters on Bob Newhart that his nose practically disappeared.

Bud is just tryin' to follow the same freewheelin' instincts that worked down South to make the show a big hit. Up here they're doing what he calls "a fear-based production." They're afraid of losing the youth audience, or losing the young mother audience, or afraid of "offending some audience if we do that," or being too silly, or the worst—afraid of booking a guest who's got "nothing to plug."

The staff sure is scheduling stuff they want to plug, and afterward haulin' home suitcases full of payback for themselves. Every month there's a plus-size fashion segment, and—what a coincidence—Erica just happens to walk away with six new outfits after each show.

Mort, the kid who's gonna win gold if masturbating replaces air pistol in the Olympics, puts together a product demo on the new anal-care aisle at drugstores. For this, he scores a six-pack of the new and improved Handjob Helper and forty samples of Ream and Clean exfoliation gel.

The worst is Goldfarb.

He buys a house in the Vinegar Hill section of Brooklyn, which they say has one of the highest violent crime rates in the city. To hike up his property value, he's producing pieces that make Vinegar Hill look like Beverly Hills.

He's got models walking down a street, but you can't see the burned-out buildings all around them. The models are carrying giant shopping bags from Armani, Bergdorf's, and Chanel, like those stores are right next to the bodega on the corner with the bars on the windows. The third time he goes there, the camera crew gets robbed and beaten. Goldfarb ends up hiding in the van surrounded by a gang of kids who're whacking the hubcaps with baseball bats like they're auditioning for *Stomp*.

15

BENNY AND SOME JETS

Donna Hanover's away again. Bud thinks she might be at a secret camp run by Mary Carillo, where Donna's tryin' to learn about baseball for an audition at NBC. Can't figure out why she doesn't play to her natural skill set and get a job proclaiming the benefits of binge drinking for intoxication ecstasy.

Little Benny the chihuahua gets put with me, or Uber-ed to a cousin on the West Side, or picked up by Donna's parents and hauled to Montclair, New Jersey. The dog's almost sixteen years old, and he's moving around like a piece of forwarded mail.

One afternoon, it's just me and Benny lying on the floor. We're enjoying the warmth of the sun and listening to music comin' through the wall. The guy next door has a new live-in boyfriend named Gabriel. To celebrate, he's playing a bouncy little number called "Blow, Gabriel, Blow."

As it's ending on a big note about Gabriel blowing, Benny looks at me and starts vibrating like that massage wand thing under our bed. His eyes close and he's gasping for breath. Either he's playing an Andy Kaufman practical joke, or something bad's happening to little Benny. I'm scared, maybe watchin' the death of my closest dog pal. We need a vet or he's gonna bark the big one. "Keep calm and carry on," I tell myself, but how do I get 'im outta here?

First, I turn on the TV and get the sound blasting. It's *The Dr. Oz Show*, and he's talking about how a husband and wife can "explore new depths of intimacy at a couples colonoscopy retreat."

Next, I stand at the door and bark loud, real loud. I'm hopin' all the racket is gonna bring Fernando, the skinny, chain-smoking superintendent guy who's always tellin' Bud that I'm making too much noise.

I'm barking, barking, barking. Fernando finally comes in. He sees the grim sight of Benny rolling around with his little pink tongue hangin' out. But Oz is now warning of the dangers of women puttin' talcum powder on their private parts, so Fernando sits down to watch, hoping maybe there's gonna be a private-parts demo. When Oz throws to a commercial, he gets on his walkie-talkie for Wendy, the office girl downstairs. He wants Donna's cell phone number, but Wendy's out getting a stuffed garlic knots pizza for their TGIF office celebration.

I figure by the time these clowns either get Donna off the base-ball field or pry her away from some noon happy hour, Benny'll be four paws up. So I grab him by his neck and run down to the eleva-tor, while Fernando's yelling, "Halt!" like he's an ICE agent about to shoot me at the border.

I hit the elevator button with my nose and get lucky, 'cause it's there fast. We're movin' down—ten, nine, eight, seven, six—but it stops at five. Coming on are Mary and her little girl Cathy, who've always been friendly to me, even when I threw up in the elevator after eating some leftover garlic knot pizza from the lobby trash.

"We'll hold it for you," Mary calls to her neighbor, Mrs. Jones, a retired middle school health teacher who has a knee brace, uses two canes, and is possibly the slowest-walking person on earth.

My heart's pounding. Every second feels like ten minutes. "Get in here, Mrs. Jones; hurry the hell up, old lady." Gotta take a breath, 'cause I realize I'm acting like an authentic rushing-everywhere New Yorker, who'd be happy to let the elevator door close in your face if that gets them to the lobby just a tiny bit faster.

We start back down—four, three. Cathy's asking, "Did a puppy just come out of Spike's mouth? Is he a father now?"

The door slowly opens in the lobby while Mrs. Jones is explaining the fertilization and birth process to little Cathy.

"What's a penis?" Cathy asks as I charge to the street.

All I got to do is race straight to Lexington and the pet store with the sign in the window sayin', "Man Dressed Like a Vet on Premises."

Can't remember much about the run over there except hearing people screaming I'd killed an old squirrel.

I force the pet store door open and go to the counter. Benny's drooping from my jaws. The sales guy's standing there with his mouth open gaping at me. He yells to somebody in the back, "I think this dog's returning something!"

That's the moment when I know the educational bar for pet shop employees is way lower than I thought.

They take Benny to the guy who's dressed like a vet, and while life-saving measures are underway, I decide to stroll around the store and do some fantasy bargain shopping. The only special is a discount and a hundred-thousand-mile guarantee on little Michelin tires for those wagons dogs need 'cause they can't use their back legs. There's also a three-for-five-dollars sale on large bags of

Chinese dog food, but they've got an expiration date around the time Nixon went to China.

After a week, little Benny comes home and Donna takes us to Nello to celebrate that I saved his life. Benny still has to recover from some severe neck trauma that must have happened during his treatment, 'cause I was very careful while carrying him. And if people need me to feel guilty because Benny's in a miniature neck brace, can't rotate his head, and is slowly getting addicted to canine painkillers, that's their problem.

Until he's stronger and this neck thing clears up, Benny'll be "going" at home on a Wee-Wee pad—an invention I put up there with air-conditioning and sedation during canine anal gland releasing.

Donna's not gonna be takin' me and Benny out like before, so Bud signs a deal with Walkin' 'n' Waggin', an exclusive Madison

Avenue dog walkin' operation. They pitch him a Platinum Birth-
to-Death Excretion Needs contract. He opts for the à la carte
package—guaranteed six leaks and two dumps a day, photographed
and downloaded on the Wag-Walk app for owner review. He vetoes
the option of live drone coverage of each walk. Way more complicated than strolling out the back door to the yard in Thomasville.

These dog walkin' guys work about as hard as Michael Moore's
wardrobe adviser.

The first walker they send comes in, turns on the television,
goes to Bud's closet, puts on one of Bud's sport coats, and sits there
fondling himself while watchin' Bud on the show interviewing a
woman who's the head of an organization campaigning for longer
sexual foreplay on TV.

She's explaining that a survey of twenty R-rated cable dramas
reveals that the average "first kiss to coitus interval" during consen-
sual sex is only thirty-one seconds. She announces that *The Affair* set
the record, at 18.2. "This kind of rushing to make love sets a terrible
example for the impressionable youth of America," she warns.

My second walker ends up being a sweet little twenty-year-
old kid named Larry David Seinfeld Garcia. You can figure how
his family learned English, 'cause his sister's name is Mary Tyler
Garcia. I hope nobody's out there rocking an innocent baby named
Wonder Dog Lopez.

Larry David Seinfeld Garcia is on the challenging career path of
dedicating his life to dog walking.

He's practicing barking for better client communication, and
takin' an online course in stoolology. He studies everything that
comes out of my body like he's in the Smithsonian peering through
bulletproof glass at fragments of the Dead Sea Scrolls.

Bud likes him 'cause he's on time, neat, and has artistic talent. He
says some of his close-up stool shots are better than stuff hangin' on

the wall of MoMA. The kid's so calm all the time, he calls himself "the Hispanic who never panics."

It's only later we learn that he stays placid by exploiting the daily benefits of Thorazine to manage the anger issues that started to plague him in seventh grade. The first sign was when he bit his math teacher's thigh outta frustration over long division.

As soon as word gets out in his neighborhood that Larry David Seinfeld Garcia is walking the Wonder Dog from TV, my fame starts growin'. I gotta say it; get ready: The Hispanics love me!

I get asked by a committee saving homeless dogs in Puerto Rico to show up at the dock for a photo op for local news. A pack of street dogs famous in Puerto Rico as The Jets is being delivered on a ship from San Juan. Some shelter in Southampton's gonna take The Jets and switch them from their diet of sun-ripened San Juan street garbage to bowls of kale and quinoa served in Martha Stewart dog bowls in air-conditioned cages.

It's a cool, drizzly day with wind from the Hudson River blowin' my ears back. I'll try to greet 'em with the new Spanish-accent bark Larry David Seinfeld Garcia's taught me. I'm next to Roscoe The Bedbug Beagle from the TV ads. Also part of this made-for-TV-event are six transit-police German shepherds, who'd rather be back at work ripping the pants off turnstile jumpers. Of course, there's a bunch of publicity-hungry politicians who rented dogs for the photo op.

Slowly descending the gangplank are San Juan city officials who must have suddenly made a commitment to help homeless dogs to get a free cruise to New York. There's also a bunch of dolled-up Hamptons women. The whole thing's being covered by *Extra*. Christie Brinkley, Kelly Ripa, Donna Karan, Jane Rothchild, and a few others have to walk down the steps with a dog on a leash.

The dogs were never leashed before. They're pulling and straining and leapin' so much that even that Dog Whisperer guy who's leading the procession is havin' a rough time not being dragged down headfirst.

The mayor of San Juan and his wife are beaming with joy that these filthy-looking dogs aren't still back home terrorizing tourists. Unfortunately they forgot one minor detail: They shoulda hosed down the cargo. The first sign of trouble is when my new pal Roscoe's tail flies up in a "Bedbugs ho!" alert.

I see flies and fleas, gnats, mosquitoes all buzzing happily, celebrating arriving in a country where DDT's illegal. Christie and Jane are wavin' off big green flies. Someone's yelling, "I got mites in my Manolos."

"We're infested!" the mayor's wife starts screamin', "*Hormigas en mis pantalones! Hormigas en mis pantalones!*"

I hear the sound of twelve leashes hittin' the ground. The Jets charge by us and run up Twelfth Avenue, dodging taxis and draggin' leashes on their way to a new life of feasting on the pollution-enriched garbage of New York.

That night, *Extra* ran the escape in slow motion.

16

The Gaze

I finally get something to look forward to other than "Spike at Noon," marching in the Dominican Day Parade, and leftover Taco Bell Volcano Nachos at the office.

Buffy is comin' up for a stay and bringing Daisy!

There's some kind of affiliate meeting she's gotta go to, but maybe it's an excuse for a visit, 'cause she's always tellin' Bud how much she misses us and the old days.

The last time I was this happy is a toss-up. It's either when I heard the Eat It Live restaurant was closed by the Board of Health for what happened with a live sautéed owl they were serving. The *Daily News* said the owl was served unconscious 'cause of electro-shocks from the chef but somehow woke up after being put on the table. The report said that "diners recoiled in horror as the bird began flapping its wings, lifted off the platter, and started flying around, drenching the live-food connoisseurs crowded below with smoldering olive oil."

The other time I was this happy is when the bum on the corner won the lottery with a ticket he bought with the ten dollars Bud gave him for food.

The bum immediately moves to Trump Tower, where there's no board approval during something they're calling "a bail sale." On the ten o'clock news, he announces he's using his Mega Millions money to buy more Trump Tower condos for other bums and realize his dream of carbon-neutral bum communal living there.

Sometimes he comes strolling back to Sixty-Third and Madison in his same filthy clothes but wearin' a new bowler hat. He gives the replacement bum advice on how to work the corner and gleefully tells Bud about his new PC campaign to relabel homeless people.

"First we were hobos; next, bums," he says. "Then homeless. Now we're 'outdoorsmen!'"

The plan is that Buffy and Daisy'll be next door at The Lowell Hotel until they come stay in our place. Bud can't be here for her whole visit, 'cause the TV show is going on location, recording a show from some new cruise ship sailing around the Atlantic.

The cruise is the biggest comp deal Erica and Goldfarb pull off since her free full-body liposuction and his failed robotic hair transplants, where he ended up with something that looked like a palm tree sprouting out of the top of his head.

Bud's not happy about being trapped at sea for three days with people he can't stand on land. He was gonna drag me along, but when he notices my glee when I heard Daisy's on her way, he somehow figures I'd rather be home than floating around on a ship taking mambo lessons with him.

She's comin' up right after the weekend when Bud's goin' to a meditation and mindfulness class. He got invited by a guy named Yogi Bob, who's been on *Noonday* showin' people at home how to breathe and relax.

This is something dogs do naturally, but I guess humans need special training. It musta worked, 'cause viewers call the next day tellin' Bud they fell asleep and they can usually only do that by scrolling Lindsey Graham's Instagram feeds.

So Bud, thinkin' maybe some meditation will calm him down from his battles at work, decides to go.

Yogi Bob lets Bud bring me along 'cause, he tells Bud, he thinks I'm very centered. I guess he can't see that the only thing I'm centered on is tryin' to calculate whether Daisy's now old enough to be willing for a little "action in the afternoon" when Buffy's off shopping.

We show up on a rainy Saturday at the Hunter College Spirituality and Wellness Festival. I'm hoping to attend the Advanced Body Worship workshop and spend an hour with twenty people who're breathing deeply while admiring themselves in mirrors, but as usual, I gotta stay with Bud. We're on the floor next to a couple of women in the Lotus position who got their BlackBerries strapped to their thighs in case they get the familiar urge to scroll Facebook while meditating.

Yogi Bob's on a raised platform. He's wearin' a white robe. He's got a long, flowing hairstyle like Jesus has in the *Dolly Parton with Jesus* black velvet painting in the Smiths' trailer. Sitting next to Yogi Bob is a guy I think I remember seein' at Joy Behar's party.

"Just a few notes on some other things before we get started," Yogi Bob says. "From now on, a helmet is required in my Hyperventilating for Inner Peace workshop, and—hee, hee—small commercial message—ha, ha—if you'd like some body work done, please consider my wife, Tammy. In addition to being a laughter therapist and a professional cuddler, she's also a certified equine masseuse. If she can relax a Times Square police horse, she's going to relax you.

"Now, I don't profess to have magical powers," Yogi Bob says, "although some of you may think so when our session today is over."

The class is so eager to please, they laugh like he's doing a Colbert monologue, not just makin' a dumb remark.

Bud gives me side eye that says, "Cut the crap, swami, and calm me down."

"I've asked the very funny Gilbert Gottfried to sit here with me, hoping that his close proximity to the emanation of the energy from private aura will finally help him," Yogi Bob says. "This is his third class, and he's having a most difficult time advancing to a meditative state. Mister Gottfried is a comedian who rants and raves onstage but can't return to relaxation after a performance. Correct, Mister Gottfried?"

"Yes, oh holy one. I'm desperate to calm down, but when I sit here trying to meditate, I can't stop thinkin' of jokes and ways to insult you. Like, does your ass get embarrassed because of all the shit coming out of your mouth?"

The class is howling but notice that Yogi Bob's upset and slam on the brakes.

"Now, Gilbert…" Yogi Bob starts to say.

"Can I tell you something about this guy, classmates?" Gilbert continues. "Yogi Bob's name is Todd Balderston, and he makes a living selling aquarium pumps to pet stores in New Jersey."

"Yes, but I'm also The Yogi Baba Shanana, a Walgreens-trained master of meditation mindfulness," Yogi Bob says, "and I can help anyone achieve a deep meditative state—even you, Gilbert. Let us begin. Today we will practice open-eye meditation with the key being visual fixation, so find an object in front of you and follow my lead."

I got no interest in this; I can't focus on anything but the copulation clinic I'm gonna be inviting Daisy to, so I figure I'll just gaze straight ahead in my typical super-relaxed state of natural bliss. I notice that Gilbert Gottfried's little brown eyes are zoomed in on me, so, 'cause I got absolutely nothing better to do, I stare back at him.

Over and over, Yogi Bob is sayin', "Breathe deeply, relax, breathe deeply, relax…. Follow your breath to the path of your vision, breathe deeply, relax, breathe deeply, relax…. The path of your vision is a blue light taking you to the next depth of awareness, breathe deeply…"

I'm thinkin' if this is all he learned at the drugstore, he should've saved his money and been a stock boy, but I gotta admit, I'm actually having a good time staring at Gilbert Gottfried. I'm using my canine power to concentrate on him. Ever see a spaniel standing like a statue in the park pointing to a bird like nothing else exists in the world? That's canine focus, and Gilbert Gottfried must be absorbin' some of mine, 'cause he's gradually looking like a different person. His mouth is smiling and hangin' open; his body is going limp; his eyes are sparkling.

But Yogi Bob's crap isn't working on Bud. His fingers are tapping on his leg, which is what he does when some song is going through his head. From the taps, it sounds like either Dylan's "Nashville Skyline Rag," the theme song on our old show, or "Oh, What a Night!" 'cause he saw the musical *Jersey Boys* last week.

After about thirty minutes, Yogi Bob says, "All right, close your eyes, imagine you're in an elevator going from the basement to the tenth floor, and when we get to the tenth floor, the door will open and you'll walk out in a relaxed state of refreshed mindfulness eager to book several private sessions with me." And he starts counting: "One, two, three, four…"

"Sure, Yogi Bob," I'm thinking, "but one question. What about when other people get on the elevator with you? Like delivery guys with smelly bags of Korean food. Maybe next stop, there are three drunk teenagers laughing and shrieking at each other, like they're all by themselves on a beach and not around your tranced-up elevator people."

"Here we are, ten," Yogi Bob says. "Everyone, let's share. Gilbert, any success this time?"

"My God, amazing, I haven't been this relaxed since after the first time I got laid. I was staring at the dog's eyes; he took me so deep, it was like going to the center of the earth on steroids, which makes no sense," Gilbert says, "but that's what it was like."

"Well, I'm actually not surprised," Yogi Bob says, "because I felt the pure force of his power, too. I was studying him, and he seems to have the kind of riveting gaze that could help many people. Bud, would you consider allowing me to take him on here as an adjunct professor of meditation as, shall we call him, say, Swami Spike?"

Bud laughs and starts scratchin' my head with his nails, which feels as good to me as I bet getting a seventy-five-dollar cranial massage feels to you. I'm just hopin' to hell Bud doesn't agree and make me go to workshops to stare at nervous people every Saturday.

"That's interesting," Bud says, "but if you and Gilbert are right, I think I've got another idea for a good way to use him."

"Very well," Yogi Bob says, "but as long as we're with you, your feedback please. Bud, did you achieve the benefits of a meditative state?"

"No," Bud says, "but you know, that first act of *Jersey Boys* is terrific."

"Not sure where you're going with that, Bud," Yogi Bob says, "but good luck with Spike; his eyes can be a window of refuge to help many people. In fact, upon further reflection, I believe he may be the reincarnation of the seventeenth Himalayan monk, Baba Do

Ram Ram Baba, who was able to create unconsciousness in his followers with a single glance."

"Probably," Bud says.

I've heard enough of Yogi Bob to figure his last incarnation was as someone wandering around unsupervised in a mental hospital. I wanna get out of this class and go across the hall to the Calling All Carnivores Meat-Eating Clinic. Try staring at Gilbert Gottfried for a half hour without blinking. Raw meat should be part of the deal.

So Bud calls Andy about putting a meditation video on our YouTube channel. He wants to record me staring straight at the camera for a long while. Andy will use keywords for meditation and mindfulness to get people to find the channel and stare back at me and relax. This is a way more lofty use of my talent than the video of me painted green running around scaring children in the park.

Bud's paying Andy to post all kinds of Wonder Dog videos. Andy says the channel's getting thousands of viewers a day. He claims I'm achieving vast popularity in foreign lands. He says I'm so popular in France that I'm now "the Jerry Lewis of dogs" over there. There's even a big fan club that's formed in Ukraine. Maybe if Bud gets some time off, I can go on a goodwill tour of the region, and take an afternoon and show Putin's dog who's boss.

Back at our place, Bud's all business—the camera's set up about a foot away from my face. He tries something new on me, Doggie Bright Eye Drops. He got 'em from the canine Reiki guru at the festival.

The guy guarantees that the drops'll make my eyes sparkle and my body super relaxed while I'm lookin' at the camera. Hopefully, they'll be better for me than the guy's Reiki fingers were poking all over the terrified Wheaten terrier he had muzzled and strapped to his Reiki table.

Bud tells me to stare straight at the lens. We start rolling and I'm doing my job when I hear Bud sayin', "Breathe deeply, relax, breathe deeply, relax…. The path of your vision is a blue light…" I turn away, lookin' at him like, "Are you fuckin' nuts, too?"

"All right, Spike, let's start again. I know it's weird hearing me talk like Yogi Bob, but this will be fun, and maybe you're gonna help some people."

We roll. The drops kick in, and they get me right in the zone. I'm starin' at the camera like it's two pounds of fresh bologna piled on a Lassie souvenir plate being held by Cher wearin' hot pants and a tight T-shirt sayin', "These Wonder Dogs Bark."

Bud's giving me his reassuring "Good dog, I love you" strokes up and down my back. They always remind me how much I love him, too, 'cause even in this real unhappy phase we're both in right now, the guy's still like James Bond to me. The poodle at Clem's gas station thought Bud had something called savoir faire, and just the other night watchin' the French channel with subtitles, I got what it means. Everybody's always amazed at the stuff Bud's capable of pullin' off when he wants to—like the time back home when he raised a pile of money for a three-year-old orphan.

I got a lot of downtime staring at the camera, so here's what happened.

There's a car crash near our house in Thomasville. A little boy gets pulled out of the wreck by Pledge, the family dog—a big black female mixed breed. Both parents got killed, and Pledge is hurt bad and dying. But she's using her last energy snarling and snapping to guard the crying little boy lying next to her.

Bud and I pull up as they're carrying off the parents. He jumps out of the car. It's a horrible scene. The cops are aiming to shoot Pledge. Bud acts fast. He gets them to hold up by asking if they really want to kill the dog that saved the little boy from a fiery wreck, and then have the kid remembering for the rest of his life how his pet got shot by the police right after his parents were burned to death in a car crash.

"Roger, OK, confirming a possibly accurate citizen communication, duly noted," the officer says loudly and slowly, like he's reading a manual. "Gunfire at dog could induce possible juvenile stress, sensitivity required, plus, men, more important, be viligent, I mean vigilant—all of the citizens watching are recording video of us right now. So stand down, and gentlemen—as noted in the new appendix to your in-public conduct training—at all times, big, wide smiles; big, wide, happy smiles for the cameras."

He turns to the crowd and announces through a bullhorn, "The canine perpetrator is injured and possibly has anger issues. Dog might turn on the juvenile. If said dog starts to attack said juvenile, we'll be justified to use full force available."

Judging by the assault rifles, teargas canisters, and the three Glock G20 pistols pointed at Pledge, I figure that for the cops, it's gonna be like Operation Desert Storm takin' down an unarmed black dog.

"Let's see what we can do to help," Bud says. He then invents a crazy story for the police captain. He tells him that I work for Kibbles 'n Bits as a board-certified dog-to-dog therapist. He suggests maybe I can reduce tension by having a roadside session with Pledge.

"You're taking a risk here, young man," the officer says. "Can't guarantee the therapist won't be victim of collateral damage by friendly fire."

"Go in, Spike," Bud says. So I walk slowly to Pledge and the boy.

As if the other cops next to him can't see what's happening, the captain says, "Continue smiling but stand down, men; a large, white, board-certified dog-to-dog therapist approaching accident scene."

Pledge welcomes me, and I slide right next to her. The little boy is wailing away, sobbing big tears, so I start flickin' my tail in front of his face, and after a couple of minutes he's calmed down and is swatting away at the tail.

Pledge is only alive for a little while. She lived a good life and had two litters of puppies. She was a pet for a family of crop pickers who lived in a tiny rented house on a big farm near Asheville. Just before she let out a couple of long, deep breaths and closed her eyes, she let me know she'd always wondered, what happens when you die? Is there really that dog heaven people are always talking about? Or do you get to be back with your owners in the big human heaven? Or is there nothing? "Now," she tells me, "I'm goin' to find out."

The next day the boy's only relative shows up. He's a sturdy-looking guy named Jack, a twenty-two-year-old from Orlando, Florida, who's tryin' to be a house painter. He's only got about $140 in the bank but says he's committed to raise the little boy, who's got the unfortunate name of Igor.

Bud goes into action and creates The Igor Fund. He's driving all over the Piedmont Triad begging for money from big tobacco and furniture companies. He's singing at charity shows at country clubs, arranging sports auctions with stuff from the Panthers, Hornets, and Hurricanes.

Lombardo lets us do a live TV fundraiser called The Igor-a-Thon, with local TV personalities and athletes dressed as characters in horror movies.

The big star is Danny the Dwarf as Chuckie, holding a giant knife and scarin' people into donating by threatening to climb through their bedroom window at night and stab 'em if they don't.

Lombardo comes on as Norman Bates, and a couple of weirdos livin' with their old mothers call in big pledges. If we'd known about that gainer-feeder eating thing then, the mayor could've been The Blob.

We haul in almost two hundred thousand dollars. Bud goes to Lombardo seekin' advice on what to do with the money, 'cause Bud's idea of managing money is earn, spend, pick up the check, send a hundred a week home for mother to enjoy. Lombardo puts some money in tax-free bonds, then makes another one of his smart moves by buyin' them a wad of Google stock on a big market plunge.

The last time Bud gets news, Jack's working as a fundraiser for Mothers Against Drunk Driving and is married to a restaurant manager at Epcot. They got a couple of million in the bank, and Igor's in private school saying he wants to own a farm someday.

Anyway, that's one story about the Budster. There's a lot—like the one featuring two dancers who came to the house on Friday night and spent the weekend. But that's his tale to tell.

Seein' my reflection in the camera lens, I'm rememberin' at The Igor-a-Thon, where I was the great white shark from *Jaws*; Jack gave me the bright red collar Pledge was wearing the day of the accident. Bud slid it on me this morning, 'cause he knows I appreciate a regular change of neckwear.

Finally, Bud says, "OK, Spike, that's it. Good dog. Want some more Doggy Bright Eye Drops? They sure make your eyes sparkle."

Of course they do. Read the label, Bud—they're made in Fiji, with kava, poppy oil, and coca leaf juice. Your whole body goes numb; the eyes are bright 'cause you got no feelin' below the neck. How do you think I'm able to stand dead still for forty-five minutes lookin' at a camera tryin' to put people in a trance—'cause of the flax in my Alpo?

The FDA doesn't check dog stuff, so nobody's figured out why sometimes ten minutes after the eye drops go in, their jolly pet topples over on his back in the middle of a crowded sidewalk to blissfully watch clouds roll by.

I gratefully hold up my head for Bud to hit me with another round.

The next day, I'm countin' the hours till Monday, when Buffy and Daisy get here. All I got to do is get photographed for the cover of *Big Apple Dog*, which is proclaimin' itself to be the new *People* magazine for celebrities' dogs. It's sad the print industry is goin' down, 'cause a publication like this is long overdue.

The magazine woman comes to our place wearin' a bright red dress and new black Jimmy Choo shoes. She must've sprayed on a pint of Angel perfume, 'cause she's smelled up the entire apartment, the hallway, the elevator, and everything she touched on the way.

A big fuss is made over me, but I can tell she does that to all the dogs. Her name's Shelly, and three years ago she left Great Neck on Long Island, to move to the city to be a journalist. She's actin' like she thinks she made it to the pinnacle of the fourth estate by doin' penetrating interviews about dogs and owners.

"I consider myself the Christiane Amanpour of dogs," she announces. I notice that her face doesn't move when she talks.

I think that's 'cause no face naturally ends up lookin' like it's got a pound of heavy-duty wood filler in it. Shelly looks like a lot of the women and men I see on Madison Avenue every day—no wrinkles, big cheekbone lumps, puffed-out lips, and ultrawide-open eyes with the "Nancy Pelosi staring into a TV camera" expression.

She takes photos of me leapin' almost six feet in the air to hang onto the rope Bud attached to the ceiling. When it's time for the interview, she's suddenly got the somber tone of Chuck Todd sitting down with a frail and ailing Bob Dole, who could be dead by the time you read this, but you get the idea.

"You both came here from High Point, ha, ha, ha—OK for the dog, I guess, but Bud, really, how could you stand living there? What do you do after the furniture mart closes? Ha, ha, ha, ha."

She's one of those people who, for whatever strange reason, laugh all the time at their own nonfunny statements. Why, humans? Why?

The always polite Bud is gently explaining that New York and High Point are totally different, wonderful places, and he enjoyed success and enormous satisfaction at WGHP-TV.

"The show down there was quite popular, and we had a lot of fun," Bud tells her.

"Yes, ha ha, that's sweet, Bud," she says, "but it was only North Carolina after all, and what could any of that fun, satisfaction, or popularity really mean if you had to be living down there and not New York? Ha, ha, ha."

I'm thinkin', "Bud, maybe let her know you had a big house with a huge swimming pool and if there was a pool here in this storage-space-sized ripoff one-bedroom apartment, I would be tryin' to drag her over and throw her in."

"OK, let's get to some questions about young Spike here. He's a pit bull, correct?"

"No," Bud says, "way off. Actually, he's an English Bull Terrier."

"Oh, sorry," she says. "Now I notice he has a slight resemblance to a dinosaur; any reason for that? Ha, ha, ha. Seriously, explain to me, were they bred to look like prehistoric creatures as companions for small children during that dinosaur phase all kids go through?"

"Ha. No, that's a good idea," Bud answers. "They were actually bred for dogfighting, and dominated it before it was banned in England."

"My God," she says, "dogfighting?"

"Of course, they're great pets; they won't start a fight, but they sure won't run from one. It's a really interesting breeding story. It took the breeders decades to get exactly what they wanted, which they say is a combination of strength, tenacity, agility, speed, fearlessness, and outstanding musical ability."

There goes my boy Bud, throwin' in musical ability just to see if the Christiane Amanpour of dogs is paying attention, but of course, she's not.

"He looks dangerous," she says.

"No more than pot tourism in North Korea."

"Oh…but fighting, Bud. My word," she says, "has he had a lot of fights? If there's a police record, we really can't put him on the cover, just list him in the monthly 'Bad Dog, Bad Dog Report.' Ha, ha, ha."

"No," Bud says, "Spike's never been in any scrape; he's a lover, not a fighter. In fact, his girlfriend's due in town tomorrow."

"Wonderful," she says. "Maybe we could do a sidebar for our 'Doggies Who Date' column, if I can get back here to spend time and watch the lovebirds together. Ha, Ha."

That's when I give her my meanest "You could hit me over the head with a two-by-four and I'll still keep looking at you like this" look.

"Now, Bud," she says, "let's get into some specifics."

She starts rattling off questions that would only be interesting to someone in solitary confinement at Attica who's gotta choose between reading an issue of *Big Apple Dog* or studying the patterns on the one roll of toilet paper they get each week.

Do I like wet or dry food? How many times a day do I get walked? Do I prefer a bath or a shower, ha, ha, ha, ha? Squeaky or nonsqueaky chew toys? Where do I get my nails done?

Then she says to Bud, "How do you think you, as an owner, have influenced Spike?"

Bud says he makes sure I can get lots of exercise, and how he thinks I like bein' on TV and meeting fans on the street. He's not close to the real answer: The guy's given me something not all dogs got—confidence. Great confidence. "You could knock down a wall if you wanted to, Spike," he tells me all the time. "You're a great dog, strong as an ox." "You can do anything you put that dog mind of yours to, Spike; you are The Wonder Dog."

I don't know what a lot of other dogs get from their owners, but he's made me feel invincible, and that's a fine spirit to have in your head as you're walkin' down the street. Now that's the dullest speech you're ever gonna hear from me, but I had to say it 'cause he didn't, and even if he did, I know you wouldn't have bothered to read it in *Big Apple Dog*.

"Let's take him out for a walk. I'd like to see his on-street manners, ha, ha, ha. But oh wait. First, you're in show business; maybe you know someone in Hollywood who could help my niece? She's gone to L.A. to be an actress. Ha, ha, ha."

She shows Bud pictures of the girl, who's wearing the mandatory uniform for amateur porn stars—extra-short, extra-tight ripped denim skirt, cutoff white tank top, tramp tat, and red stilettos.

"Cute," Bud says. "I don't think I can help her, but tell her not to wear herself out auditioning."

We go over to Park Avenue, and I'm striding briskly up the block. She's watching me greet other dogs with a friendly sniff and fast tail wags. When a fan calls my name, I use my Ronald Reagan nod—like the one he'd do when he'd pretend he couldn't hear questions yelled at him.

I spot a crushed Slurpee cup, pick it up, and give it to Bud.

"Is that a trick?" she asks.

"No, he doesn't like stuff on the pavement, so he'll give it to me to throw away," Bud says. "He's not used to litter, 'cause he never saw it on the sidewalks in High Point."

"That's rather gallant of him. I never really thought about picking up cups or anything dropped on the sidewalk. Ha, ha, ha…. What else do you think's been difficult for him in the transition to Manhattan from the rural life you were able to escape?" she asks.

"Well," Bud says, "if he doesn't see them coming, there's a problem with squads of phone zombie kids; last week a texting teenager tripped over him. The kid was lyin' on the sidewalk. I asked if he was OK. He said, 'Yeah,' and kept just pecking away at his phone, even though he was just texting another kid in the group."

"Oh my," Shelly says, slowly looking up from her phone.

We're havin' a lovely stroll when I notice two Park Avenue women doing something I see all too frequently. I call these the "Oh my God women."

A lady walking by is surprised as she sees another lady she thinks she knows.

"Eileen? Eileen? Oh my God!" she calls out, real loud. "Is that you?"

"Sharon? Oh my God…Sharon?" Eileen yells back at her, as they walk toward each other.

Then it happens.

They go through this odd greeting ritual. You think it's weird that sometimes dogs smell each other's ass when they meet? What about this?

First, Eileen and Sharon wave and yell more "Oh my Gods" as they approach each other. Once close, they momentarily stop shrieking "Oh my God" and rear back with mouths and eyes wide open. Their hands fly up by their heads, makin' them look like two frozen people of Pompeii.

Then over and over it's: "Oh my God, Eileen!" "Oh my God, Sharon" "How are you?" "How are you?"

This is followed by: "We have to get together!" "Oh my God, yes! We have to get together!" "Oh my God!" "Yes!" "Yes!"

But they're both already standing there together. This is where I get confused.

"Yes, we'll get together. I'll call you," Eileen says.

"Yes, call; we'll make plans. Oh my God, this was great," Sharon says.

But how come they didn't make plans just then, when they were together?

They walk off in different directions, each looking kinda happy they hadn't wasted any more time Oh-my-God-ing with the other.

This is the strange way that some humans got of saying hello and, I guess, planning to not really make plans.

Who started this custom?

Bud thinks he first saw it on *Sex and the City*. It's sure not the way I'm going to greet Daisy.

17

DAISY

Buffy and Daisy are supposed to be at our place at ten a.m., but it comes to this—I gotta lick Bud to wake him, 'cause he'd been out late. He's tellin' me he shouldn'ta gone to a club called Flash Factory.

"Never let yourself get hooked on electronic dance music, Spike," he's groaning.

"Don't worry, Bud," I'm thinkin'. "I'm having enough trouble fighting off a growing Marilyn Maye music addiction 'cause of the tender ballads I'm hearin' through the wall."

Buffy comes in, but no Daisy. Buffy's cousin Gail, the nuclear physicist from Rutgers, is walkin' her in the park. So I gotta keep calm and carry on, and control my excitement. I'll be cool when she gets here, not act like one of those overeager jerks on *The Bachelor* who get thrown off on the first show.

"Wow," Buffy says, "this is the apartment? I wanted to see Central Park. I thought the ad said you'd have a partial view of the park."

"Yeah, well," Bud says, "if you risk your life a little bit by leaning way out the bathroom window—I can hold your feet if you want to try it—you can see a couple of branches of a tree, that's if the wind's blowing in the right direction."

"Very rustic, and look at Spike," she says, massaging my head the way she did when I'd be lying next to her desk and licking the tasty body lotion off her ankles. "How about you! You're bigger and even more handsome than ever."

Buffy turns to Bud, who's standing and squinting at her in the bright morning light reflected in from the building across the street. That half hour of light coming in is what made it OK for them to advertise the place as sun-drenched, even though it's mostly dark and gloomy the rest of the day.

"And Bud, you…"

"Yes?" he says, maybe expecting a compliment from Buffy, who used to greet him every morning at work with "Well hello, handsome!" But there's this long, strange pause before she clears her throat like people do when they got bad news coming at you.

"Well remember how Lombardo told us he thinks a person is never more interesting than when they're being totally honest?" she says.

"Why do I suddenly feel like you're about to hit me over the head with a baseball bat being interesting?" Bud asks.

"No, you know I love you, and maybe I'm just worried, but you're looking older and kind of ravaged, or dissipated, or peaked. Are you OK?"

"Don't mince words, Buffy. Let me know what you think. You're saying I look like Jim Morrison near the end?"

"Not the morgue shot," Buffy says, "but close."

"Well, I was out a little late, didn't get the jog in this morning."

And I'm thinkin', "No jog yesterday morning or the day before that either."

"But I'm OK," he says. "We got this stupid cruise thing coming up tomorrow, so I'll get some rest there."

"Hey, here's something you're really going to like," Buffy says, as she spreads out a big feature story on me in the *High Point Enterprise*. It's all about the gazing into the camera, and how Bud's voice and my face and some soft piano music from Bud's old friend Bernard are sending people on YouTube into a trance. The caption under my picture says, "The Wonder Dog Way to Relax."

"I know a lot of people who're trying this," Buffy says, "and they can't believe that peering into Spike's beady little eyes is actually helping them to meditate, but it is."

"Buff," Bud says, "Andy, who's helping me with this, says it's going big. How about the power of our buddy Spike!"

"You and The Wonder Dog," she says.

All I know is my staring into the camera thing was only great 'cause of those kava eye drops Bud plunked in me. So it's just another inspiring case of drugs and the creative process—probably like maybe every episode of *Bob's Burgers*.

Bud and Buffy sit down to enjoy a few minutes of the remaining reflected sunlight. It's good to see them together again. He's unwrapping a gift from her, and while he's doin' it, she takes out a little speaker and plays, "It's a Wonderful World," the song Bud would use at the end of every Friday show under the credits.

"This is terrific! Oh, I love this," he says, looking at a big framed color photo of the going-away party we had on our lawn.

All the channel eight people are there. Lombardo's in his blue blazer with the gold buttons, and he's raising a glass to Bud and me. Buff's got one arm over Bud's shoulder and is holding little Daisy with the other. There's a Frisbee flyin' in the air, which I'm chasin', hopin' to catch it to impress Daisy. It's a real happy photo, except I remember jumpin' for the Frisbee and the thing whackin' me hard in the head. It's OK, 'cause at the time, Daisy was lookin' at a plate of nachos, plus, as you know, I didn't feel a thing. My head's like a two-pound stone with eyes.

Underneath the photo, Buff's neatly written in bright blue ink, "The value of things is not the time they exist but the intensity with which they occur." Bud reads it and has one of his emotional reactions where he's choked up with feelings and can't talk. I cover for him by barking with delight, 'cause no matter how sentimental I get, I got no problem barking.

"So how's your chase for fame, fortune, and creative control coming along up here?" Buffy asks.

"I don't know about the first two, but the third, no progress."

"What about going to Skrill, the station manager, about creative differences with Erica? It's the sort of conversation Lombardo would always want to have."

"Yeah, well, I was having a meeting about that with Skrill once. What happened was, you know that desk JFK had that you see in the pictures and little John John's crawling around under it? Well, Skrill had a bigger version of that desk made but with a swinging panel in the front. Anyway, as I'm talking to him, I happen to glance down and see one of Erica's red Van sneakers under the panel. She was most likely giving him a blowjob, 'cause his eyes started to cross while he was talking about my ratings, and they stayed that way for about thirty seconds. The ratings are good, but not that good."

"Oh my," Buffy says.

"That was kind of like the moment when I realized Erica had the upper hand, shall we say, on the creative control issue," Bud says.

"If it makes you feel any better," Buffy says, "Lombardo's actually been complaining about control himself. He told me ABC's pressuring him to make stupid daytime changes, and he said that the only way to run things the right way is to probably own the station."

The door swings open, and Buffy's cousin Gail says, "Hey guys, here we are! The park is gorgeous today; you gotta get outside."

And there's Daisy, all grown up!

What can I say about being in love that hasn't already been covered by literary greats like E. L. James and Shakespeare? I'm just another typical case of a guy swooning over a nonconsummated, long-distance, one-way relationship with a female he doesn't really know. In fact, my friend Mr. Boggs once wrote a novel about that. I'd better read it to see how it turns out, 'cause I'm exploding with doubts as Daisy is slowly makin' her way toward me.

Will she remember me? Is there another dog? High Point is loaded with eligible dogs. Is all the extra exercising I've been doing to get my body ready for her going to pay off? Could she be gay? Benny was crazy about Liz, a fox terrier on our third floor who turned out to be nuts about Iris, a Bedlington terrier with a cool spiked haircut on the fifth floor.

Maybe I'm possibly smelling too human? Bud uses a dab of Crest in his mouth before he goes out, so I bit into the tube and accidentally squirted toothpaste all over my face and neck, had to stick my head in the toilet to get it off this morning. Maybe I'm givin' away a big dog secret here, but you got no idea how often your dog plunges his head in the toilet. It's quite refreshing.

All at once, we're nose to nose. She sniffs me. I sniff her. I remember her smell. Does she remember mine? My heart's pounding, but I'm telling you, I'm ultracool—just letting it flow, like I'm Idris Elba greeting a fan.

"I'm back!" she says.

At the exact moment that I'm realizin' "Thank God everything's OK," I hear a long-short-long SOS signal on the door buzzer. This means Donna Hanover's desperate to come in and get a bottle from the stash of her emergency booze that she asks Bud to hide from her.

She comes charging in and, not noticing another large white dog and Gail and Buffy, she asks, "Bud, do you still have my limoncello? I must have it now."

After she takes two long drinks from the bottle and lets out an "ahhhh!" a couple of times, Bud introduces her to Buffy and Gail. Daisy impresses me by barking politely at Donna. I get a little sense that Buffy may be jealous of Donna—not for limoncello drinking at ten thirty in the morning, but just for barging in on Bud. There's a bunch of small talk about TV work, and Donna explains she's got a new job being a sideline reporter for the Yankees' triple-A team.

"I'm the left side of the field-line girl," she says, "so all I need to know about is third base, shortstop, left field, and plays at the plate, but it's really hard to figure out that new no-collision rule with the catcher. The main thing is, I'm just hoping they don't overload me and assign me balks, too."

She takes a small swig. "Ahhh…limoncello, anybody? Better cold, but so good anyway, whooo!"

"Maybe you'll just handle balks on right-handed pitchers," Buffy tells her. "I played college ball, shortstop at UNC."

"Really? Wow, that's impressive," Donna says, taking another gulp while leaning on a chair for support and eyeing Buffy's fingernails, maybe to check out possible softball-linked sexual identity clues.

"Balks are mystical. Think of the balk as the foot fault of tennis transferred to the pitcher's mound," Buffy says, a little like the way she'd mock mansplaining dimwit anchorman Sam Holloway in High Point.

"Brilliant, Buffy. Any advice on that home-plate rule?"

"Think of the catcher building a fence he's not supposed to build, and because of the fence, the cow can't get back to the barn."

"Oh, wow! Now I get it. So what are you guys all doing? Want to go to Nello?" she asks. "They'll make me Ketel One oatmeal as an eye-opener!"

"Nello's is closed now," Bud says.

"Yes, but the bartender's there. I checked with binoculars before I came down. So let's get going. Whoo! Whoo! Whoo!" she says, jumping up and down, clapping her hands over her head. "Come on, you guys, you guys, you guys, let's go, go, go!"

Bud tells her that they'd better not have a boozy breakfast, 'cause they got a dinner that night with Bud's old boss Lombardo as part of the ABC upfront meetings, and Lombardo's good friend the police commissioner is gonna be at the table, too.

"No sense showing up drunk in front of the police," Bud says.

"Believe me," Donna says, "I know what that's like. OK, well, I'm headed over there, and if anything changes, you know where I'll be today."

She takes a last, slow drink of limoncello. "This stuff is great! Try it this morning on corn flakes with raisins and ground flax seeds. Finish the bottle, please, my treat. Bye-bye, everybody."

"Remember, Donna," Buffy's cousin Gail calls out, "the distance between past, present, and future is only an illusion, however persistent."

Donna stops with the door open. "Huh? Er…right…er…ah, yeah, and that's just the sort of thing I hear the manager and home-plate umpire arguing about a lot, I think. Bye! Bye! Whoo! Whoo! Whoo! Oh, I'm a little bombed," she says, stumbling off.

I'm tryin' to figure out if what Gail just said is an explanation of the thing Buffy wrote at the bottom of the party picture. My brain's hurting exploring the subject, so I focus on Daisy curled up in Buffy's lap. The last bit of sun is shining on her nose. I'm wishin' they'd all go to Nello, get bombed, and leave me and Daisy here for some possible romance.

"Gail," Buffy asks, "why did you say that Einstein thing to her?"

"'Cause in my experience, only a drunk at a bar can make any sense of it," Gail says.

That night Daisy and me finally get to be alone. I'm missing my chance for fatherhood with her. The special scent's not there to tell me she's in the mood for some mutually assured pleasure. It's not like with people. Dogs have a way more organized approach.

Daisy's really smart and curious, and a history expert, 'cause Buffy's listening to all kinds of audiobooks on the morning drives to the station. She lets me know that General Patton had an English Bull Terrier named Willie that she heard about in a book on Generals Patton, Marshall, and MacArthur. With my vast knowledge of pop culture, I'm able to tell her the same guy who wrote *The Generals* also wrote *Forrest Gump*.

She tells me she was sorry to hear I'd been painted green, and then wonders what I've been thinking about recently.

I immediately start explaining my dilemma over the controversy reported on *Extra* about the dwarf Dopey and fears of how he's gonna offend millions of people if they remake the movie *Snow White*. I point out they're organizing woke rallies in Times Square to make it *Snow Person and Six Others*, with Dopey in a spa for slow learners, who's visited by Doc on a regular basis. The others will give him high-fives while they're singing, "Heigh-Ho, Heigh-Ho, It's Off to Stagnant Wages We Go."

For Daisy and me, it's a night of hope and longing and sadness, 'cause we know we can't plan a life together. We're just dogs. We won't be flying back and forth between New York and High Point for visits. Yeah, maybe Bud'll go down South to see friends, or Buffy might come up here with her a few times. If we're really lucky with timing, maybe we'd even be able to swing a mating session. But we can't plan a life together.

Buffy and Daisy will be in town while Bud's away. These couple of intense days with each other might be the happiest time we will ever have. Buffy's handwriting under the photo is making sense.

These are the crazy, sad things you let yourself contemplate when you're in love. My heart is aching. I gotta stick my head in the toilet.

18
Gone Dog

The bad day starts like a good day. Bud takes me for an early-morning walk in the park. Andy comes over and gets Bud, and they go to the dock to board the cruise ship.

Buffy checks out of the Lowell and comes up to our place with her suitcase and Daisy. She leaves Daisy and me together and heads off to her ABC thing. As soon as Buffy leaves, we wrestle around for a while in that nimble way only bull terriers can do together. Then we jump on the couch and curl up. She's got her head pressed under my jaw, rubbin' against the red collar from Pledge.

It's the first time either of us is sleepin' with another dog. She smells so great. We're blissed out. Hope you in your life have felt like this—not about sleepin' with a dog but, you know, the bliss part. Unfortunately it wasn't gonna last.

Larry David Seinfield Garcia wakes us when he comes to get me for the noon walk. He's takin' Daisy, too, but to get his company's permission for Daisy to go, Buffy has to sign three different release forms, an insurance waiver, and give out so much personal information, that a kindergarten student with a toy computer in Moscow has probably already stolen her identity.

We leave The Cheshire Gardens Mews and turn left. We cross Madison and are halfway down the street toward Central Park when I smell the heavy scent of Ike "I Got Money" Piles' cologne blowin' up from behind. I'm wonderin' why anybody in this fancy neighborhood would want to smell like cooked peas and gardenias? Daisy's wrinklin' her nose, 'cause the cologne smell's getting stronger.

I'm figurin' some handyman or doorman saw the new TV ad saying, "Wear this and smell like piles of money" when…

I hear a crack. Larry David Seinfield Garcia gets smashed on the head and falls face first onto the pavement. A man leaps out of a car next to me. He and the cologne guy behind me grab my leash and start tryin' to drag me into the car. Daisy takes a bite out of one guy's ankle, as I realize I'm being abducted by James One and Five Plus. I lunge to bite Five Plus but miss just as he whacks Daisy straight in the face with a little club.

I'm snappin', tryin' to get to Plus when James One shoves something up my ass, and I got horrible pain. There's blood gushing from Daisy's mouth, but she comes right back at them and gets whacked again. I'm twisting to get the thing out of my ass as I get dragged on my back by my leash and pulled up into the car by a smelly guy they're callin' Julio, who's one of those guys who'd been following us on the walks and feeling my muscles. He throws a heavy metal mesh cover over my body. I'm trapped, can't move.

The car skids off while Daisy's yelping and cryin'.

Whatever they shoved inside me is starting to knock me out.

"Don't take this personal, Spike," Plus says.

Of course not, Plus…. You just smashed my girlfriend in the face, maybe killed my dog walker, and kidnapped me; nothing personal at all…

"This business. We always like you. You fun, but you got too famous. Ike 'I Got Money' Piles want you fight for him. He and rich, flabby, baggy-suit-wearin' banking dudes in Greenwich got big dogfight operation, and you gonna be new headline attraction."

The only headline I want to read is "Wonder Dog Throws Man With Plus Tattoo on Face out of Car Window."

"It go like this—you be cool. You win your fights, all be good. You win big and are great, Money take you to mansion in Greenwich. Money introduce you to those bad rich dudes."

Can I then introduce those bad rich dudes to the police?

"But after a while, if you not win one, Money Piles get bored. He bored, but you still OK, then Money Piles ship you to Costa Rica, you fight for his cousin. They got dogs fightin' boars down there, tusks tear old slow dogs to pieces."

Cancel that trip, Plus. I got zero interest in Costa Rican tourism. Forget boar tusks; who wants black sand on a beach?

"But he bored and you not OK, like last big star Mean Brenda who took too many bites and all them cuts not healin' fast enough, then 'cause you male, Money get you jerked off. He sell Wonder sperm to fight-dog breeders."

Actually, Plus, I'm not plannin' to lose my virginity hooked to some machine operated by Money Piles. Clamp the thing on your own dick.

"He sell Wonder sperm to fight-dog breeders. Then he fatten you up for Spike dog dinner in Thailand. You get froze alive, and he ship you to Bangkok."

You know, Plus, somehow you've finally managed to convince me that I actually don't like what I'm hearing, so if I gotta chew through ten steel cages and knock down walls, you're not getting me.

"Over there, they be watchin' your dogfights on close-circuit network Greenwich got rigged up in Thailand. Crazy people there pay to eat star dog. They make Spike stew of you. Watch videos of you fightin', eat stew, and smoke great hash. They bad."

The car's bumping along to who knows where. James One and the Julio guy are laughing and drinking tequila. Plus is on the phone with Money Piles. I'm worrying about Daisy and Larry David Seinfeld Garcia lying on the pavement. The worrying only stops when the drugs they shoved in my ass finally get me. I pass out.

Part Three

19

The Hour Shall Come

Remember when I said, "You don't like flyin'? Try it as a dog"? You don't like hard-core rap music? Try waking up trapped in a cage on a dirty cement floor with a guy screaming about pumpin' a gat fulla' slugs into someone's cheddar.

Last night, instead of relaxing my way to sleep by calculatin' the number of times I think Conan O'Brien's audience has to be cued to applaud, I'm countin' the number of "motherfuckers" blasting from "N. W. A."

By the way, if you're thinkin' I'm gonna stop with the light-hearted moments of saucy jest because I'm now part of a massive dog fighting syndicate in mortal danger of bein' frozen to death and stewed—forget it. Somebody told Bud, "Never lose your sense of humor; it's the most valuable possession you have." I'm probably the only dog in here doin' a monologue in my head to keep from goin' *completely nuts. Because this sucks!*

So here's what's goin' on:

First, I'm calm. I got my emotions under control, and I'm focused on doin' what I need to do to prevail, like Lombardo always says. He loves the word "prevail."

I woke up really sore from that cigar-sized tranquilizer James Plus shoved in me. My achin' ass makes me question the vast popularity of anal sex and the consequences for half the people involved.

I got no idea where I am, but it feels like a long walk from anywhere. Judgin' by the little bit of horn honkin' I hear, I figure it's city, not country. Escape's only possible through one door, and there's a guard on it day and night. From what I see when the door opens, it leads to another larger area.

I'm in a corner in what might be a VIP space just for me. There's a "Wonder Dog" sign on the wall. I'm in a big cage lookin' out at a huge steel space that's probably specially built inside a warehouse. It has its own ventilation system, which it needs, 'cause the guys workin' here smell like they've been rolling around for two days in mounds of salsa-covered dog shit.

They got a couple of dozen dogs in small kennel cages set pretty far apart. In the middle of all of this, there's a circular steel fighting cage, bigger than a boxing ring. It's got a dirt floor, and in the center, hanging down, is a cord and an announcer's microphone, just like they had in Vegas. The drone almost got caught up in that cord one time when we were doing landing rehearsals. They got bleacher seats circled around the fighting cage.

Flashing on one wall is a big electronic betting board with pictures of dogfight match-ups and betting odds. Above that is a giant, massively retouched photo of Ike "I Got Money" Piles, and over his head he's holding his boxing belts with wads of money dropping from them. Mounted on the walls are flat-screen monitors with tapes of past dogfights. If I'm lucky, I'm gonna be able to see the styles of dogs I might be fightin'.

Hidden in a corner, making it look like part of the wall, is the freezer. I woke up seein' the ugly sight of a dead pit bull being dragged out by her frozen-solid tail. She got packed in a container full of ice and covered with fish for shipping halfway round the world. *Monde Cane.*

They give me a good breakfast of a lot of raw meat. There're a couple of red pills jammed in the ground steak. I don't think these are vet-prescribed holistic vitamins, so I hide 'em in the back of the cage. Gotta keep a clear head.

Julio from yesterday and another even smellier guy named Julio are in charge of me. They took me out of the cage, and walked me around on a chain leash they attached to my collar. Every dog is lungin' and snarlin' at me, biting the metal and shaking their cages, wantin' to tear me apart. They got a crazed look in their eyes, 'cause of the loads of steroids bein' fed to them.

A couple of other workers stop by to look at me, and James Plus shows them my big mouth and gleamin' white teeth and my long, sharp fangs. It'd be real easy to bite off a finger when James Plus has my cheeks pulled back and his hand in my mouth, but that's not gonna do me any good right now.

Money Piles isn't around, but everybody's always calling him by the full Ike "I Got Money" Piles name. They talk about him in the same hushed tones people use in cramped dining rooms in small New England bed-and-breakfasts. They act as if Money, this crooked, sleazy, sex-addict hustler, is a member of the royal family.

What about Daisy and the two smashes to the face, and Larry David Seinfield Garcia? Has he got brain damage from that whackin' he took? Did he even wake up and tell people what happened? Any witnesses? Surveillance video?

This has gotta be real, real bad for Buffy, I don't even know if she can contact Bud on the ship. Most of all, I'm scared of how Bud's gonna explode when he finds out somebody stole me. How's he gonna get back and find me? He's trapped on a ship not making any port stops. They're sailin' around in the Atlantic on a press cruise to nowhere.

I spend part of the first day on a treadmill, which has got to be the most boring way to get exercise ever invented. I'm eatin' more meat, hidin' pills. I'm just playin' things as cool as possible and actin' like I'm lookin' forward to goin' into the ring.

My only goal is preserving myself and, if possible, not hurting my competition. I gotta see what develops so I can figure out a way to escape. Or maybe I'll get rescued. I'm hopin' real hard there's some clues back on Sixty-Third Street. This looks like a totally hidden operation, or the cops would've found it a long time ago.

Fight One: Mad Max

"Today, you got first fight, Spike," James Plus says. "You go in against Mad Max, who not lose no fight yet. You got big odds against you, so you win, you make more piles a money for Ike 'I Got Money' Piles. You lose, you off to bad start, have to give you easier fights and lower odds, mean less money for Ike 'I Got Money' Piles. Ev'ybody wanta see The Wonder Dog. You first fight a night, gonna be full house."

All afternoon I'm watchin' videos of Mad Max in action. He's a lumbering, black and gray, muscle-bound dog who looks like he's part Staffordshire terrier, part Great Dane, and part mentally challenged. He probably outweighs me by around thirty pounds. Max has only one way of fightin'. He's a "swarmer." He comes straight at you snapping and biting. He forces you against the cage, then drags you away to pin you and go for the throat. He killed one dog, and in the other fights he won 'cause he had 'em down and helpless.

He wins fast, 'cause when he charges, the other dogs make the mistake of charging him, too. I'm rememberin' things from the ESPN classic fights I watched with Bud, and I see that Max fights the way Joe Frasier did against George Foreman. Smokin' Joe came chargin' right in, got knocked out, and lost the title. And I spot something else—in Max's one fight that lasted more than two minutes against a fast, smaller dog named Big Larry, Max's tongue is hangin' out. So I'm figurin' he's also like early "Big George" Foreman, who came out throwin' punches but got tired fast 'cause of bein' too tight and lack of stamina. That's how Ali beat "Big George," by takin' him to eight rounds and usin' the "Rope-a-Dope."

The bleachers are packed with greasy gang members who look like they got into the U.S. by wading through a sewage tunnel but haven't bothered to shower yet. Up in the VIP box behind a window is Money Piles with a couple of rich-lookin' guys in blue suits and long red ties, who I figure are the big, bad dudes from Greenwich.

I'm being paraded around in front of the circle of bleachers and bombarded with words of encouragement like, "Wonder Dog's a pussy!" "You ain't on TV now!" "Glad that faggot Bud's not here!" "Mad Max gonna put you to sleep like them stupid YouTube people you puttin' to sleep."

I'm calmly struttin' around doin' a dog's version of "Walk Like a Man." I show 'em the slow-motion walk, and a guy in the crowd yells, "He playin' with us now, oh yeah, he playin' that Wonder Dog shit now."

I get the clue Mad Max is more of the crowd favorite when they give him a standing ovation, yelling, "*Olé! Olé!*"

I don't care.

Ever since I woke up yesterday, the smell of the other dogs, the cages, the ring—everything here—set my fighting instincts on fire. My jaws are twitching with feelings my ancestors had.

When they took off my red collar and threw it in the back of the cage and put the chain around my neck to bring me out tonight, everything was sharp and focused. Inbred powers are turned on.

I'm gonna fight, and I'm gonna win.

Sergio, the announcer, finishes and runs outta the cage. A bell rings. Like I figured, Mad Max charges across the ring straight at me. He's faster than I thought. His eyes are yellow from drugs. His big mouth is wide open. I let him almost bite me before I bounce to the left and start bouncing around in a wide circle, just like I did a million times in the big backyard in Thomasville. But now, I'm bouncing faster than I ever thought I could. Max is runnin' after me. I shift and bounce to the left. Then I bounce right. Left, right.

He's confused and stops chasin' me, and stands in the middle of the ring panting and barking at me.

The crowd's booing. Not sure if it's about me, or Max, or both of us.

Then he crouches. Lunges. I jump over him.

The crowd roars.

I hurdle him again, and I'm thinkin', "Thank you, Mister Ali for the 'Jump-a-Dope.'"

He twists and charges. His sloppy tongue's flapping around, and he's foaming and drooling. I time it right and jump one more time. He's mad, tense, frustrated, and burnin' energy, so I jump over him again. He leaps straight up to get me but tips backward and falls over.

The crowd's goin' crazy booing Max after his clumsy fall.

As he's getting up, I pounce on him, and I get his hot, wet throat locked in my jaws. I don't hear the crowd. I'm feelin' weird, like I'm not really me, but like I'm another dog in another time and place. Something's driving me I never felt before. I'm all-powerful. I got Max where I want him. I can win by bearing down and crushing his throat. I want to do it, so I slowly start to tighten the grip.

Everybody is standing and screaming.

The only other time I clamped this hard on anything was when I was racing around the ice rink at the Greensboro Coliseum tryin' to hold Donald Duck's head in my mouth by the beak. I remember the kids laughing and yelling, "Spike! Spike!"

Now I'm hearing, "Kill! Kill!"

My teeth are going deeper into Max's throat. But I stop. NO! I don't kill dogs for a master.

A little whimper comes out of Max, like he's a puppy again.

I use all the force I got to flip him in the air like he's a big furry truck tire. He lands hard on his back. I pin him to the floor and pretend to be as menacing as possible while waitin' for somebody to come in to save him.

A handler comes in. I let Max go and back off. He still wants a fight—he lunges at me groggily, but they get the chain around his neck and drag him out of the ring.

I won. My skull's pounding from what just happened. Max was trying to kill me.

Back in my cage, I'm chewin' on another pile of lean raw meat. I taste some of the blood that's oozing onto my tongue. I'm glad to know the killer instinct is still in me, 'cause before I get outta here, I'm gonna need all of it that I've got.

Fight Two: Big Nipper

As I'm tryin' to drift to sleep that night to the haunting refrains of some guy rappin' about how mad he is 'cause his bitch got the wrong tattoo on her bottom, James Plus shows up. He gets down on his knees and is shouting at me through the wire on my cage door.

"Today you do so good, tomorrow Ike 'I Got Money' Piles set you up against Big Nipper. He tough, he fast. You watch your paws, Spike; he specialist on winnin' by munchin' real fast on legs and paws."

Oh that's encouraging news, thank you, Plus. By the way, have you considered brushing your teeth this week? Your breath smells like a smoldering pile of jockstraps in the Yankees laundry room after a Labor Day doubleheader.

"Big Nipper personally trained by Ike 'I Got Money' Piles. He got some of the same Money Piles strategy that make Money Piles champion."

Really, Plus, you mean Big Nipper is giving away cars to judges? I stay up watching videos of Big Nipper fights.

He's light gray and mostly a pit bull, but 'cause he's got a smaller head, longer mouth, and longer legs, I figure he's got a little greyhound in him. He's an "in and out" fighter like Roy Jones Jr. He's lightning fast, even faster than me. He never wins on power like Mad Max. His style is first nippin' at your legs, then biting your legs, and when he's got you bleeding and you're slower, he's able to get in and chew your paws. He doesn't have jaw power to kill on the throat. He wins by damaging you bad. The pit pull I saw bein' dragged out of the freezer was the last dog he fought. The Big Nipper has dozens of ugly scars all over his back from where dogs were bitin' to stop him from chewin' on their paws.

I need a different approach to fightin' him, 'cause he'll catch me if I'm movin' around in a circle, and he's gonna be able to jump high enough to get my leg if I try leaping over him.

I go to sleep remembering another Friday-night ESPN show where a young "Hands of Stone" Roberto Duran charged the other guys and knocked them out early with raw punching power.

The next day is hours of waiting around to fight the Nipper. I'm the main event, so I gotta sit in my cage during all the other fights, 'cause I'm on last. When they finally get me, I'm stiff and nervous. Gotta control the mind, gotta prevail, gotta impose my will on Big Nipper.

The worst thing would be to realize what could happen to me in the fight. Sometimes, for an instant, I do. It's then that I have fear. But like Evander Holyfield told Bud in an interview on boxing, "Fear can be your friend." Back then I didn't know what he meant. Now I understand.

There's a lot of bettin', and the odds are against me, 'cause Nipper has never lost. He's got a perfect record of every dog he fights bein' put to sleep afterward.

They parade me around. To loosen up, I do jumps. I hop. The crowd's applauding. I snarl at the guys in the front row calling Bud names.

The Big Nipper makes his usual entrance. He strides around chewing some kind of leg. There's a small hoof on the leg, so I'd say it's more leg of lamb than leg of dog.

Since I got here, can you kind of tell that nothing in this place is "nice"?

The bell rings, and we charge each other. He's lookin' to take a quick nip at my leg, so he comes in low. All the other dogs can't get their teeth in him when he attacks—they miss 'cause he's too low and too quick. I'm runnin' at full speed like I'm going to plow right through him. I lower my head to slam him. There's a loud crack as I hit his head, and he spills off sideways.

He's charging me again; this time he's slower. I sprint and smash him with another headbutt.

Crashing into his skull at full speed is not a pain-free experience, but it's a small price to pay for not getting my paw chewed off. Besides, it confirms that I *am* "Head of Stone."

Can't say the same for the Nipper. He's showin' the effects of two smashes. He's shaky. He's runnin' away, maybe expecting me to tire out by chasin' him round and round but, like Duran would, I cut off the ring. I charge at an angle and slam into him as hard as I can under his little cropped ear. He rolls over a couple of times and hits the cage wall. He's ten feet away and getting up slowly. I close in to grab him by the neck. All I gotta do is hold him down till somebody runs in to save him.

But I make a mistake.

Money's girlfriend Ra'sheed'duh? is in the front row. An instant before I have him, she takes a photo of me. I wasn't stopping to pose, but the flash throws me off, and the Big Nipper's able to get my leg. He's dizzy from the butts, and he's probably not chewin' as hard as normal, but I still got only about fifteen seconds before I get serious leg damage.

On his back, probably from that last fight with the pit bull, is a pink and raw open wound. It's like an arrow pointing to a "Bite Here to Win" sign. I nip him there a couple of times, and soon blood is pourin' down his sides and he's screechin' in pain.

I back off—like Larry "The Easton Assassin" Holmes did in his fight with Ali, when Holmes tried to get the ref to stop it. But like in that fight, nobody's stopping anything. So I grab the Nipper by the neck, shake him, and drag him over to the cage door for them to come and take him out. The Big Nipper has surrendered to me. He's lyin' quietly, quivering and bleeding all over the dirt.

'Cause I suddenly got the urge, I try something I saw Tarzan do in the movies after he pretended to kill a lion. It always worked great, 'cause all the lions knew how to play along with Tarzan; otherwise there'd be a lot of dead Tarzans. I put my leg on the Nipper, raise my head high, and let out a long howl of victory.

I'm resting in my cage when James Plus comes with what he thinks is great news for me.

"Spike, Ike 'I Got Money' Piles watch you closed circuit from his VIP den. Money Piles no like be around ring crowd; he get pissed off by fans who shake Money hand too hard. No good for fighter hand. He here now, and he personally gonna bran you with the Money dollar-sign bran he put on best dogs. Your leg gonna be sizzling, but you be branded as best, also increase your value if you frozen. Eatin' the branded leg of mighty champion dog get special ceremony in Thailand."

"Terrific," I'm thinkin'. "It's like you get an Academy Award and then cannibals rush onstage to boil you during the commercial break."

James Plus walks me over to Money Piles, who I coulda found blindfolded, 'cause of him smelling of the Money Piles cologne he probably uses instead of water in his hot tub. There's a branding iron stuck in burning charcoal on top of a small grill.

I'm lookin' at him with the kind of distain I reserve for big-game hunters, terrorists, and people who don't believe in global warming.

"Spike, you Wonder Dog. That stupid Bud be wastin' you on TV. If he sold you to Ike 'I Got Money' Piles, Ike 'I Got Money' Piles woulda give him a cut a your winnings, but now he gotta find a new Wonder dog, 'cause Ike 'I Got Money' Piles now brandin' you mine for all time.

I look at him and give him my big, original, TV-show yawn.

"He so bad, he bored," Money Piles says.

"Oh yeah, he so bad, he bored," the Jameses standing by him echo.

I yawn again, this time even wider.

"Look at that mouth; look at them gleamin' teeth," Money Piles says.

"Come on," I'm thinkin', "you know what you want to do now, Money, so just do it."

"Let me see them teeth, James Plus. Let me see teeth of a Money Piles champion."

James Plus lifts my cheeks, and Ike "I Got Money" Piles bends down and sticks his hand in my mouth and rubs his fingers along my teeth.

"He got fangs like tiger," he says, just before I bite down as hard as I can.

Money Piles is screamin' like James Brown except there's no music or words comin' after the screams. James Six is beatin' me to stop, 'cause I got Money's middle finger between my back teeth. I twist my head from side to side, jerkin' on the finger, and I feel the bone crack. I bite it loose and spit it at him. It bounces off one of his red Monster Fendi fur-trimmed high-top sneakers and rolls into the dark.

The two Julios are crawling around screamin', "Find the finger."

"You be OK, Money," James Plus says. "You be OK; it real easy to sew finger back on hand these days."

"Oh sure, Plus," I'd like to tell him. "There must be an old Italian shoemaker right down the block who'd be happy to do it while you wait."

"We take Ike 'I Got Money' Piles and the official Money Piles finger in for repair, and you be good as new tomorrow," James Plus says.

"Not really, Plus," I'm thinkin'. "Tell the champ to enjoy the rest of his nine-finger boxing career."

The two Julios are kickin' me as hard as they can all the way back to my cage.

I got revenge, like Bruce Willis after an entertaining night on the town happily executing people in that feeble remake of *Death Wish*.

I'm calmly waitin' for whatever they got in store for me. I've been blockin' out how much I miss Bud. How I'll never see him and Daisy again, 'cause after three days here, I'm kinda sure the cavalry is not chargin' in to save me. If Bud ever finds out what I did to Money Piles, he's gonna be proud. I just wanna settle down and get some rest.

But first, I gotta get the sickening taste of gardenias and peas outta my mouth from the Ike "I Got Money" Piles cologne on the finger. The crap tastes even worse than it smells.

Around midnight James Plus kicks my cage.

"Countdown to frozen Spike now goin' on," Plus announces. "Money hand ruined. Money boxing career done. Money girlfriends Ra'sheed'duh? and Cartier mad 'cause Money now missin' special pleasure finger he use when he bein' double extra bad with them. You in deep shit, Spike."

"Oh yeah, bet that finger's been in some, too," I think. I'm wonderin' how long Cartier and Ra'sheed'duh? are gonna hang around once their orgasm count drops below the women they compete with on the Money's Bitches' Climax Count tote board at his Vegas gym.

"You be happy to hear Money Piles' agent already sold Money Piles' finger for a wad a cash to guy in Red Bank who collect celebrity fingers. Guy proud owner of Count Basie thumb. He say celebrity fingers now fastest-growin' collectible market since Smurfs."

"Well, Plus," I'm thinking, "anytime Money Piles wants a little spending money, he can just stick a hand in my cage."

"So let me give you good news now, Spike. Tomorrow at high noon, you opening attraction, and you know who you be fighting, Spike?"

Neil Patrick Harris, maybe? Or how about Cher? I want her oiled up in a bikini, knocking me unconscious by whackin' me senseless with a double-wired, no-padding, push-up bra.

"You be fighting new dog team arrived fresh from killing wild boars in the big cage fights in Costa Rica. You goin' in against Monstro and Little Tiger. They kill every boar they fight, and they got shipped up here for novelty shows, maybe killin' old racehorses Money's friends own, but you be first dog they kill. Closed-circuit show start at noon so Thailand see you nighttime there, and that make your frozen-Spike price be higher."

I don't think I could possibly hear more comforting news before drifting off for a relaxing sleep.

"We be playin' nonstop video of Monstro and Little Tiger to promote the pay-per-view, so you go to sleep and you wake up watchin' them rippin' four-hundred-pound male boars to shreds. They great team, just like you and TV Bud be, but he not here to help you. Sleep tight, Spike. No way you can win."

I watch Monstro and Little Tiger on the big screens. Monstro is the size of a miniature horse—a purebred English mastiff, the toughest breed us bull terriers had to fight back in the day. Little Tiger is a female Doberman, and they did some kind of bionic Tommy John surgery on her jaw that gives her tremendous biting power—she's got 328 pounds of bite pressure, way stronger than mine.

I watch the way they're trained to attack a boar. She charges first and goes for a front leg. If she misses, she darts behind the boar to latch onto a rear leg. Monstro lumbers in weaving left and right. The bobbing and weaving makes the boar miss every time he lunges with his tusks. Once Little Tiger gets those jaws on a leg, the boar spins around tryin' to get at her, and Monstro draws blood by bitin' away all over him.

It doesn't take 'em long. It's sad to see a mighty boar lyin' helpless with back legs that don't work while Monstro and Tiger finish him off.

The boar's dyin' in the prime of life. There's fear and pain in his big black boar eyes. Gives me the same bad feelin' I had watchin' a documentary about bullfights. The way they stuck in those swords to weaken the bull's neck muscles. I was always hoping to see a bull shove one of his horns up the matador's ass, but it never happened. Bulls got dragged outta the ring, like I'm scared they'll be doin' with me tomorrow.

Just before fallin' to sleep, I spot something interesting about Monstro and Little Tiger. They may be a team, but they sure don't like each other. They gotta be released from separate cages. Once the boar's dead, they start growlin' at each other. Monstro bares his fangs, and she curls her mouth and snarls at him. As soon as that happens, the handlers run in and hurry 'em away in different directions. They're probably like Johnny Depp and Amber Heard at the end.

Around three thirty, I wake up. The only sounds are a few dogs barking in their sleep, probably dreamin' of a master they never had. Bud says, "Everything always seems twice as bad in the middle of the night." Never understood what he meant, 'cause I always sleep straight through. But now it's easy to know—I'm low, real low, and embarrassed that I'm so frightened.

How would you feel if you knew you were gonna die in nine hours? Which would you want—bein' ripped to death by two dogs or slowly bein' frozen to death in an eight-by-six freezer? Tomorrow it's one or the other, or worse, maybe a combo where they stick me in the freezer half dead.

Where's Bud? Where's Buffy? Where are all my fans? How could this happen to me?

Death's waitin' for everybody, and I got a noon appointment. OK, I know I went a little noir there, but that's how it seems.

I know lyin' here feelin' lonely and sad and sorry for myself's not gonna do any good. I could end it now by eating the sixteen steroid pills I hid. It would be fast and pretty stimulating at the start, but that's bein' a coward. If I'm goin' down, I'm goin' down with valor like great-grandfather Brick.

I'm staring out into total dark and something from the office in High Point comes to mind. On the wall was a picture of John Wayne and his quote:

"Courage is being scared to death but going out and saddling up anyway."

Tomorrow, I'm just gonna saddle up.

Maybe there is a dog heaven and I'll be up there runnin' around with Pledge and Brick and every dog that ever died. Probably pretty crowded up there by now, but feels good to think of that. My guess about death? It's a simple fade to black. Whattaya think it is?

If this is the kind of crap I gotta dwell on in the middle of the night, I'm goin' back to sleep.

Final Fight: Monstro & Little Tiger

Sergio the announcer stands in the middle of the cage. He's about six feet tall with black, wavy hair. He's had plastic surgery to make himself look like Michael Buffer, the famous ring announcer, who's had plastic surgery to keep himself looking like Michael Buffer.

Directly across the fighting cage, I see Ike "I Got Money" Piles surrounded by Cartier, Ra'sheed'duh?, and the rest of his female pleasure squad. He's wearin' a New York Knicks basketball uniform, big wide white hat, and he's got five different-size gold dollar signs dangling from his neck. I spot a tiny dot of blood on one of his Fendi sneakers from where his finger bounced off. There's a giant white bandage on his right hand. With his left, he's givin' me thumbs down over and over like the emperor at the Roman Colosseum.

"Not quite yet, Money," I think. "Not quite yet. I got a plan."

Sergio has the mic in his hand, doin' his usual booming Michael Buffer imitation: "Before we begin our savage encounter between these mighty beasts, let's acknowledge the acclaimed accomplishments of the man who makes this all possible…because…today… Ike…"I…Got…Money"…Piles…entered the book of world records…not for his outstanding work in the boxing ring…but for his activities outside of it…. Today, Ike Piles went down in the record book…"

Sergio is yelling and pointing at Money Piles ringside.

"…with more sexual assault accusations than any living athlete in the world!"

Booming cheers.

"Money! Money! Money!" the crowd screams.

Money Piles stands up, beaming like he's been given the Nobel Peace Prize for flashing his member. He's so proud of himself, he accidentally pounds his chest with the bandaged hand and doubles over gasping in pain. But he straightens up and quiets his audience.

"Money Piles so bad," he says, "that most a my hashtag MeToos oughta been MeThrees and MeFours!"

Roars of approval.

"Money be so bad, Money make Harvey Weinstein look like clean-as-a-marble-statue Mike Pence."

The crowd goes silent trying to figure who those guys are.

Sensing a lull, Sergio interrupts: "And now...dogfight fans around the world, let's get ready to bark and...growllllllll!

"In cage one, tipping the scales at a burly, fighting-ready 220 pounds, our latest attraction, the Costa Rican mauler, the tough and savage...Monstroooooo!

"And in cage two, his partner, weighing in at a trim and fast fifty-two pounds...our new lean and mean, jaws-of-steel, leg-crushing machine...Little Ti-grrrrr.

"And...across the ring...in cage three, their opponent.

"A star outside the ring with his own YouTube channel, who proudly joined the Money Piles Mean Time syndicate just this week. He immediately demolished Mad Max and battled Big Nipper into bloody retirement. And now, he's single-handedly taking on the undefeated Central American boar-fighting champions Monstro and Little Tiger.... Weighing in at a rock-solid seventy pounds... Spike...The Wonder...Dogggg!"

Odd that in this dire situation I'd be pissed that he announces my name wrong—it's "Spike...The Wonder Dog." There's no pause after "Wonder," Sergio, you moron.

He lets go of the microphone and runs outta the cage. My heart's pounding, muscles twitching, jaws clenching. I figure I got one chance, and it's this—I gotta make a vertical leap higher than ever before to catch the ball end of that dangling mic, and then hang on up there.

Monstro and Little Tiger are wild-eyed, snarling; each one's in a rage to kill. They're rattling their cages to get out and attack. And if Monstro's as dumb as he seems, he's probably just now starting to wonder why the boar is white.

The bell rings.

I'm first to the center of the ring. I crouch to jump, but Little Tiger's right on me. She goes for my left leg. I grab her by the neck and throw her as far as I can. Monstro's confused. He stops comin' at me to enjoy watchin' Little Tiger fly head over paws through the air and crash into the side of the cage.

I crouch. I launch. Up I go. Crowd is screamin' the instant I leave the dirt. Straight up…three feet, up…four feet, up…five feet. I'm starting to slow. I'm scared I'm not gonna make it. Up…six feet…. The mic's three inches away. I stretch…stretch…

I'm at the moment in every big jump where I'm as high as I'm gonna go, and there's a fraction of a second when I'm motionless—floating—before falling back. In that instant, I clamp on the mic. It tastes like Money cologne from Sergio's hand, and I chip two small front teeth grabbing the metal ball, but I got it. I'm hanging above the middle of the ring.

Booming over the big sound system is my breathing, 'cause the microphone in my mouth is still turned on. To get payback for the bad music they blast all day, I start growling as loud as I can.

The growls are roaring louder than anything they play. Every dog in every cage is barking back at me. The place is shaking with noise. But below, Monstro and Little Tiger are snarling quietly.

They're facing each other for the first time in a ring, and as I hoped, they're looking to have a fight.

Maybe they've just spent too much time working together. Maybe, like every woman who ever worked with Regis, Little Tiger thinks she's not getting the credit she deserves. Maybe, like Anderson Cooper and Kathy Griffith, their bosses put them together but they were never really cut out to be a team in the first place. Whatever the reason, Little Tiger and Monstro now want to kill each other. I'm happy to give them the chance, but hope I don't slip off this thing and crash down on them while they're at it.

They attack. She makes a mistake by goin' directly for his throat instead of a leg. He smashes her with his head and gets his teeth into her neck and shakes her, but she gets away. Little Tiger's already bleeding. She knows she's no match for him, but there's nowhere to hide.

One of the Julios races in to save her. When he tries to get a chain around her neck, Monstro bites Julio's leg and chases him out. He's growlin' as loud as he can, and he slowly turns toward her. Little Tiger's scared—panicking—running left, running right, running everywhere, but he's got the size to block her. He pounces, bites into her back, holds her, and shakes her. She twists away, pouring steroid-colored blood that looks like purple rain.

Little Tiger's dead, and Monstro is struttin' around the cage like a man who just got out of a bad marriage without paying alimony. The crowd's just happy to see anything get killed, so they give him a standing ovation.

As the noise is dyin' down, he looks up at me with purple blood dripping off his long tongue. Good thing I don't have tongue envy, 'cause he's got a whopper. Monstro wants to fight, which gets me wondering if he can jump high enough to bite my tail.

The answer is yes.

It's OK, 'cause as you mighta figured, the plan is not to hang up there forever. I knew I'd end up fightin' one or the other. Monstro's leaping and nipping little tufts of hair outta the end of my tail. I roar into the mic a couple of times to distract him, and then as light as I can, drop to the floor of the cage.

I wasn't real eager to be fightin' Little Tiger. If she got my leg, that's it, I'm finished. She was great, but she shoulda fought Monstro like he was a boar, not a dog. Glad she didn't, 'cause I'm hoping Monstro's gonna be a more user-friendly opponent. Sure, he's the size of one of those annoying strollers for twin babies that take up half a subway car, but he's also just about as nimble. He's slow, very slow. Plus, I'm figurin' he's stupid, 'cause of the way his tongue is always hangin' out. You walk around with your tongue hangin' out all day and I guarantee you're gonna look more like a simpleton than the editor of *The Atlantic*.

All I gotta do is use a combo of my strategies with Mad Max and Big Nipper, and I got 'im easy.

I hear Sergio yell, "Here they go, everybody."

I start with a headbutt to daze and slow him. I plow in but bounce off his head, like when I tried to escape and slammed into the metal door of the Smiths' trailer. I figure I musta run at the wrong angle or something, so I charge even faster and butt again. I bounce off, fall over, and get up and start looking for a plate of bologna Mrs. Smith was about to give me. I feel his fat tongue and slobbering mouth on my neck and wake up, realizin' I just knocked myself out and was havin' another one of my bologna dreams. I wrestle away an instant before his jaws lock on me.

"Head of Stone" has failed me.

"Spike goin' down," Money Piles is yelling. "You not so Wonder Doggy now. He make you look like little old squirrel tryin' to fight

225

mighty King Kong. How 'bout we just freeze your ass now, get this over with?"

My head clears. I start hoppin' around the ring to get him to chase me and tire out like Mad Max did. I'm bouncing left, bouncing right, bouncing all over. But he just stands there looking at me like a bored parent who'd rather be checking Instagram than watch his kid doing triple somersaults on a trampoline.

I see a fire in his eyes. He snarls, bares his fangs, and attacks. I go leaping over him, but he rears up and swats me down like he's blocking a volleyball at the net.

I got no tricks left.

I'm standing my ground.

If I'm going to show valor, this is it.

Come on, Monstro, bring it on; let's fight.

We tangle. I'm faster, way faster. He's stronger, but maybe not so much stronger that I can't take him. His bobbin'-and-weaving tactic with the boar isn't workin' on me. I can get in short bites to his throat almost at will. I'm using those bites like Ali used his jab. But 'cause Monstro's above me, he counters with chomps on my back each time I jab, and they're hard bites. Hurts, stings bad—but I'm bred to handle pain. Is he?

I'm moving my head in and out, taking quick, nasty little nips. His chest is dripping blood on the dirt.

We tangle again. He gets the side of my face, and I taste my blood for the first time. I dart in and land a hard nip under his throat. He lets out a small screech. I nip him again. He screeches again. He's feeling pain—good.

He doesn't like what I'm doing, so he starts using his power to bulldoze me. I resist just enough to make it hard work to move me. I wanna tire his legs; that'll give me a big advantage. He's struggling to push me all around the ring.

The crowd starts booing.

This clinch would be broken up by the referee if we were boxers, but nobody's separating us, and nobody's stopping this on a TKO; one of us is going to bark the big one.

The crowd's booing louder, 'cause it's boring.

Monstro's panting real heavy, so I drop back quick, then charge with two head fakes that make him just miss nipping another piece off my ear. I maneuver inside and get a small chunk of his skin. I back off and spit it out. He's mad and runs straight at me.

"They be fightin' like Hearns-Hagler," Money Piles yells. "It's Hearns-Hagler of dogs."

I remember bein' with Bud watching the video of that fight over and over. It was three of the greatest rounds in boxing ever, and comin' to mind is the powerful Tommy "The Hit Man" Hearns' uppercut.

Monstro's charging again, and this time, my counter's gonna be like an uppercut. I come in low, duck even lower, and spring for a clean grab on his neck. I've got him in the bull terrier throat-hold position—the one we were bred and trained to do. All I gotta do is hold on, slowly tighten down, and he's finished. But like he's a UFC fighter, he flips sideways and rolls over twice. Monstro's not as stupid as I figured—it's a brilliant move, 'cause he stops at an angle that makes me drop the grip; otherwise, his body weight's gonna break my leg.

I'm off balance and stretching my leg as he moves at me way quicker than I ever thought he could. He gets my throat, flips me, and pins me under all of his 220 pounds. He clenches down to crush my windpipe. No big pain, but he's slowly cuttin' off my breathing, so I'm only able to suck little bits of air through my nose. I'm panicking for air. Lungs are burning. Mind's calm. I'll fight to

my last breath, but which breath is it gonna be? I'm being killed....
This is it.... Goodbye, Bud.... Goodbye, Daisy...

For what happens next, you gotta credit the UFC, 'cause
Monstro's obviously been watching round after round of UFC
battles. Instead of just takin' another ten seconds and finishing me
off like he coulda easily done, he decides to entertain everybody by
grandstanding and smashing my head against the dirt floor.

The crowd roars, so he smashes it again, and again, and again...
and again...and...

Mr. and Mrs. Smith are singing a Christmas song about a flyin'
reindeer....

Mr. Smith's got his oxygen mask off and takes a deep drag on
an unfiltered Camel cigarette as he's singing. The only difference
between how Sinatra looks while he's smoking and singing and Mr.
Smith is that Frank has teeth.

They finish real loud, "You'll go down in hiss...torr...reee!"

"OK, Rudolph," Mrs. Smith says. "Here's a little Christmas
treat."

She tosses a piece of bologna at me that looks like a limp Frisbee
floating through the haze of smoke in their trailer. I catch it. She
starts throwin' pieces at me as fast as she can, like it's the annual
bologna speed-heaving competition at the trailer park. Slices are
bouncing off my head, my chest, my everywhere; it's piling on the
floor. I'm gobbling them down as quick as they're comin' in. I'm
chewin' as hard and fast as I can. My mouth's full, and I'm rushing
to chew more, and I bite my tongue. *Mistake.* I got the worst pain I
ever felt. "Ahhhh!" This hurts...torture...torture.... Oh my God,
bad pain, bad, bad pain.... Horrible, horrible, tongue-biting agony
accident pain."

My eyes open. I musta got knocked out again and woke up
when I bit my tongue dreamin' I was chewin' bologna. Tongue is

throbbin'. And what's that dangling an inch in front of me? Bologna? Am I gazing at the world's biggest, thickest slice of delicious pink bologna? Maybe I'm unconscious again? But I hear a crowd chanting, "Kill! Kill!"

No! I'm wide awake, and what I'm looking at isn't a piece of bologna—it's Monstro's tongue.

The instant he feels my right fang sinking into that tongue, his body tightens like a Slinky snapping back into place. He's rigid. Small high-pitched squeals start deep in his throat and fade to squeaks when they get to his mouth. The crowd hears nothing. They don't know what I'm doing. To them, it still looks like he's got me down and is choking me.

"Kill him, Monstro! Kill him, kill him!" they're screaming.

"He dead yet?" Money Piles shouts to the crowd. "What you think? What you think? Spike dead yet?"

Monstro's breathing is gettin' slower and slower and slower. His eyes are crossed, which is kinda rare for a dog, unless they got astigmatism like that Boston terrier in Thomasville who wore yellow corrective goggles. I'm bearin' down on the tongue as hard as possible. Can't imagine the pain he's got right now. Even though I'm doin' this to save my life, I'm not happy hurting him, so it's good when he lets out a gasp and passes out. His body's in shock; not unusual to pass out 'cause a pain.

I get loose from his slack jaws and slowly back out from under him. I hate to make a victory appearance ass first, but it's the only way I can exit. As more and more of my body appears, the yelling gets louder and louder. By the time I'm standing in the middle of the ring, with Little Tiger in a pool of blood on one side of me and Monstro in a massive heap on the other, everyone is standing and chanting, "Spike, Spike, Spike!"

My moment of triumph with what I'm calling "The Tasmanian Tongue Hold," lasts about ten seconds before a Julio, James Two, and James Plus run in and throw that heavy mesh metal cover over me and get a wire on a stick around my neck. I can't move. It's like I got a melted airplane wing holding me down.

Money Piles enters, and the crowd gives him a cheer. He looks at Monstro.

"We seen Spike The Wonder Dog kill Monstro with phantom bite like Mohammad Ali use a phantom punch 'n knock out 'The Big Bear' Sonny Liston in Lewiston, Maine."

"Ohhhh, ahhhh," the crowd goes, pretendin' to know what the hell he's talking about, or that they ever even heard of the state of Maine.

"Now this Spike's last fight. He be retiring undefeated, like 'The Brockton Blockbuster,' Rocky Marciano."

"Ohhhhhhh, nooooooo," the crowd moans, like they're really gonna be thinkin' about me tomorrow, let alone doing MapQuest to find out where Brockton is.

Money Piles looks at some notes he's got written on the hand bandage, and it's the start of the dazzling raillery of his stand-up comedy.

"Spike oughta be arrested for animal abuse in here, the way he kill Monstro."

No laughs.

"Now all my James boys know how good my girlfriend Cartier is at givin' head—right, boys? Her sex trainer got her on the new Phallusal-lick-it diet."

"Strange transition," I'm thinking, as my tongue's hanging out dripping 'cause of the weight of the metal on me.

James One says, "Yeah, she bad, Money. She head-givin' champ, Champ; she love workin' in your no-fly zone."

"She better at outercourse than intercourse," Five Plus screams.

"And, Money, you know what Bible say about her," James Three says.

A gleam enters Money Piles' eye, like it's a setup line he's waiting for.

"No, Three…. What do the Bible say?"

"Your rod and your staff comfort her," Three says.

"Amen!" Cartier yells.

Five Plus shouts, "She tell me she never defy a gag order. She better than porn star; she make Stormy Daniels look like Charlie Daniels!"

"She *is* porn star, you stupid dick," Money Piles yells. "And I was thinkin' of Cartier givin' Spike head…"

Wait a minute! I get stolen, tranquilized up the ass, locked in a cage, battle multiple dogs, they're gonna freeze me and stew me, but first Cartier gives me a blowjob? No fuckin' way!

Money Piles pauses to let the crowd do some "Wow"-ing and "He bad"-ing before he delivers his punch line, but he's got the timing of an amateur comedian on open-mic night at a pop-up comedy club in Fenwick, Connecticut.

"Oh, yeah! I was thinkin' of Cartier giving Spike *head*…to a prince in Nigeria who pay ten thousand dollars if Cartier slice head off. That prince want Spike head for trophy in middle of palace dinner table. He say he pay extra five thousand for video if Cartier be oiled up and naked when she be heading to beheadin' him."

I'm seriously wondering why I didn't swallow all those steroid pills when I had the chance. Forget valor; I saw enough of *Game of Thrones* to avoid beheading whenever possible.

"But that prince crazy usin' kennel-fresh dog head for a trophy. You know why? You need to eat dog head fresh, 'cause dog head, when you add pineapple and cloves…it taste better…"

He looks down at the bandage and reads, "...than Hormel ham...your mother make...at Easter."

Because nobody else is, Money Piles starts laughing. The Jameses finally realize he's tryin' to be funny, so they burst into the loud, fake laughs employees always give their bosses.

"You funny, Money; oh, yeah, you funny," James One says.

"Oh, he so funny he make Chris Rock look like 'The Rock,'" James Two says.

A couple of laughs come from the crowd, and behind Money Piles I see Monstro's eyelids fluttering.

"But Cartier not choppin' off Spike head, 'cause Ike 'I Got Money' Piles is sendin' full head-on frozen body of Spike to Thailand to my friend Abouti...for..."

He pauses, while I get set to calculate my per-pound price by dividing seventy into...

"Fifty thousand dollars."

The crowd roars just enough to make Money Piles feel good, even though they want him to get the hell outta the ring so they can watch another fight.

The roar startles Monstro. He sees me stuck under the metal thing.

Is he gonna charge to try to finish me off while I'm trapped here? We eye each other. He nods: "You're good. I had you, but you still beat me."

Then he spots Ike "I Got Money" Piles, and Monstro's eyes go dark. His mouth curls back and uncovers long, yellow fangs.

I don't know if he did it 'cause Money Piles' cousin in Costa Rica stole Monstro from a family where he had a happy life, and forced him to fight boars with a partner he hated. I don't know if he did it 'cause Money Piles shipped him in a way-too-small crate all the way to New York on a cheap, slow freighter. Or if he did it 'cause Money Piles has him livin' here in a tiny cage in a dirty corner with no daylight.

I don't know why, and I never will, but Monstro rises, and even faster than when he took me down, leaps on Money Piles' back. He knocks him over.

Money Piles lands on his bandaged hand and screams. Monstro starts biting him, rippin' away at his leg muscle like he did to dozens of wild boars. He mangles the back of his knee and starts biting again and again on his calves.

"Kill him, kill him, kill him, shoot him, you motherfuckers!" Money Piles screams at his men.

But seeing Monstro come alive stuns the Jameses into some kind of ghost dog trance.

"Kill him, kill him, kill him, you bug-eyed bastards, shoot him!" Money Piles yells.

Monstro starts rippin' through the basketball pants to get to Money Piles' balls. Cartier runs in the cage, pulls a little pistol from her bag, and shoots Monstro, who takes the bullet and doesn't even howl. She fires again, twice into Monstro's shoulder. The bullets go through him into Money Piles' arm.

"Bitch!" Piles screams. "You shootin' me! You shootin' me!"

"My bad," she says.

Three blasts from James Plus' Beretta knock Monstro down. He crawls toward me. Collapses. His eyes close. He's dead.

Don't know who's got more blood pourin' outta him—Monstro or Ike "I Got Money" Piles.

Half the bloodthirsty crowd is standin' outside the cage carrying enough firepower to take down a special-forces platoon. They're in line, hopin' to get in on the action and have some fun pumping slugs into a twitching, dead dog.

"Call nine-one-one! Call nine-one-one!" James Plus yells.

"Fuckin' no way," Piles yells at him. "This look like animal shelter to you? We get turned in. Pick me up and drive me to Saint Mary's!"

"Who car we use, Money?" Plus says, lookin' around. "You just buy all your Jameses new SRXs with fine hand-stitched leather cargo bays; who wanta get that all bloodied up? Car still smell new."

"Fuck your cargo bays!" Piles screams.

"Maybe we just get Chicago Bob the vet take taxi over and patch you up?'"

"That horse doctor patch me up? You see the white thing down there where I suppose to have a goddamn leg? That called thighbone. Get me to fuckin' Saint Mary's, now."

"Money, how 'bout we carry you to walk-in urgent care down street near hairdresser and tell them coyote nip you? No long wait line there, plus you got no insurance anyway," James Two says.

"It called walk-in because you gotta be able to walk the fuck in," Piles yells. "Get me outta here!"

"I'll take him in my Malibu," Cartier says. "Just load him in the back, but put blankets down."

Ike "I Got Money" Piles passes out. Considering that his leg is dangling off him like a loose tooth and he's squirting blood like a fireboat, I think he'd be disappointed to learn that Cartier takes time to fix an eyelash, brush her long blond hair, and put on even more lip gloss and foundation for the trip to the hospital. She wants an armed guard with her, so the daytime security man is going along.

Just when I need it, I get lucky. Two things happen that give me a chance to escape—James Plus takes the mesh thing off me, and the security guard's helping one of the Julios carry Money Piles to Cartier's Malibu. The open door's gonna be unguarded, and after they go through it with Money Piles, it's gonna take around six seconds for it to swing back and automatically lock.

The instant they go through the door, I race out of the fight cage draggin' the stick and dogcatcher wire. I figure if I make it to the street, I'm gonna be walking around looking like an escaped convict 'cause of the stick, but I'll deal with that later.

I tear across the room running faster than I ever have. The door's slowly closing. They're chasin', but I'm way ahead. There's about six inches of space before the door closes. I wedge my head between the door and the jam, and swing it a little bit wider and wriggle through. I start runnin' but get snapped back by the wire, 'cause the door closed on the end of the long stick.

I try biting through the stick, but they got me.

James Two says, "Nice try, Spike. You faster than rabbit. But now, I takin' you back to cage."

Outta luck.

20

The Freezer

Waitin' for me in my cage is a five-thousand-calorie feeding. James Plus says, "You're gonna love this, Spike. Your last tasty meal add nice sizzling layer of fat on you by time you be shipped outta here tomorrow morning."

I got no intention of eatin' anything that makes me a better stewing dog. My red collar's the only thing here with me, so I start chewin' on it. I had that bad habit as a puppy of chewin' on collars, but Bud trained me to stop. I figure in my final hours, collar chewin's the only comfort I got, just like returning to heavy drinking's gonna be the only comfort for George W. Bush at the end. Wonder if he'll get real drunk like in the old days and admit he fucked up by invading Iraq?

I got a little time now to reflect on things at my end. I get so sad thinkin' of Bud. We had unconditional love, and that's a hard thing to find. I gotta block him out every time I see his face before me.

Just a few regrets—never got the quality time with Cher that I wanted, never really enjoyed New York, but when you sign on with an owner, you go with them. Never got that Pizza Pouch gig right, never had puppies with Daisy. Never made it to an ocean to surf. I always admired those dogs on YouTube gliding along on waves. The rest of my brothers and sisters have probably been neutered, so I guess our bloodline's dyin' with me, like *Last of the Mohicans*—regret that.

But I've been one of the lucky dogs of the world. I heard Lombardo say, "Bud, a measure of a person is what you do with the luck that's left you." I got lucky when Bud picked me out of the pen; he had his choice of other, smarter, better-lookin' dogs—like Billy, who I heard won Best in Show in Pennsylvania—but he picked me. So now, even though the freezer's waitin', I'm feelin' lucky as I'm lyin' here watchin' the trainers shove scared-looking strays in the fight cage to time how quick the new dogs can take 'em down.

I'm wonderin' about these strays. They started out like every dog—just a cute innocent little puppy. What went wrong for them? What bad luck came their way? Same kinds of questions I got about the grim-faced people I seen rooting through trash cans for food—what went wrong for them? They were once just someone's cute little baby.

I gotta let you know, from the bottom of my soon-to-be-frozen heart, how much comfort it's been telling you my story. Nothin' else to say. I'm just waiting as calm as I can to get led across to that dark corner to the freezer hidden in the wall.

I enjoy spending the next hour watching the two sparrows who somehow live here. They got a nest on a ledge, and two baby sparrows hatched this morning. Real strong possibility those little sparrows will never fly free of this place. Tomorrow, they'll be one day old, and everything they see is gonna be the usual—dog trainin', dogfights, crowds screaming—except the big white dog will be gone.

James Plus comes over and opens my cage. "OK, Spike, this is it."

He's wearin' arm-protecting gear. I bite his forearm anyway, but it's like chompin' on a giant roll of aluminum foil.

I turn to get my red collar, but he jerks my head away. "Might be able to sell that as Spike collectible."

I'm findin' no comfort in the coincidence that Tupac Shakur is rappin' "Death Around the Corner" as I'm being led to the freezer. I'm walkin' with head high and tail straight. Why make him drag me and look like a coward at the end?

The two Julios and the Jameses are leanin' against the wall getting drunk. They've emptied a cheap bottle of Jose Cuervo and are cracking open a second one.

The Julios pick up small, battered guitars.

James Two opens the freezer. "Julios have special song they sing to send you on way, Spike. They sing it to all dogs before they go in," he says.

Wonderful, this'll be like music therapy for people in hospice care. What could it be? I'm hopin' for a teary rendition of the Astaire classic "Let's Face the Music and Dance." But since the Julios barely speak English, let alone would sing lyrics about fiddlers fleeing or sharing teardrops, I get what I was expecting—a drunken rendition of "*Besame Mucho*."

In my last hour, it's like I'm alone with a bad lounge act in Cancun's Hilton Garden Inn.

If only the Zebe were here to give me a simultaneous bar mitzvah, funeral, last rites, and rabbinical certification, so those terrorist bastards over there would know they're eating a Kosher dog who's a friend to the state of Israel.

I look up at everybody—all of the Jameses with the stupid tattoos on their heads, the two scrawny Julios, a couple of the

blood-loving dog trainers, who're scratchin' their balls from fleas they got from the strays, and three puffy-lipped blonde bimbos from Money Piles' pleasure squad, who're snorting coke off their fingernails while balancing on five-inch platform stilettos on the dirt floor. The song ends on a bad, screeching high note, then they start kicking me toward the freezer.

No way they're forcing me in by kickin'. A song pops into my head—my favorite from back home in High Point. I give them the deepest, meanest growl I ever made, and jauntily stroll into the freezer singing to myself, "Nothing could be finer than to be in Carolina in the morning..."

"Look at him; he so bad, he march in there like he Denzel goin' up to get an Oscar," James Plus says.

"Yeah, he bad but he dead," someone says, and I hear a click. The door's locked.

"Turn it to eighteen," they say. "That'll take a while. Ike 'I Got Money' Piles said to make it slow, 'cause he like slow freezin' process, not dry aging like in Mexico."

"This is my 'This is it,'" I think.

I see my brother Billy's kind face. Now I remember: "*Horam expecta veniet*," he told me. "Await the hour; it shall come."

239

It's just the ordinary sound of a freezer door clicking shut. No machine guns cutting me down on the beach at Normandy, no doomed plane with screaming passengers plunging to earth, no Bud holding my paw and comforting me in my final moment—just a click.

In the first minute or so, it's not feelin' too cold; it's just makin' the wounds on my sides and face sting more than before.

Inside the freezer's a surprise. Ever go someplace and it's way smaller than you thought it would be? Like maybe that resort in Aruba, where the beach was only the size of a tennis court, not the length of a couple of fields like you were expecting from the glorious pictures on the hotel website.

The freezer's way smaller than I imagined. It's just about big enough to park a Fiat inside. You could do that if you didn't mind drivin' around later with a frozen dog stuck to your hood. Sad, though, if you were driving home on Christmas and the kids thought you were bringin' them a pet, but they had to use ice scrapers to get it off.

There's a little peephole, probably to check on me without opening the door and letting in some comforting warm air.

I figured the freezer'd be empty, but lookin' around, I see they put some stuff on the walls.

I spot a sign instructing the morons who work here to "keep fecal material away from ice cube trays." Next to that is a headshot of Nicki Minaj with pink and blonde hair, autographed to someone named Ralph. There's the mandatory-for-the-inside-of-any-freezer photo of Kim Kardashian looking over her shoulder at her ass like she spotted a pimple. A photo of Cary Grant is next to one of Judy Garland, which maybe confirms that the Julio with the thumb ring and "Judy Judy Judy" tattooed on his hand might be headed to Chelsea after work.

I'm feelin' the cold set in on my paws and tips of my ears. Gotta stay calm, which I do for three seconds before I spot a frozen-solid Scottie dog standing in the corner.

Awful sight. I never saw frozen eyes before. Frozen eyes look right through you, worse than Putin's at a press conference. There's a tag on the Scottie's neck: "Thirty-four pounds at twenty-five degrees = dead in four hours." There's a pile of other tags like that on the floor with dog weights and temperatures and times till death. If Birds Eye wants to produce frozen dog dinners for the Southeast Asia market, these guys have research.

Studying tags, I figure I got about three hours to live. You never know how valuable time is until you're runnin' out of it. Don't forget that.

Hour One: Getting Drunk

On the floor in the back are a couple of bottles of Tito's vodka. I figure getting as drunk as possible is gonna ease my—usin' the words people who never mention "death" say—"transition"; and then they act like it's just a ferry ride across a river "to a better place on the other side," like you're away on a swell vacation.

So why not show up on "the other side" really loaded? And I mean really loaded—falling-down-drunk loaded—like I'm Sid Vicious after a binge with Amy Winehouse? That'll be fun, and I've never been real, real drunk before. Yeah, OK, that one time with the Bloody Bull shots.

Also, I got an idea: Maybe if I slurp up enough booze, it'll be like antifreeze and I'll just pass out. Then they'll think I'm dead and I'll wake up packed in ice under the fish. I'd escape with only a drinking problem and a minor cut from bitin' off the top of the bottle.

I pour vodka into a stained blue plastic dog bowl and start lappin' away. One bowl later, the whole body's even more relaxed than after a tranquilizer dart. The booze is helping me stay a little warmer, even though I know I'm getting colder and colder and can't stop the base of my tail from quiverin'.

I heard there are two kinds of drunks—mean ones and happy ones. Maybe it's just the circumstances, but I'm fallin' into the mean category, 'cause I wanna ram my head through the door and go out and kill everybody I see. Maybe endless vodka drinking is how Quentin Tarantino gets inspiration for his movies?

I even feel like pickin' a fight with the frozen Scottie. If this is the way I'd been drinkin' at Nello on a normal Friday night with Donna Hanover, I'd've developed a bad reputation. I don't think wanting to rip the balls off the guy on the stool next to you is why they call it happy hour.

I'm angry they're taking my life away from me. The one and only thing I really got. I'm angry at every terrorist in the world for killin' innocent people. I'm angry at all the school shooters who ever lived, and people who club baby seals, and man's in-fuckin'-humanity to man! Why?

Life is bein' takin' away from me, and I loved life, loved every minute of it, except for dealin' with Mayor Gordon and his stupid wife, bein' painted green, and the shit they put me through in here.

But I liked bein' in those fights. Enjoyed combat, and I was fuckin' good! Fuckin' good—and you know it! If I ever get out of here, I'm gonna find some kind of friendly sparrin' partner. Maybe Daisy and me could wrestle around? Shouldn't a thought of Daisy! Oh God, now I'm cryin' over her. Cryin'.

I lap up a second bowl of vodka, and I'm slobberin' and slobberin' and dizzy. Big dizzy.

But I'll tell you this: I might only have three hours like another notable had while he was dyin', but you're not gonna hear, "Bud, Bud, why have thou forsaken me?" This shit is not his fault.

If I was a prayin' dog, this is where I'd pray to Dog God for help, but my friends who do waste their fuckin' time sayin' prayers to Dog God tell me nothing ever happens. They figure Dog God's probably always out bein' walked.

Now I'm thinkin' about God, who I never thought about, but bein' drunk is doin' wonderous things to my brain. Here's something every drunk in every Irish bar in New York oughta ask the bartender…. Hold on; I gotta drink more…

Slurping, slurping away. Lapping delicious ice-cold vodka straight outta a freezing-cold dog bowl—try it!

Ahh! Stuff's good, helpin' me fight the cold…sort of…. Anyway…so, if Jesus is God's son, why the hell does God let his only begotten kid get nailed to a cross and suffer all to prove he's "the way, the truth, and the light?" Why doesn't Jesus hold a big rally…a huuuge one? And then Jesus just says, "OK, believe in me, folks, and you can go to heaven just like this. Watch, everybody; here I go, one, two, three"—and wham, he vanishes! Like I saw Penn make Teller disappear in Vegas, except God is doin' it to Jesus at this huuuge rally and he's gone. Huh? Huh?

I'm gonna pass out. Fuck 'em all. Fuck 'em. For takin' my life from me. Fuck fuck fuck and bite them where it hurts the most, bite bite bite…. Oh God, I wanna disappear. I'm so cold.

Hour Two: Memories

Oh Christ, I'm awake, shaking, shiverin' out of control…shit! So cold, horrible cold, nose is stone cold from breathin' freezing, horrible icy air.

I vomited in my sleep. It didn't kill me, like throwin' up and suffocating on it while sleepin' killed Hendrix, Joplin, and Mama Cass and somebody else; I can't remember. Who cares? Didn't kill me 'cause it was projectile vomiting, and now barf's all over that picture of Cary Grant in the nice gray suit. Judy's OK; she's just got a little polar ice cap of it on one knee.

The vodka-as-antifreeze theory's not gonna work. Gonna fight the cold mentally. I gotta control my mind, gotta transport myself to somehow have an out-of-frozen-body experience. Or try, anyway.

I'm rememberin' Bud quoting Carson the butler on *Downton Abbey*, who said, "The business of life is the acquisition of memories. In the end that's all we'll have." I'm goin' back in time, way, way back as far as I can remember; gotta transport me away from this cold that's making my whole body shake, and then maybe I'll die with a happy memory playin' in my head…. I'd like that…so I'm thinking back, way back…

There's my dad standin' over me, and now he's pickin' me up by the back of my neck. He's got a more gentle carrying style than Mom, 'cause he's not used to doin' it, so maybe he thinks he's gotta be more careful. He's lifting me up and outside the pen.

"What's Rocky doing with Elmer?" Mrs. Erdrick, the breeder, is askin' her husband.

Yeah, my original name was Elmer. All of my litter got named after cartoon characters; we had Lulu, Minnie, Oswald, and Billy. I heard I was the only one who got a new name, 'cause Bud called me Spike.

My dad's carrying me around the living room like he's showing me off. He's so big and so strong, with rippling muscles piled on top of more muscles.

"Be careful with him, Rocky," she says.

My dad never knows when someone's gonna come and buy us and take us away from him forever. Dad works every day with Mr. Erdrick as a guard at the factory, so he's not always around to tend us, so time with Dad is precious.

He sets me down in the corner of the living room and puts his head next to me. His head's about as big as my whole body.

Dad's lookin' me straight in the eye. He's got a fierce energy about him. Could be scared of him, but I'm not, 'cause he's my dad and I know he loves me.

"You got something special, Elmer…a special property," he's telling me. "Your mother and me had three litters, fourteen pups so far, and we both see something extra in you…a force in your eyes…. You're gonna do a big thing for our breed in your life. Billy's real smart and extra handsome. He's got those brains from your mom's side of the family, and we're proud of him. But I know there's something of my great-great-grandfather Brick in you."

I'm feelin' mighty good and real surprised that Dad and Mom are thinkin' this way about me.

"Just carry this with you forever, Elmer; remember me, remember Mom, remember your brothers and sisters, and never, ever doubt yourself."

I get put back in the pen. I remember fallin' asleep bein' happy and proud of Dad and tryin' to absorb his words to me. Askin' myself if I was worthy of those words.

Later that day, Mrs. Erdrick wakes us up and we know a buyer's coming. "Time for you all to be a basket of adorables," she says.

It's Bud. He's a handsome young guy with broad shoulders and a big smile. We all like him. He looks like a guy who should own an English Bull Terrier, and not some wimp who's gonna buy one of us to make himself look more macho.

"Not sure, but I think I want a male," he says, as he looks down at us smiling at him.

Oswald, Billy, and me all want this guy to take us. Billy's practically doing a dog show routine. Oswald, who's a little on the crazy side—Mom says he's "demented but affectionate"—is leapin'

245

around and wildly shaking a toy in his mouth. I'm just standing still. I'm looking up at Bud. I feel special 'cause of what Dad just said to me. Bud looks at me. I look him right in the eye the way Dad just did to me. Next to me though, just inches away, Billy is giving off a lot of energy.

"This one's a beauty," Bud says to Mrs. Erdrick, as he leans way down looking at Billy.

"He's a brainy little fellow, too," she tells him.

Bud stands up. He looks at Billy. He looks at me. I'm gazing at him with all my might. I feel him inside me in some strange way, and I think he's somehow feeling me back—like we're absorbing each other's energy. He's linked with me, and we got that thing flowin' between us for the first time—our connection, the one we'd go on to have a million times.

"This one's got something special," Bud says, and I think, "Yes! That's it, he's gonna pick me!"

But smart little Billy gets Bud's attention by putting his paws on the pen wall, stretching up with his tongue out, tryin' to lick Bud's hand.

Bud looks at me again. I can't help it, 'cause I just woke up; I let out a big yawn.

"Oh my God, he's so cute. Can I pick him up?" Bud asks.

Now Bud's holding me in his arms, and I got an owner who I like. I'm having the greatest day of my life.

"Will he be big?" Bud asks.

"He'll be the biggest of the lot," Mrs. Erdrick says. "Take a look at his dad; he'll be even bigger."

And there's Dad off in the corner giving me a proud nod of his huge head.

I'm comin' out of the memory, and my cold body's shakin' more than that vibrator thing I had in my mouth when I ran around the block. Mr. and Mrs. Erdrick and Mom and Dad know all about the adventures of Spike The Wonder Dog. Dad was somehow right that day, and he and Mom gotta be happy with what I did, bein' on TV and all. I have a kind of peace from that memory. Thanks, Carson the butler, wherever you are. And thanks, Dad. I'm not doubting myself; I'm gonna die happy. But now, 'cause I can't take this cold anymore, I'm just closing my eyes.

Hour Three: Going to Sleep

Just woke up realizing something's different—I'm not shaking. Maybe that means "and now the end is near." I sense my heart workin' slower but harder and harder. Most of my body's numb. Can't feel my paws or ears. Tail won't move, maybe frozen solid. Does the tail get hypothermia first on dogs? I don't know much about freezing to death…. I know how to make frozen drinks from watchin' Bud. I'm makin' no sense…

…Throw a blanket on me, Mrs. Erdrick…. Now, please. Oswald's cold, too…. Mom! Mom!

I'm mixed up…like it's…like it's…it's now…what's the word? The word for…when…you're confused?…. There was a beer… Bud liked it…had that word in it? Can't think straight…oh… Delirium Tremens beer…that's what I am now, delirious.

I got songs swirling around in my head. The one about bein' a puppet or a pauper or a pirate that Lombardo played for Bud…. "Puppet, pauper, pirate" keeps singing itself to me…"pawn"… "king"…and over and over….

Now…I'm seein' Bud at that church beltin' out a baseball song about how your luck could be battin' zero…. People were cheerin' like it was…I don't know…. Whatever it was…they were goin' wild…. They were yelling and stompin' like that old song was teachin' them that they had to get their chins off the floor.

Man next to me was whistling with two fingers in his mouth.... First time I ever saw that.... Now I hear the whistle...loud...loud whistle.

Bud had heart.... I love Bud.... He shoulda' stayed in High Point and been a minister at some church. I could collect offerings with the silver plate in my mouth. What am I thinkin'? I'm confused. Sorry. Confused, and...real, real tired and heavy. Everything on me is heavy and tired, and slow and numb.

...This might be it.... Is this it? What's the song?.... Final curtain song?.... Falling asleep...irregular heartbeats...goin' to sleep...now...might be...

The Interview with Lester Holt

Boggs: (Note to reader) Spike told me that Lester Holt interviewed Bud about what he did when he learned Spike was abducted. The following is a transcript of that conversation.

Holt: The day you left for the cruise was the day Spike was stolen. When did you find out about Spike?

Bud: Thanks for this chance to talk about this, Lester.

Holt: You're welcome. It's quite a story for any pet owner.

Bud: Well, you have to go back to the morning of the first day for me to really explain this...the awful morning.

Holt: Go ahead, take your time.

Bud: I just had this horrible feeling of not wanting to leave. My friend Buffy, her dog Daisy and my old boss Lombardo were in town, and I'm going off on a cruise feeling like I shouldn't be leaving, and I had a bad feeling saying goodbye to Spike...something I never had to do before.

Holt: Of course.

Bud: So I get on the ship, and I have this lurking, empty sense of dread.

Holt: We figure Spike was taken when you were just a couple of hours at sea. When did you find out?

Bud: The ship was brand new and had no internet, no Wi-Fi, nothing working the first twenty-four hours.

Holt: So you didn't know until…?

Bud: Around three o'clock or so the next day, a text comes through from Buffy about the abduction. Larry David Seinfeld Garcia, the dog walker kid, was hurt pretty badly, but he saw enough to know that Spike was dragged into a car by someone who he thought had been stalking them. The kid just had a hunch it was a dogfight operation that nabbed Spike.

Holt: Your first reaction?

Bud: One thing, I gotta get back and find Spike. That's it. One reaction.

Holt: You didn't know about the red collar then, right?

Bud: Correct.

Holt: Why did you jump off the ship?

Bud: The captain laughed at me when I told him he had to change course to go to a port to let me off so I could find my dog. The son of a bitch laughed right in my face.

Holt: Not pleasant.

Bud: Hardly, but one way or the other, I was getting off that ship, and it was Buffy who worked it out because Buffy's brother, Quinn McQueen, was a rescue swimmer on the U.S.S. *Enterprise.* He's now part of a private evacuation-at-sea business.

Holt: What happened?

Bud: Wasn't complicated. I get a wet suit from shore excursions. We coordinate the time. I see their helicopter, they see me, and I jumped off the side of the ship around thirty miles from Bermuda.

Holt: Scared?

Bud: Not really. Spike would have done it for me, but he wouldn't have liked the wet suit, anyway…

Holt: Funny, go on.

Bud: So I'm back in New York and Lombardo's stayed in town to help, and he's leaning on his friend Police Commissioner O'Neill, who says that they heard of a sophisticated dogfighting operation in Brooklyn maybe financed out of Connecticut, but the place is well hidden.

Holt: No other leads, clues?

Bud: Nothing. I was going nuts, and then the phone rings and Igor's father, Jack, is calling from Orlando.

Holt: The collar.

Bud: Right. He tells me he saw the whole story on TV about Spike The Wonder Dog being stolen.

Holt: The NBC News story…

Bud: Bless her, our friend Donna Hanover set it up, and Chuck Scarborough did the report for WNBC and you picked it up for the *Nightly News* 'cause of the suspected national dogfighting angle to the story.

Holt: And the small news-worthy fact that you jumped into the Atlantic Ocean in December from the railing of a cruise liner going twelve knots.

Bud: Yeah, well, you know, Lester, when you buy a puppy, you got a responsibility.

Holt: Ha! So, the collar?

Bud: Yes, the Igor fund thing. Well, that day of the telethon, they gave us Pledge's red collar, but nobody mentioned the collar had a chip in it.

Holt: Isn't the chip usually in the dog?

Bud: Yes, but Pledge was so afraid of going to the vet that they put the chip in her collar. We got the code to activate it and…

Holt: Yes, you made some big news there. So tell us…

Bud: No, that's enough from me…. It's Spike's story from here on in.

21
DYIN' WITH YOUR BOOTS ON

I wake up more clear-headed than before. I was dreamin' of having a conversation about plus-size dog models with my roommate, the frozen Scottie. We were outside lyin' on our backs risking major skin damage under the hot sun in my backyard in Thomasville. Dream warmed me up a little.

Weird to be happily baskin' in the heat with the Scottie one moment and wake up and see her frozen eyes the next. The more I look at her, the more panic-stricken she seems—like Rick Perry tryin' to remember the third part of a three-part question on *Meet the Press*.

But the Scottie's standing erect; she's bold and solid as a statue. She died lookin' brave, like the tough old breed she is. She didn't wanta end it like I am now—scared and curled up in a ball tryin' to stay warm. In death she's settin' an example for me.

When it's over, and they come in and get me, they're gonna ship me outta here in whatever position I froze into. I don't want to get unpacked in Thailand and have 'em say, "Hey look, here's that

Spike The Wonder Dog all coiled up with his paws coverin' his eyes like he's a frightened little puppy."

I gotta somehow pick my chin up off the floor and stand up. I want to face the end like I'm in the show ring at the Garden. But my legs and tail and body and neck are so stiff—rigid. Never been this stiff. Real stiff—like a twenty-year-old on a Viagra drip. Not good. Can't move much of me. It's practically takin' a minute just to straighten a leg.

I just gotta stand and do my breed proud, like Dad would want.

Movin' now. Slowly movin' over to the door to look out that peephole.

Shame how most times ya never really know that when you're doin' something, it might be the last time you ever do it.

I'm groggy. Half awake, half dead. But I'm movin' my beady little eye up to see life for the last time now. Whatever those creeps might be doing—whatever dogs they got on the treadmills, whoever's walkin' around with the pail of meat for feedin', I'll be seein' the movement of life, and I'll know it's the last time I'll be seeing life.

Then I'm planning to freeze myself into the stance of a champion.

Bud's got this theory that people with those near-death experiences are just using their imaginations to give them comfort. He thinks they only imagine a long tunnel with their mother at the end of it saying, "No, don't die yet; make a U-turn; go back now." He had a big argument on the show one day where he said there's no long tunnel, no spirit's talking to you. He said it happens "because humans are employing magic brain power so when they think they're dying, they make themselves believe they're setting off to the great beyond."

I musbe using that magic brain power now. I'm lookin' through that little peephole, and what am I seein'? 'Cause of the hole, it looks like a tunnel, and at the end there's Bud and Lombardo and

Buffy and police, and they're arresting everybody. Bud's over at my cage, and he's got James Plus in a hammerlock, askin' him where I am. I'm closing my eyes and dyin' with that comforting scene in my imagination.

I'm fading to black but never thought that dying would have great sound effects. I hear sirens. Like police cars are pulling up outside. Makes sense though. The biggest emergency of your life and you got police aiding you in your imaginary transition.

Now it's quiet again. Dark inside my head but eyes frozen open, like the Scottie's. Hope I got a brave look in those eyes. Numb all over. Can't feel a heart beating. Must be dead. Yep. But it's all so peaceful because I got an imaginary comfort out that hole, in that long white tunnel.

I'm seein' Bud lookin' around, like he's trying to find me and save me. He can't see the hidden freezer. He's real upset, 'cause they musta lied that I'm not here, but he's acting like he knows I am. He's got both arms up and his palms out, trying to sense where I might be. He looks like he did when we'd play mentalist together in the woods in Thomasville.

Talk about dying happy. I got great comfort now, 'cause of how good it feels imagining that I could use the dog powers to link up with him…. He's there at the end of the tunnel. Can I tune in with him? Tryin'. Sending forth the brainwaves from my frost-covered old skull. Tryin' to connect with my master…

I did it! Oh, yeah, this is a quality death for me.

I made the old Spike-and-Bud connection. We had it at the house in Thomasville. We had it first time we met. When it's working right, it's like we're so twined up together that he's looking through my eyes and I'm looking through his.

Oh boy, what a way to go! I'm pretending to think that I see him staring over here at this unlit corner, like he's able to sense me through the dark and through the wall and…wow! Now he's walkin' toward the freezer. Walkin' straight toward me. It's wonderful…. What a calming final thought…your master coming over to give you one goodbye pat on the head, or one long tummy rub, and then send you on your way to nowhere…or maybe somewhere… 'cause even though I'm dead, I'm enjoying myself.

Death is good, 'cause it's not feeling much different than life. Wanting this reassuring comfort is why people pile money into the church collection plates every Sunday.

But now I'm thinking I might be experiencing a new-wave type of dying, 'cause I hear the door click open. Warm air's pouring in. Bud's pulling me out of the freezer. Wow! I'm having a Jesus style of death—they'll be coming to my frozen tomb, and my body won't be in it. Feed me an Easter egg.

Bud's actually lifted me off the ground and is hugging me. I feel his warm hands on my ears. This is my first clue that all my senses will be working here in the afterlife.

Bud's tellin' me, "Oh my God, Spike, you're cold, you're almost frozen…but you're OK now; we got you."

Here's Lombardo greeting me: "Well, Spike, you finally stopped pissing on my tires in the parking lot, so I figured I'd return the favor and stick around to help find you."

And Buffy, too! She's holding Daisy up, and Daisy's licking my nose. This is heaven. I'm actually feeling licks on my nose. Somebody's got to tell Joel Osteen about this place or at least Jerry Falwell Jr. Let them know they have a brand new, highly profitable afterlife concept to sell—"Living Death," 'cause nobody here with me in heaven is dead yet.

I'm telling you, when you die—if you get the kind of deal I was offered—expect to be surrounded by people who are still alive. You get to love them even though you're dead! Maybe that's what heaven actually is? You just live on in the hearts of people who are living, but in my case, I'm actually with the living people, too.

I'm slowly warming up. I just licked Bud's face, and my tongue felt that he hadn't shaved today. I smell his smell. This gives me reason to maybe question where I am and what's going on. Life after death could actually be a massive VR experience without a headset.

Am I dead? Am I alive? Is this nirvana? I thought nirvana was really just an empty restaurant on Fifty-Sixth Street with an all-you-can-eat Indian buffet. This is a better deal, and Bud's feeding me nicely warmed, good old American beef, not red-dyed tandoori chicken.

Is my brain still frozen? Am I gonna be like Andy Kaufman trying to fool people about bein' dead? 'Cause I think I see Andy standing over in the corner watching me. Oh yeah, Andy's there. Am I in some alternate universe where I'm gonna be living now? Is this the bardo that the Tibetan monk on Bud's show was talking about? Where am I going?

Four Hours Later

I'm curled by the radiator in the apartment, and Daisy's lyin' next me helpin' to warm me up. Bits of ice are still frozen to my skin. The wounds on my body and face were bad. But they're mending extra fast, 'cause Bud got some pills from a trainer for a local football team. I heard him say it's a blend of andro, HGH, DMSO, steroids, and musk oil specially designed to heal serious injuries during halftime.

Whatever it's doing, one gash on my side is closing so fast, it looks like time-lapse photography. Or am I just imagining I'm watching it heal?

Dazed and confused now. Don't know if what's going on here is real. Is my dead body back in the freezer? Is what's happening now the long white tunnel thing going into extra innings?

I'm just takin' it all in, listenin' carefully for clues that might hint if I'm dead or alive, 'cause I feel like half of each.

Bud tells Buffy he had something called an epiphany on the ship 'cause of what he heard from a guy on board givin' a lecture.

"If Lombardo will take me, I wanta go back to High Point and our show," he says.

When I hear this, as frozen solid as I'm still feeling, I get a hot flash of happiness. Daisy looks at me as only a girlfriend could look at a guy if she suddenly knew there weren't going to be seven hundred miles separating their doghouses anymore.

"What happened? Why do you want to come back?" Buffy asks.

"Pure and simple thing about truth from a speaker on the ship, and I wrote it down, so I'll read it. He says, 'I'm trying to guide people to the truth of who they really are, and once they recognize that truth and accept the fact that they want to live a life based in that truth, the truth will set them free.'"

Bud looks at me. He looks at Buffy and then at the picture she gave us of our house in Thomasville. His eyes mist and he says, "Truth is, the 'who I really am' is that happy guy up there in the picture standing on his lawn, not the guy living here crawling all over New York at night because I don't like the work I'm doing during the day."

"The going up?" Buffy suggests.

"The going up?" Bud asks.

"Your song, the Kristofferson song you love," she tells him.

"Got it," Bud says. "Found out in my case up here, not worth the comin' down.

257

I want to go back to High Point and try to host the most success-ful daytime show of the decade. Or you know what? Maybe not. But at least I'm going to enjoy life and work again."

Right now my ears are still numb, and I got no feeling yet in the paws, but I'm trying to remember all the words of that Kristof-ferson song, "The Pilgrim." Bud played it all the time down South, but stopped listening to it here after Erica the producer wouldn't let Kristofferson on the show 'cause management said he was too old. It's the song Billy analyzed, but I don't remember, 'cause I'm still not thinkin' straight; it's like I'm in this happy dream.

His phone rings, and Bud answers and listens and then screams as loud as I've ever heard him yell, "What? No way, Andy, Spike did that? No! Impossible. Impossible!" Bud hardly ever screams outside of the bedroom, but he was doin' it just then.

And that's how he learned that Andy had somehow attached a dollar fee for everybody around the world who logged on to my "Stare" meditation video on our YouTube channel. That's how Bud learned he had enough money to throw in with Lombardo to buy WGHP and go back to High Point as an owner in total control.

That's how I learned that ten million people around the world settle into a low-blood-pressure state of relaxation every day because of me. I'm responsible for low productivity in the labor force. I've become the over-the-counter tranquilizer of dogs.

Five Days Later

I gotta share a bit of a troubling personal development. Accord-ing to everything I heard and saw on TV, I'm supposed to be alive 'cause Bud jumped off a ship and then got the red-collar code, and they tracked me down and arrested dozens of people for dogfight-ing. The case is still bein' investigated, and there're clues that some big-deal financial guys might be bankrolling a worldwide dogfighting operation.

The good news is, Money Piles is goin' to be standing trial, except he won't be standing too well, 'cause they had to amputate his leg. Wherever I am now, if I run into Monstro, I'll let him know. See, that's my problem; I'm not really sure where I am.

I got a complete physical examination. My wounds are mostly healed, and I lost a little bit of an ear 'cause of frostbite—adds a touch of character to my profile.

The vet gives me an A-plus checkup, except she finds rectal damage from that thing they shoved up me, so I gotta issue yet another friendly caution for everybody out there planning on plunging away at anal sex tonight. Talk to your vet first.

After the exam, I'm convinced I'm alive, and the long white tunnel thing was a hoax. Who wouldn't figure you got rescued and you're actually still in the real world, right? But here's the trouble— I think I see Andy Kaufman peering in the vet's window, and he's holding Igor's dog Pledge. OK, so maybe you're saying that a bit of Spike's brain still needs defrosting. Maybe.

But it gets worse. I don't know if when I wake up, I'm actually starting to dream, or if when I fall asleep, I'm actually waking up? I can't tell the difference between dreaming and what's supposed to be life, 'cause every night I got exactly the same dream: I'm in the freezer; it's as real as could be. There's the frozen barf spot on Judy Garland's knee, the bottles of vodka, the brave Scottie. Am I still alive in the freezer waitin' to die, and all this is a dream? Is my whole story gonna end like "Who shot J. R.?" Or am I dead and this is what I get—like it's God's way of rewarding me for finally getting housebroken? Did Bud really rescue me, or am I still in the freezer making it all up? It's way more complicated than dying by fading to black, like I always thought I would.

For all the advanced twenty-first-century crap they got for dogs—like, and I'm not kidding, a dog collar that shouts obscenities when dogs bark, so, you're yappin' away, happily greeting your owner as he opens the door, while the collar's screamin', "you ugly shithead"—even with modern marvels like that—nobody's providing me with what I need, which is intense canine dream therapy.

Anyway, "the bottom line," as Lombardo says, is that I'm savoring each precious moment of what's supposed to be the life part, and staying up later and later trying to avoid going to sleep and the returning-to-the-freezer part.

22

A Month Later: The Orange Doghouse

Bud stored my beloved orange doghouse with all the other stuff we had in Thomasville that we didn't need 'cause of the turnkey apartment in New York. I'm in the house now, lying on fresh cedar chips here in a big back yard, behind our great new house. I'm a little outta breath, 'cause I was just tossin' truck tires around.

Things are mighty perfect in life, and when they're good like this, you gotta experience the intensity of it. I know dogs who're way more likely to be complainin' about how bad things are than ever letting you know about the good times—should be the opposite. I'm gaining this new spiritual outlook on life, 'cause Bud's playing a lot of personal-empowerment babbling on DVDs from that speaker on the boat.

The guy says, "You are very powerful provided you know how powerful you are." I coulda told him that. That's the whole deal with me and my breed. OK, so I'm bragging, but I'm flyin' sky high. Let me tell you why, and I'll wrap up my story for you.

First off, Buffy's been over at our new place almost every night. I don't know if she and Bud are in the erotic zone yet, but judging by the look in their eyes, I'm thinkin' this could be the start of something big. She and Daisy are inside. I came out to get some fresh North Carolina air and tire-toss for a couple of minutes to burn a few calories, 'cause I ate nineteen Christmas cookies before Bud's mother started to yell at me 'cause I was wolfing them down while standing on the table.

Pip's here! Bud flew his mother and Pip down for Christmas. They came in some private airline that Bud bought timeshares in. Do you think Pip's got any idea he's flying first class 'cause Yogi Bob saw me relax Gilbert Gottfried and then told Bud I had a unique gift? No! Pip would've come down here locked in the trunk of a '63 Pinto. He just wants to go huntin' with me tomorrow. He's left squirrels for badgers, and he bets we got some out there in the woods behind us.

Only negative I'm facing in my life is that Daisy doesn't like Pip. Thinks he's "a bloodthirsty, self-involved little dachshund with a Napoleonic complex." Pip's got no idea about this. He thinks Daisy's goin' badger hunting with us tomorrow, but she can hardly wait for him to get out of the house. Ever have a problem like this— you get a girlfriend, and she doesn't like your pal?

Happy to relate that I got a lot of media coverage on the dogfight thing. It was about the fights and all they put me through and the police rescue. Today I wanted more press. I was wishin' *The New York Times* would do that feature-story thing on me about "How I Spend My Sunday." Usually people just make up a fictional bagel-filled, dreamlike version of what their Sunday routine is but never actually admit what they normally do, which is get high and watch TV in their pajamas all day.

Anyway, today I would've told them that my Sunday was really simple—after we had our bagels, I spent the whole day standin' next to my doghouse goin' at it big time, pounding away with Daisy. "Action in the afternoon!" Oh yeah, we did the deed multiple times. Everybody knows I'd been a virgin for way too long. That ended today.

And you know what else ended? The mix-up about if I was just dreamin' life while still in the freezer. The first time I felt the pleasure of a year's worth of lust for Daisy shooting outta my body, I knew there was no way it could be my imagination. I'm feeling more alive than ever! And if we get lucky and have a litter, I'm naming one of them Monstro, outta respect for a great combatant, who took five slugs and died with his boots on. There was a lotta dog in that dog.

Unfortunately, with all this happiness, a bad thought keeps entering my mind. If we have pups, Pip's gonna wanta play with them, and Daisy's not gonna like that.

Yeah, I got minor relationship tension already. Bachelor days were way more simple, except, of course, now I'm getting laid.

Had stress last night over her givin' me a hard time about drinking a Bloody Bullshot during the Budster's cocktail hour. At least I'm not scarfin' down croissants in the morning like she is. Do I say a thing about it—even though that junk can really expand the waistline? No, 'cause look, I'm getting laid.

Another issue: She's got this strange thing she does, wrinklin' her nose when she sniffs. Bad habit and she looks weird. It embarrasses me in front of Pip. But when I try to tell her to try to sniff with a relaxed nose, she gets pissed and runs outside. Won't let me near her for ten minutes.

Oh, and speaking of outside—she wants to get rid of my orange doghouse.

"Not big enough," she says. She wants a green and white junior one-bedroom doghouse. What the hell is a junior one-bedroom doghouse? Where do I get one? Pressure. And she's demanding to change the cedar chips on the floor to hay. It's a doghouse, Daisy, not a manger. You wake up on hay smellin' like Mr. Ed. She's also spouting off about replacing my pictures of Cher and Lassie with shots of winners from *Dancing with the Stars*. No way! They say relationships are a lot of work. I already got a job on TV. But then I remember—I'm getting laid, so maybe this is part of the proposition, like the price you gotta pay to have sex.

Maybe I need a male dog support group?

But you know what? I can't worry about this stuff now. It's makin' me lose my bliss. Gotta take a breath and Yogi-Bob my head a little.

Breathe…relax…breathe…be here now…. Breathe…relax… be here now…and…

Now…

Now is a beautiful, starry, crisp December night in North Carolina. Bud has a big Christmas tree glowing in the living room. His mom brought some of the old decorations from when he was a little boy. There's a fire in the fireplace. It smells like the best of winter. Christmas music is floating out of the windows.

A year ago we were drivin' away from Thomasville headed to New York. Bud had Christmas music on the radio, and Frank was singin' about how through the years we're all gonna be together if somehow the fates will allow it. I had my head on the car seat thinkin', "What is this crap? This song's complete holiday bullshit!"

I was real, real wrong about that.

I hear Frank singin' that same song and those same words now, and you know what happened?

The fates got it right.

THAT'S IT.

Thanks for reading.

Oh, P.S. If this gets optioned and made into a movie, please don't include the scene of me taking that big dump on the street with all the people in line for *The Tonight Show* watching. By then, Daisy and me might have pups and it'd be embarrassing for them to see old Dad like that.

Think I'm too sensitive? If fifty people cheered you on while you took a dump on Sixth Avenue, you'd feel the same way.

Who knows where time and tide will take us? But I gotta figure, I'll be back when I got more adventures to tell Mr. Boggs. Shouldn't be a problem getting the connection again, 'cause Bud got a handy six-pack of shrooms by givin' the nurse at NBC tickets to see Taylor Swift at Radio City Music Hall.

Let's pause there....

SPIKE

You will be remembered by the tracks you leave.

Special thanks to:

Jane Rothchild
Trevor Boggs
Barry Dougherty
Derek Pell
Jeff Leibowitz
John Hedlund
Bernard Weinstock
Zach Simmons
Stacy Slotnick, Esq.

About the Author

Bill Boggs is an Emmy Award-winning TV talk show host and producer, author, and professional speaker. His Off-Broadway play, *Talk Show Confidential*, and his first novel, *At First Sight*, were optioned together for a screenplay inspired by his life.

He began his career as a comedy writer/producer, and *The Adventures of Spike the Wonder Dog* reflects his strong observational comedy chops. He has written essays for *The New York Times Sunday Magazine*, travel articles for *The Times*, and a well-received self-help book, *Got What it Takes?* for HarperCollins, based on his interviews with highly successful people.

A true industry insider, Bill has interviewed many of the most notable personalities of our time—cultural icons, comedy and music legends, presidents, writers, athletes, celebrity chefs, and a movie star or two.

His TV credits include the long-running "Midday Live" on Fox, and programs on Showtime, The Travel Channel, NBC, ABC, CBS, PBS, and ESPN. Bill spent a decade hosting and producing "Bill Boggs Corner Table" on Food Network. He has displayed unique versatility—as a game show host for CBS, a news anchor for WNBC-TV, and as host and co-executive producer of the syndicated series, "Comedy Tonight." Bill was also the executive producer for the ground-breaking Morton Downey Jr. Show.

BILLBOGGSTV on YouTube features hundreds of Bill's notable interviews from different shows over the years. He is an officer of the Friars Club in New York, a graduate of The University of Pennsylvania, with a B.A. and M.A. He is an inductee into the Northeast Philadelphia Hall of Fame. In 2000, he was selected a Father of the Year. He lives on the tranquil island of Manhattan, in East Hampton, and Palm Beach with long-suffering girlfriend, "Lady Jane.